Nine little wizards snickered at fate
One wizard laughed aloud—and
then there were eight!

The floor was still tacky, as Lord Darcy verified by pressing the side of his hand against it. He knelt down by the body and looked it over carefully. After a few moments Master Sean joined him. "What do you think?" Lord Darcy asked.

"I think he's dead," Master Sean replied. "Look at his face, my lord; it is an expression of terror frozen at the moment of death. I think Master Paul was in mortal terror of someone—or some*thing*—and it chased him in here and killed him . . ."

"Lord Darcy and Master Sean O Lochlainn, Sorcerer, are characters who have become as real to me as my neighbors, and of whom I never grow tired. I owe a deep debt to Mr. Garrett for bringing them into our time world."

—Andre Norton

RANDALL GARRETT'S LORD DARCY

— IN —

TEN LITTLE WIZARDS

BY MICHAEL KURLAND

ACE BOOKS, NEW YORK

This book is an Ace
original edition, and has never
been previously published.

TEN LITTLE WIZARDS

An Ace Book / published by arrangement with
the author

PRINTING HISTORY
Ace edition / March 1988

ISBN: 0-441-80057-2

Ace Books are published by The Berkley Publishing Group,
200 Madison Avenue, New York, New York 10016.
The name "ACE" and the "A" logo
are trademarks belonging to Charter Communications, Inc.

PRINTED IN THE UNITED STATES OF AMERICA

10 9 8 7 6 5 4 3 2 1

1

THE AGENT KNOWN AS Pyat tiptoed down the dark second-floor hallway, stocking feet silently moving along the margins of the polished hardwood floor. It was three o'clock of a cold, wet April morning and throughout the *Gryphon d'Or*, and indeed for ten leagues in any direction from the old inn, not another soul was awake. Even the hostlers snoring in their cots above the stable had another hour before they pushed themselves into semiconsciousness and began feeding and grooming the early post mounts.

Pyat paused before one of the row of doors and felt the brass numbers with a delicate touch. A door too soon: the next room was the one he looked for. Five more steps, fingers lightly following the wall in the pitch-black corridor, and here it was.

The door was locked, of course; even here in the middle of the peaceful Duchy of Normandy, in the midst of the Angevin Empire, in the Year of Grace 1988, there were still sneak thieves and burglars. But the lock on an inn room door was no problem for a skilled picklock, and the commercial lock spell was no match for a counterspell woven by a master wizard.

Pyat crouched before the door for ten minutes, his hands moving in intricate patterns, his voice intoning precisely pronounced, harsh syllables. There was a flash of light, and then another, and the pungent smell of wormwood arose, to quickly dissipate in the cold air. Carefully he inserted a slender silver key into the keyhole and then gently rotated it clockwise. The wards cleared, the lands raised, and the lock clicked open.

Silently, Pyat pulled open the door. The room was as ink-black as the corridor. He stood and listened, hearing only the regular, slightly asthmatic breathing of the man sleeping within the room and the steady drumming of the rain hitting the window. Satisfied, he stepped inside and closed the door. Feeling his way cautiously, he approached the bed. With a delicate touch, he located the great feather pillow at the head of the bed and, a moment later, the head of the man sleeping on it.

He removed a thin wire from his tunic, and in one motion had it around the sleeping man's neck. He pulled firmly at both ends. There was a slight gargling sound, pushed through the man's constricted windpipe; his body convulsed once, twice, kicked at the covers, and then was still.

The bedclothes on the far side of the double bed rustled; the unmistakable sound of someone sitting up. "My lord? Is something wrong?"

Pyat froze. It was a woman's voice. His target had a female companion. Whence had she come? No time for reflection. Pyat dove across the corpse and felt the body of a woman under the coverlet on the far side. She giggled for a second as Pyat's hands ran up her body. "Really, my lord," she whispered, "at this time of night!"

Pyat found her throat and his fingers tightened.

"My lord!" the woman gasped, her hands grabbing Pyat's wrists and trying to pull them away. "What are you——" And then some horrible realization came to her, and with her last breath she screamed; a shrill, penetrating scream. And then she fell back on the bed, and she, too, was still.

Pyat lay there, over one corpse, his hands still clutching another, and tried to catch his breath. Had anyone within heard the scream? It would not have carried outside, over the rain. Would anyone rise from the comfort of their bed for a predawn investigation of the noise?

Nothing stirred.

Pyat rose and went to the door. Opening it, he stood silent and listened for the slightest sound elsewhere in the large inn. Aside from the creaks of an old house settling, there was no sound.

Pyat went about his work. Two bodies would complicate things, but not unduly. His plans were made; his preparations in place. In half an hour of hard, wet work the bodies were disposed of and he was in the bed they had vacated. He slept well.

2

MASTER SORCERER RAIMUN DEPLESSIS could not escape the feeling that something was wrong. A large man who used his great bulk to insulate himself from the world around him, Master Raimun seldom suffered from such a feeling. Now that he had it, he wasn't sure exactly what to do about it. He sat in his corner of the compartment in the first-class railway carriage that bore him away from Tournadotte and the really excellent breakfast supplied by the *Gryphon d'Or,* and tried to analyze what was bothering him.

In normal times Castle Cristobel, Master Raimun's destination, would have been about a three-hour train ride; but with the heavy rains, they had been warned it might take as much as two or three hours longer. But time was not a constraint on Master Raimun. He had several good books: two works of historical fiction and a treatise on topological magic that he had been meaning to read for some time. No—it was something else nagging at the edge of his mind.

Master Raimun tucked his powder-blue Master Sorcerer's robes around him and leaned back farther in his seat, taking on the appearance of a round, balding, jowly head perched on the back of a blue beach ball. He surveyed his fellow compartment-mates. They had all been to breakfast at the inn with him, so presumably they had all stayed overnight at the inn as he had, although he couldn't remember seeing any of them prior to breakfast.

Opposite them, perched like a slender bird on the very edge of the seat next to the window, was a young nobleman wearing a black traveling cape and a wide-brim black hat. He had the look about him, from the cut of his boots to the strategically placed leather patches on his breeches, of a young man who would much rather be on a horse. His light blue eyes darted about the compartment, fastening first on one thing and then another. The expression on his face suggested that he expected one of the compartment's inanimate objects to suddenly come to life and spring at him, and he didn't want to be surprised.

The dispatch case clutched between his legs looked to be official, which marked the youth as a courier of some sort and explained his horsey look. The train network through the Empire was not yet extensive enough, and couriers still spent much of their travel time on horseback.

To that young nobleman's right was a short, stocky man in the garb of a commercial traveler, sitting well back in the seat, his feet together, his arms at his side. He was staring unseeingly at the wall a foot from Master Raimun's right ear, and was obviously deep in his own thoughts. The man had a strange lack of unnecessary motion; no fidgets, no twitches, no readjusting the shoulders or hands or legs. It was as though he were waiting to be turned on.

And to his right, in the corner seat by the door to the corridor, was a small, neat man with a spade beard and piercing brown eyes. His clothes had that vaguely over-exuberent look of the southern tailor; perhaps Rome or Pisa. The luggage over his seat, Master Raimun noted, was of fine Italian leather. He noticed Master Raimun looking at him, and smiled and nodded politely before turning again to the copy of the *Paris Courier* that he was reading.

On the seat next to Master Raimun was a serious-looking young man with a round face and a well-developed bushy mustache, who was deeply engrossed in a book on fly fishing, full of color plates of dry flies that you could make yourself out of bits of twine and an occasional feather. His clothing had a well-worn look, suggestive of streams and marshes.

The only other person in the car was an elderly lady with a high-collared dark red dress, who clutched a rolled umbrella possessively. She looked as though, with the slightest encouragement, she would tell you all about each of her grandchildren. Or, possibly, her pet cats.

After observing his five compartment-mates, Master Raimun turned to stare out the window. It was a cold and rainy morning, and the window was fogged over enough so that vision was restricted to a view of the trees and bushes by the edge of the roadway as they whipped past. He let his mind go blank as he stared at the repetitive scene. Somewhere, at the edge of volition, the thing bothering him was struggling to be heard. But its shrill but faint voice was too easily overpowered by the day-to-day thoughts that came unbidden.

The fog swirled and thickened, and the carriage bumped gently over the rail points. Master Raimun's breathing steadied, and his mind slowly cleared of the minute-to-minute trivia and became receptive.

Receptive—that was it! It wasn't his own feeling nagging at him, it was someone else's. Master Raimun was a healer and a sensitive, although not a priest. Most of his work was theoretical these days, and his mind was no longer accustomed to being receptive to another's thoughts.

But here was a soul in torment. It was heavily masked, but it came through clearly now that his mind was jerked away from its own preoccupation. One of the persons in this carriage, he realized, was in great psychic pain. Was he being nosy? It was very improper and impolite for a sensitive to intrude unbidden on another's feelings. Even though he couldn't actually *read* someone else's mind, like those mental entertainers in the music halls claimed to do, feeling someone else's emotions could be a violation of privacy.

But such pain—

He would merely establish which of the five it was, and then privately take them aside and suggest that they see a qualified priest-healer. The sufferer might object even to that, but he felt it his duty.

He concentrated, his eyes closed, and let the feelings wash over him.

What? But that was impossible! Master Raimun's eyes flew open, and he felt as though he had been punched in his expansive gut. The air whooshed out of his mouth with explosive force as his stomach muscles contracted in response to his mind's commands.

The pain—the anger that he felt—was directed at *him!* One of the five persons in this carriage with him was carrying around a load of hatred so strong that it was almost physical. It was well masked under layers of tight control, but Master Raimun could feel it like a physical blast. Aimed at him! One of the persons in this carriage hated him.

He kept staring out the window for a minute, getting his physical reactions back under control, afraid to turn around. His feelings would show on his face. He must mask them. He must find out which of his fellow passengers was this poor, warped soul. He must get him professional help. Perhaps one of the healing fathers at the Stephainite Monastery at Castle Cristobel. But he must not let it be seen that he knew. It would embarrass the person and serve no useful purpose. Especially since the emotion was directed at him. That would never do.

Slowly, casually, he turned around to face back into the compartment. None of his companions was looking at him. None of them was showing on the surface the turmoil that Master Raimun recognized underneath.

A true professional consecrated healer, a priest with the Talent, dedicated to his calling, would have been able to tell in an instant which of the five it was. But Master Raimun was not a priest, and his Talent had been trained and practiced along other lines.

He looked them over carefully; the man in black, the stocky man, the man with the spade beard, the young man with the mustache, the elderly lady—he could not recall ever having seen any of them before that day. None of them could he conceivably have injured in any way. And yet one of them hated him. It was a puzzle.

But it was also a deucedly awkward situation. He couldn't stay in the compartment. Not with that wash of emotion around. By the time they got to Castle Cristobel, he'd be a nervous wreck.

He pushed himself to his feet, smiled blandly to the others, and waddled past the several pair of feet out into the corridor. There must be vacant space in one of the other compartments.

Ah, he was in luck! Here, two compartments down, was his old friend Master Sir Darryl Longuert, a fine sorcerer and a boon companion. Even though he had recently been appointed the Wizard Laureate of England, Master Sir Darryl still traveled alone and without fuss. Master Raimun knocked on the compartment door and entered. "Sir Darryl!" he said, relaxing into a corner seat. "How lucky to run into you here. I've just had the strangest experience."

Sir Darryl, a kindly man with a smile-creased face and a healthy twinkle in his hazel eyes, sighed and closed his book. "Tell me about it," he said.

3

Two weeks had passed.

The Chevalier Raoul d'Espergnan reined in his mount and paused to stare at the distant spires of Castle Cristobel, which rose, gleaming and sparkling, above the morning mist. He could not help thinking of legendary Camelot, which must have looked much like this to questing knights back in the mythical days of Arthur Pendragon. But the Camelot of King Arthur would recede into the distance the harder one tried to reach it, whereas Castle Cristobel had better stay where it was.

D'Espergnan was a courier in the King's Service. He carried the London dispatches, which were already a full day late due to the cursed heavy spring rains flooding the countryside and washing out roads. This part of the trip was usually done by rail, but since he had last made the trip two weeks before, a section of track had washed out and would be another full day being repaired.

He had been delayed four hours at the station before they discovered the cause of the holdup, and another three hours before he could get a horse from the relay station at Tournadotte. He would have a lot of explaining to do, and His Most Dread Sovereign John IV disliked listening to explanations. D'Espergnan pulled back the cuff of his leather glove and checked his watch. It was already after ten.

The Chevalier cursed fluently and imaginatively for so young a man, and spurred his horse on through the foot-deep water that covered the road.

Castle Cristobel, which spread its vast acreage over a high hill in the otherwise flat Norman coastal valley, was one of the oldest of the royal palaces of the Plantagenet kings. Built by the first Arthur—not the mythical King Arthur, but the flesh-and-blood nephew and heir of the first Richard—as the principal redoubt and keep in his Normandy dominion, it had been the strongest of a web of strong points during the contentious battling of that boisterous and undecided age.

It was yet, as it had been, a fortress, a seat of law and government, a royal residence, the Main Depository of the Royal Archives, and the principal headquarters (in a small monastery within the castle grounds) of the Stephainites, a monastic order of healers founded by the legendary St. Stephain d'Aviss in the thirteenth century.

Though the principal site of government, and the chief residence of the Plantagenet kings, had long since moved to London, there was still one ceremony that was, as it had been for six hundred years, performed only at Castle Cristobel.

Gwiliam Richard Arthur Plantagenet, Baron Ambrey, Duke of Lancaster, the twenty-seven-year-old younger son of King John IV, was about to be raised to the title and station of Prince of Gaul. His great uncle, Charles, having held the title for sixty-three years, had died the year before, and Gwiliam was the logical and traditional successor. And, as his older brother John, Prince of Britain, was of a monastic and scholarly turn of mind, there was every chance that the to-be annointed Prince of Gaul would someday be elected the next King of England and France and Emperor of the Angevin Empire.

But John IV was still young for a Plantagenet, who are of a notoriously long-lived stock; so Prince Gwiliam could look forward to many years of letting his father worry about the reins of government before he would have to gather them in to himself.

It was eleven-thirty when the hooves of the Chevalier d'Espergnan's mount clattered over the wooden bridge leading to the Knight's Gate to Castle Cristobel. The rain had commenced again, and the sky was a leaden gray. An armsman in a red rain cape stopped him at the portcullis.

"From London on the King's business," d'Espergnan told the armsman. He pulled back the rubberized canvas hood of his rain cape and leaned over in his saddle to display the silver greyhound device that was the insignia of the Imperial Courier Service. "Let me pass!"

The armsman regarded the tall, slender young nobleman who sat rapier-straight in his saddle. Young men on the King's business were always in a hurry. But that, the armsman supposed, was why the King picked them for his business. "Pass," he said, stepping aside. "But leave your mount in the stableyard in the Great Cristobel outer bailey. They will see to it there. No horses allowed past that point for the next few weeks."

D'Espergnan nodded. "Thank you, armsman," he said. Gentlemen on the King's business were always polite, when time permitted. Anything less would be an abuse of power. He wheeled his mount and clattered and splashed his way through into the outer bailey. The stable and stableyard were up against the inner wall, across several hundred yards of open ground decorated with a smattering of tents, booths, and less-identifiable structures. The outer bailey of Great Cristobel, the newest and outermost keep of the Castle Cristobel complex, was the largest cleared area within the castle walls. It held a year-round open market, and twice a year an entire traveling circus pitched its tents along the wall. Showing admirable self-restraint, d'Espergnan crossed the field at something less than an outright trot.

Ten minutes later, after pausing only to remove his rain garment and towel his face and hair, the young courier was handing his leather dispatch case over to the holder of the golden greyhound: Lord Peter Whiss, a short, slender man with receding blond hair, who was the personal Secretary of Marquis Sherrinford, the King's Equerry. The silver greyhound couriers were bound by oath to give up their dispatches only to holders of the golden greyhound, or to the person of the King or a Royal Duke directly.

"Thank you, Sir Raoul," the secretary said from behind the antique walnut desk in his office as he took the bulging brown case and hefted it in his well-scrubbed hands. "And only twenty-seven hours late. We consider that, given the state of the roads, you have done very well."

"Thank you, my lord," Raoul said, breathing a sigh of relief that Lord Peter had considered the weather.

"But see that it never happens again," Lord Peter added, smiling.

"Yes, my lord."

"Were there any private messages?"

"None, my lord," d'Espergnan said.

"I'm glad of that," Lord Peter said. A private message was not, in this context, a love note from a lady in London, or any other nonofficial mail. Rather it was the one exception to the oath of delivery: a message from a highly placed source which was so confidential that it could only be delivered to the one to whom it was addressed. As such, it was usually not good news. Its existence, although not its contents, had to be divulged to Lord Peter.

"Have the seneschal assign you to a room," Lord Peter told the young man. "Dry off, eat something, and get some sleep. From now on report to me once a day, in the morning, and see whether I have any instructions for you. Aside from that, stay out of the way of the coronation preparations and have a good time."

"Thank you, Lord Peter," d'Espergnan said. He saluted, and then retreated rapidly from the secretary's presence. D'Espergnan, had you asked him, would have expressed the opinion that, although His Dread Majesty John IV reigned over the Angevin Empire with a kind but firm hand, the person who *ruled* over the Empire was Lord Peter Whiss, private secretary to the Marquis Sherrinford.

Lord Peter held a slightly different view of the true state of affairs. Although it was a fact that among his duties were some of much more moment to the Empire than that of Royal Postmaster, still he regarded himself as but a cog in the complex and far-reaching mechanism of the King's Government. An important cog, perhaps, but a cog nonetheless. He turned the dispatch case over and examined the seal. It had not been disturbed. On completing his examination, Lord Peter knew that the case had not been opened since the seal was affixed. He didn't merely think so, he *knew*. It was part of his one talent. Other holders of the gold greyhound, who were not themselves sorcerers, would use a government sorcerer to assure that the privacy spell on the packet had not been violated; but Lord Peter had no need of that. The dispatch case could have been sealed without using a privacy spell, and he still would have known if it had been opened, no matter how carefully it was done. Of course, the spells were still used; there was no point in being foolhardy.

The other part of his talent, which King John made good use

of, was, so far as was known, unique. Lord Peter knew when someone was lying. He couldn't tell what the other was lying *about*—just the fact that some part of what the other said was not true.

Lord Peter opened the dispatch case and dumped the envelopes within onto the desk. Then he ran his hand around the inside to make sure none had somehow got caught in the stitching. He was not by nature a careful man, but he had trained himself well over the years. Eternal vigilance and a nervous stomach were the costs of his job.

He sorted the forty-two envelopes into three different stacks, routinely checking the seals on each as he did so. The first stack he tied with a red ribbon for delivery to the Lord Chamberlain; the second he tied with a blue ribbon for delivery to the Foreign Minister; and the third he slit open with an ivory letter opener and read, one by one. He uncapped his fountain pen and initialed each as he read it, sometimes with a comment and sometimes not. At the next-to-last one he paused thoughtfully, then reread each of its three pages as though to be sure he had understood it the first time. Then he folded it and put it in an inside pocket of his russet-and-gold jacket. He quickly read the last letter, then bundled the stack of opened mail together and tied it with a green ribbon.

He put all three bundles into his own gold-stitched leather shoulder bag for delivery. He could have assigned this part of the job to another, but it was not in his conception of his duties to do so. The shorter the chain, the less chance for a broken link. He left his office, carefully locking the door behind him.

The throne room, Lord Peter's eventual goal, was down a long hallway called the Gallery of Kings, off of which most of the royal and imperial offices had their temporary homes. The seat of government moved with the King, so when he had come last week to prepare for his son's coronation, the critical government offices had come with him. But a heavy communication between the two places was a necessity; the decisions made in Castle Cristobel still had to be implemented from London.

Lord Peter walked slowly down the Gallery of Kings; one week's residence was not long enough for him to have become inured to its symbolism. Here along the right-hand wall were the official portraits of the Plantagenet kings, from Geoffrey of Anjou, who was called "Plantagenet" for the sprig of "genet" broom plant he wore in his cap, to John IV, who was the direct descendant of a royal line called "Plantagenet" for most of the last millennium.

Here was Henry II, Geoffrey's son, who already held the title of Duke of Normandy when his father died in 1151 and he took over the throne of England. He looked slightly cross-eyed and very somber in the portrait, but Lord Peter decided that the first was probably the artist's attempt at perspective, and the second due to the fact that the painting probably hadn't been cleaned in the past three hundred years.

Lord Peter stopped at the next door, delivered the red-beribboned bundle to the Chamberlain's secretary-in-chief, and then went on.

Here, next, was Henry's son, Richard the Lion-Hearted, glaring paternally down in his old age. On the wall across from Richard's portrait was the famous nineteenth century Jan Etyacht painting of the Siege of Chaluz, reproduced in every school history book. Twenty feet wide by ten feet high, it showed the full field of battle before the walls of Chaluz. In the right-hand corner was the crossbowman on the battlement who had just fired his bolt. Slightly to the left of center Richard was sinking to his knees as the crossbow bolt penetrated his shoulder.

The luckiest wound in the history of the Angevin Empire, Lord Peter thought. Had Richard not had the time for reflection provided by his long bout with the infection and fever caused by the wound, and perhaps its intimations of mortality, then he might have remained the good but profligate king who spent his time and energy on foreign crusades instead of wisely ruling his kingdom and his people. Had Richard instead died of the wound in 1199, then his younger brother John Lackland would have ascended the throne, and probably would have proved as stupid and evil a king as he had been a prince.

But Richard had lived and ruled wisely and well until his death in 1219, when the scepter passed to his nephew Arthur. Lord Peter stared up at the portrait of Arthur I, "Good King Arthur," whose history was mixed in the popular mind with the legends of the mythical King Arthur of the Round Table. How would history have been changed if Arthur had not reigned? What would John Lackland's stewardship have done to the kingdom and to the Plantagenet line? Lord Peter shook his head as he continued down the line of portraits. That was the sort of speculation best left to the writers of phantasmagorical fiction.

Here they were in order: the Geoffreys, Johns, Gwiliams, Richards, and Arthurs; rulers who had kept together their British and Norman holdings and, for the most part, ruled them wisely and well. At the foot of each painting, set into the frame, were the personal arms of the King, which changed slightly with each reign, but which, in every case, joined inexorably the lions of England and the lilies of France.

Each of the Plantagenets had expanded these holdings slowly, carefully, by marriage, diplomacy, and the sword, until the Anglo-French Empire now ruled over more land than the Roman Empire at its height, and had lasted more than twice as long. And showed no signs of lessening now; with an intelligent and vigorous king at the head of a loyal and vigorous people, administered by a well-schooled, capable, and absolutely faithful civil service. If God willed, there was no reason why there should not be a Plantagenet on the throne of the Angevin Empire for another thousand years. With that thought, Lord Peter crossed himself, and reminded himself that the way to keep the will of God was to continue to do God's will on Earth to the best of one's ability.

As Lord Peter reached the throne room, he resolved to leave by the opposite door, so that he could walk down the Gallery of Queens on the far side. Portraits of the Plantagenet queens, from Eleanor of Aquitaine to the present Marie of Roumania, graced those walls. The queens consort showed the eye for beauty of the Plantagenet men, and the strength and intelligence that was, generation after generation, infused into the Plantagenet bloodline. And the five queens regent: Anne, Mary I, Edith, Stephanie, and Mary II, had proved during their reigns that the Plantagenet skills ran as deeply in the female line as in the male.

Lord Peter nodded to the two guards flanking the doors, and entered the throne room. The King was not present; the two hours of public audience did not begin until two o'clock. But Marquis Sherrinford, resplendant in his forest-green and silver court costume, was already at his small desk to the side of the ancient oak throne, sorting dockets, perusing files, listening to urgent pleas, deciding who would get to see His Majesty today and who would not. Harbleury, the gnomelike ancient who was his personal assistant and was privy to more of the secrets of state than many a duke, stood behind him.

Lord Peter looked with concern at his master as he approached. Marquis Sherrinford suffered from headaches. For the past year they had been growing more frequent and stronger, and had proved beyond the reach of the healer's arts. He refused to consider easing up on his duties, and indeed, the headaches did not seem to be affecting his judgment; but at times these days he was difficult to work with. Besides, above everything else, he was Lord Peter's good friend, and being impotently unable to help a friend in pain is not a good feeling.

"Ah, good day, Lord Peter," His Lordship said, taking his spectacles off and looking up as his private secretary approached. He rubbed at his temples briefly with his thumbs, then replaced the wire-rim spectacles. "You bring the day's post from London, I presume. Anything of note?"

Lord Peter removed the blue-tied bundle from his shoulder bag. "For His Lordship, the Duke of Clarence," he said. Then, removing the remaining green-tied bundle: "For Your Lordship."

"I shall pass this on to His Lordship of Clarence immediately," Marquis Sherrinford said. "Harbleury, see to it. Now, is there anything in our pile that demands our immediate attention?"

Lord Peter took the letter from his inside pocket and passed it over to the King's Equerry. "I fancy Your Lordship will agree that this merits such," he said.

Marquis Sherrinford took his spectacles off, wiped them with a bit of white linen, carefully hooked them back behind his ears, and then unfolded the three sheets of stiff paper. "Ha," he said. "Hmm."

Lord Peter looked up at Harbleury, who had passed the blue-tied bundle of documents on to an aide and was once again standing at his master's back. He raised an eyebrow slightly, and Harbleury shook his head. The nonverbal exchange of information was complete. Is His Lordship suffering from one of his attacks? Not at the moment, as far as Harbleury could tell. Lord Peter nodded his thanks to the old man.

Marquis Sherrinford stared at each page of the letter long enough to have read it several times, and then gathered them together and laid the letter on the table, neatly and precisely. A frown formed across his brow. "What do you think, Peter?" he asked without looking up.

"I think we must treat it as though it is true," Lord Peter said. "Although I will at once, of course, try to check through my own sources."

"Yes," the Marquis said impatiently, "but what do you *think*? Is it true?"

"I can only say that I'll investigate," Lord Peter repeated. "I have heard nothing of it. It is very hard to establish a negative, so if it is not true, we may be some time in proving it. In the meantime, we must proceed as though it were fact."

Marquis Sherrinford tapped the end of his pen impatiently on the desk top. "Why have none of your sources picked it up?"

Lord Peter shrugged. "Perhaps because it isn't true. Perhaps because it is well hidden. Perhaps because I am incompetent, Your Lordship."

The Marquis glanced up sharply, looking over his wire-rim spectacles. "Take this seriously, Lord Peter, but not personally. Somewhere in this kingdom there must be a man more competent and more loyal than yourself, and more able at his job, but I have not met him." He picked up the stiff sheets of paper and shook them, making them rattle. "We must act. Go find His Grace the Archbishop of Paris, Richard of Normandy, Sir Darryl Longuert, and Lord Darcy, and ask them to do me the honor of meeting with me in the Map Room at four o'clock. Do it personally; we want as few ears and mouths privy to this as possible. And return yourself, of course."

"Of course, my lord," Lord Peter said. He bowed and turned away, his footsteps ringing hollowly on the tile floor as he strode toward the ceremonial doors of state, the fastest way to the private quarters where he would probably find His Grace the Archbishop. His perusal of the Queen's Corridor would have to wait.

"Now," Marquis Sherrinford said, sticking the offending letter in the inner pocket of his dress tunic and turning back to the other papers on his table. "I have an appointment with that Italian healer fellow at one o'clock. Probably can't help me, but I'd better go. Which gives us twenty more minutes to devote to this, Harbleury; let's get to it."

Twenty minutes later Harbleury tapped his master on the shoulder. "It is time for your appointment, my lord," he said.

"What? Oh, yes. Suppose I'd better go. Damn nuisance, though. This fellow—what's his name. . . ?"

"Count d'Alberra, my lord. Very highly recommended, my lord."

"Yes. Well, I suppose anything's better than the damn headaches. It's just that I can't afford the time right now."

"You never can, my lord," Harbleury told him. "Your cloak, my lord."

"You're right as usual, Harbleury," Marquis Sherrinford said, rising and letting his assistant help him on with the ornate cloak. "Tidy things up here and go prepare the Map Room for our four o'clock meeting. And—thank you."

Marquis Sherrinford left the throne room, traversed the Great Hall, and buttoning his cloak around him against the rain, left the main building. He crossed the outer bailey of Arthur Keep—which was now actually an inner bailey, as construction over the centuries had surrounded Arthur Keep with new layers of castle. He was pleased to see that the drainage system was working well and the bailey was staying fairly puddle-free even under this heavy assault of spring flooding. He must remember to commend the Castle maintenance crew.

Against what had been the bailey's outer wall nestled the monastery of Saint Stephain, where pious, dedicated, and Talented men had studied and advanced the healing arts for the past five hundred years. He approached it and knocked at the tiny front door, over which, deeply chiseled, were the words SED LIBRA NOS A MALO—"but deliver us from evil." After a moment a lay brother opened the door and admitted him.

Some of the greatest healers of the past centuries had been Stephainites. In the fourteenth century the Stephainite monk Saint Hilary Robert had the flash of insight that showed a mathematical relationship within certain healing arts. Then he spent the next twenty years of his life working out exactly what that relationship was. When he was done, he published the *Mathematicka Manticka*, establishing the logical basis for the laws of magic, and the physical world was never again the same.

Not everyone had the Talent, for unknown reasons, but those who did could study his principles and achieve consistent, reproducible results. Healers could practice the Laying On of Hands, and with the license of the Mother Church, confidently expect to help many, if not most, of their patients. The art of healing was the first of the magical arts to be exploited, and perhaps was the best understood to this very day.

Over the centuries men and women had come to the Stephainite monastery at Walsingham, where Saint Hilary

Robert had lived, or to the other centers at Liverno, Geneva, and here at Castle Cristobel, to be trained in the healing arts.

But some ills lay outside the skills of the healers. A broken bone, for example, had to be reset by a chirurgeon before the Laying of Hands would speed the recovery. And some ills seemed to lay outside the art of healing.

The cure for most headaches lay within the healing arts. A headache caused by tension, by anxiety, by the retreat of an overly worried mind into pain, could be eased even by lay healers. Of course, the underlying cause would have to be treated or the pain would recur, but it could be eased. A headache caused by a complex sickness of the mind, or a headache with an underlying physical cause, such as a brain tumor, called for the services of professional healers, usually priests, who were well trained in the specialty in question. But usually these, too, gave way before the healer's art; sometimes combined with the chirurgeon's skill.

But magic and healing were human arts, and thus imperfect; miracles remained the province of the Divine. Some broken arms failed, for unknown reasons, to heal properly; some infections spread and worsened despite the most accomplished healer's hands; some headaches refused to depart.

Marquis Sherrinford's headaches had at first been minor and easily abated by his family healer. But as they grew more frequent, and more extreme, they proved intractable to the Laying On of Hands. Some of the best sensitives in the Empire had examined him, and all agreed that they could find no underlying physical or mental cause.

The Marquis bore his affliction with dignity and disdain, refusing to allow it to interfere with his work or his private life. But he also was wise enough not to allow himself to become a martyr. When the possibility of a new cure came along, he was willing to try it, provided it did not sound too silly or take up too much of his time.

Father Phillip, the elderly abbot who was in temporal charge of the monastery, met Marquis Sherrinford at the door to his small, uncluttered office, where the lay brother brought him. "Good to see you again, my lord," he said, waving the Marquis to one of the two hard-backed chairs. "Let us pray that we can do something for you this time."

"Visiting you is always a welcome pause in a too-hectic day, Father," Marquis Sherrinford said, lowering himself into the chair. "And the additional possibility of some alleviation of these headaches makes this a haven indeed. Tell me about this Count d'Alberra. Do you think he can do anything?''

Father Phillip shook his head. "I would not like to guess," he said. "He helps some. More than I would have guessed. His record of success in Rome and Como and Verona is very impressive, and is attested by His Holiness himself. So there is no question that this method of his has merit. But he has only been here a few weeks—hardly long enough for me to judge what his system can or cannot do.''

"Tell me about the man himself," Marquis Sherrinford said, taking his glasses off and polishing them with a cloth.

"A very nice, soft-spoken gentleman from the north of Italy. Count d'Alberra is attached to the court of King Pietro and is a professor of something they call 'Mental Science' at the University of Verona. His theories of healing come from his studies of the mind. He has written a book called *Non-Physical Symptomology of the Mind and its Possible Non-Magical Treatment*. He is not, himself, a healer, you know.''

"No, I didn't.''

"It is true." Father Phillip sighed. "One should not attempt to explain the ways of God to man, for life itself is enough of a wonder to spend a lifetime considering.''

"Well, if he isn't a healer, than what does he do?" Marquis Sherrinford asked.

"Count d'Alberra talks and listens," Father Phillip said. "As far as I can see, that's what he does.''

"And he cures people?''

"In many cases. He seems to.''

Marquis Sherrinford took off his glasses and rubbed his temples with his thumbs. "I'm not surprised that the man is a scientist," he said. "His method sounds decidedly unmagical. But if it works, who am I to argue?''

"I'll take you in to see him now, my lord," Father Phillip said. "He was delighted that you decided to come. He says he hopes he can help you.''

"So do I," Marquis Sherrinford told the good father, sounding a bit doubtful. "So do I.''

Count d'Alberra was a small, dark-haired man with a closely trimmed beard and mustache. The beard came to a point, emphasizing the angularity of his head. He dressed in the somewhat more ornate costume common to central Italy, all blues, yellows, and tasseled gold fringes. He met them at the door to his treatment room. "It is a pleasure—a pleasure—to meet you, my lord marquis," he said, taking Marquis Sherrinford by the hand and wringing it firmly. "Thank you, Father, for recommending me. I shall most sincerely try to help."

"I can ask no more than that," Marquis Sherrinford said, allowing himself to be pulled into the small room.

"I'll leave you now," Father Phillip said. "God bless." He smiled, nodded, and walked away.

"Just what is it that you do here?" Marquis Sherrinford asked, looking around the small room. It contained a desk, a chair, and a leather couch.

"Nothing mysterious," Count d'Alberra assured him. "I will start by taking a patient history, and then we will talk. You, actually, will do most of the talking. I will ask you to lie on the couch, since I have found that most patients are able to relax better lying down. But if that bothers you, I can have another chair brought in."

"No, no," Marquis Sherrinford said. "I have no objection to lying down. Quite the contrary. You'll have a job keeping me talking, though. I'm liable to drift off to sleep. It's been a busy day, and it's only half over." A look of concern suddenly crossed his face. "You don't ask me about my work, do you? You know I can't discuss—"

"I assure you," Count d'Alberra interrupted, holding up his hand. "I have no concern with your lordship's work. Our conversations will revolve mostly about your childhood, your relations with your parents, things of that sort. We may also touch upon how you feel about, ah, the ladies, or what sports you like and why."

"That's all?"

"That is all."

"And this may cure my headaches? Asking questions about my childhood?"

"If, indeed, as the healer's say, there is nothing organically wrong that they can find, it well may."

Marquis Sherrinford lay back on the black leather couch. "Go ahead, friend Count, ask away."

"First the history," Count d'Alberra said, uncapping his fountain pen. "Where were you born?"

4

THE SKINNY COUNTY ARMSMAN refused to sit, and instead shifted uneasily from foot to foot as he waited; looking and feeling out of place in the elaborate drawing room of this sumptuous suite. Lord Darcy could sympathize with him; the ornate, cane-bottomed Gwiliam II chairs did look as though they would break under anything but the most delicate behind. He was not entirely at home here himself, but the seneschal had assigned him these quarters, and with the hundreds of people arriving for the coronation, it would not be fair to ask the the seneschal to do a musical-chairs act because Lord Darcy would have been happier in plainer surroundings. At least they had found a large desk and comfortable chair for him.

The armsman kept making surreptitious moves to doff his hat in the presence of so much finery. But he would remember that he was in uniform and under arms, and in the presence of the Chief Investigator of the King's Court of Chivalry, and his hands would snap back down to his sides. Then he would try to polish the sole of one boot against the heel of the other, distributing even more drying mud onto the plum carpet in the process. Lord Darcy found the series of motions annoying, and he almost snapped at the man before realizing how unfair that would be. Instead he looked up from the letter the armsman had brought and twisted his lips into a smile, hoping the smile didn't look as artificial as it felt.

"I'll be about ten minutes or so composing a reply to this letter," Lord Darcy said. "Why don't you go inside, through that door, and have my man Ciardi fix you a drink, er, of caffe, since you are still on duty."

"Very good, my lord. Thank you," the armsman said with evident relief, and he retreated hastily through the indicated door.

One of our country cousins, Lord Darcy thought. Then he did smile, recognizing the expression as one that his good friend and companion Mary, Duchess of Cumberland, used to describe the inept or the unsophisticated.

The message the armsman had brought was from another old friend of Lord Darcy's, from the days when he was merely the chief investigator of the Duchy of Normandy, instead of Investigator in Chief of the Court of Chivalry for the whole Angevin Empire. It was short and to the point, but the unwritten subtext went on at some length.

Dear Lord Darcy,

I hope you won't think it presumptuous of me to write you after all this time. I heard you were at the Castle Cristobel in charge of security for the coming coronation. His Majesty could not have picked a better man.

There has been a double murder here in the small town of Tournadotte, at an inn named the *Gryphon d'Or*. The killings had no motive that anyone here can determine. The identity of one of the victims is also still a mystery. I thought this might interest you, since you are, so to speak, in the neighborhood. The village of Tournadotte is but two stops farther down the Paris-Le Havre line, at the Calais junction.

It would be good to see you again. I remember fondly how you helped me in the matter of the disappearance of the late Marquis of Cherbourg.

Your Friend,
Henri Vert
Prefect of Police
Duchy of Normandy

Lord Darcy remembered the case of the missing marquis well. It had been a long time ago, when life had been less complex. Or, perhaps, it had only seemed less complex.

What Darcy's old friend Henri Vert, who was now the highest uniformed police official for the whole duchy, wanted from Darcy was clear: He needed help—or thought he did—in solving these two murders. The fact that he sent an armsman to deliver the letter personally showed that. He could not ask for aid from the Court of Chivalry directly unless one of those killed was noble, or a noble was suspected of complicity in the killings, or the murders were somehow of importance to the Empire. And, clearly, he could not demonstrate that.

But does not any man's death diminish us? came the quote, unbidden, into Lord Darcy's thoughts. And, after all, he *was* in the neighborhood—less than three hours by train to the *Gryphon d'Or*, according to the note. Unsolved murders were not good for the soul of the people. When he could get time off from his present duties, Lord Darcy decided, he would go down and see if he could give Chief Henri a hand; if the spring flooding did not close down the railway line, as it was threatening to. He was sure that Master Sean O Lochlainn, the Angevin Empire's Chief Forensic Sorcerer and Darcy's good right hand, would also volunteer to accompany him.

Lord Darcy spent the whole ten minutes composing his answer. He would have to speak to Coronel Lord Waybusch, commander of the Castle Guard, to see if he could get free for a couple of days. He couldn't just leave, even though he was not in charge of security, as Chief Henri thought, but merely on hand to observe and advise on security for the coronation. But there was no point in antagonizing the Coronel, a friendly, hard-working trooper who welcomed his advice. And in case he *couldn't* get free, or the railroad did stop running, he didn't want Master Henri to have been waiting for him instead of investigating on his own.

When Lord Darcy was happy with the reply, he made a clean copy, then folded it and sealed it with his signet, and called the armsman back into the room. "Tell Prefect Henri that I will look forward to working with him, if I can get away," he said, handing the paper to the armsman.

Ciardi came to the door as the armsman was leaving. "Lord Peter Whiss to see you, Your Lordship," he said.

"Lord Peter? At midday? How strange. What does he want?" Lord Darcy asked.

"He didn't say," Ciardi replied. "And it is well past midday, my lord. It is almost four o'clock."

"So it is," Lord Darcy agreed. "Show His Lordship in, please, Ciardi." He stood up and slipped into his jacket, which had been hanging over the back of his chair.

"Sorry to bother you, Lord Darcy," Lord Peter said, barely sticking his head around the door. "But, much as I regret it, I must drag you away from all this."

"If you must," Lord Darcy said, buttoning his jacket and adjusting the lace cuffs of his shirt. "Are we going outdoors? No? Good, then I won't need my rain cape or overboots. Lead the way!"

A minute later they were bustling together down the long castle corridor. "You are the last of the invited guests to be notified," Lord Peter explained. "And we're running a few minutes late, as it took me longer than expected to locate His Grace the Archbishop. I must say, Darcy, that you are surprisingly uninquisitive for a man who has just been suddenly pulled away from his work. I expected at least a couple of questions, if not an argument."

"You said that you *must* drag me away," Lord Darcy pointed out. "I took you at your word. You are not frivolous with language."

"That is so," Lord Peter admitted. "These days I will admit I seldom feel frivolous about anything." He stopped at the Map Room door, which, Lord Darcy noted, had an armed guard from the King's Own standing at attention beside it. "Well, here we are. After you, my lord."

Lord Darcy entered the Map Room ahead of Lord Peter and greeted the five people already there: His Grace Archbishop Maximilian of Paris; His Highness Duke Richard of Normandy, the King's brother; Master Sir Darryl Longuert, the Wizard Laureate of England; His Lordship the Marquis Sherrinford, the King's Equerry; and Goodman Harbleury, the Marquis Sherrinford's amanuensis and shadow.

"Good day, Lord Darcy," Marquis Sherrinford said. "Please sit down, and we'll begin."

The Map Room, a part of the Royal Archives, was a fourteen-by-twenty-foot room, equipped, as its name indicated, to store, display, and examine maps. The rear wall was one vast walnut cabinet of long, wide, flat drawers for storing unfolded maps. Along the wall to the right of that, below the high-set windows, were rows of oblong bins, crafted of the same wood, for storing rolled-up maps. The front wall contained devices for hanging maps for study, and the large, walnut table that dominated the room was inlaid with a complex set of brass fittings that would enable one to hold down, examine, magnify, or pantographically duplicate or enlarge a map.

Lord Darcy dropped into the nearest straight-back walnut chair and rested his hands on the table. He had spent many hours in this room during the years he was Chief Investigator for the Duke of Normandy, examining and committing to memory the plans of the kingdom's major castles and many of the minor ones. It was a knowledge that had proven useful more than once.

Marquis Sherrinford pushed himself out of his chair. "Thank your lordships all for coming," he said. "I'll be as brief as possible, as I know you all have important duties that you put aside to come here."

"And without a word of explanation too," Duke Richard said. "It is a mark of the esteem in which we all hold you, my lord marquis."

"I would not abuse your confidence, I assure Your Highness," Marquis Sherrinford said. "I wish to read you a letter that arrived this noon, addressed to me." He took the letter from the table and unfolded it. "It was first opened by Lord Peter, and he passed it directly on," he said, then began reading.

> To His Lordship, the Right Honorable the Marquis Sherrinford.
> From His Lordship the Marquis of London.
> On Monday, the 25th of April, in the Year of Our Lord 1988.
>
> Greetings Noble Cousin.
> I hesitate to bother Your Lordship, busy as you must be with plans for the impending coronation of His Royal Highness. I would be there myself but, as you know, pressing business keeps me in London—

"Pressing business!" Duke Richard interrupted, laughing, "pressing weight is more like it. He hasn't left that palace of his in something like thirteen years. There isn't a carriage that would hold him; he'd have to hire a dray. He must weigh thirty stone."

"Nonetheless," Marquis Sherrinford pointed out, "he carries out his duties as Chief Magistrate for the City of London very well."

"That's so," Sir Darryl agreed, nodding his angular, bony head. "The man never leaves his house, and yet he knows more about what goes on in London than if he ran about all day peering around corners. And the inferences he can make from the merest speck of dust or spot of food on a waistcoat are truly astonishing."

"Oh, yes," Duke Richard agreed. "The man is a brilliant investigator, no question about that. A relative of yours, I believe, Darcy?"

"Distant cousin," Lord Darcy said.

"Just so," Marquis Sherrinford said. "Now, if Your Highness will permit me to continue—"

"Of course," Duke Richard said. "Sorry."

" '—pressing business keeps me in London,' " the Marquis picked up where he had left off.

A certain piece of information has come to my attention during the routine investigation of a series of bizarre robberies. Since you are concerned with the safety of our beloved King John, I thought I had better pass it on. It is probably of no moment, but you are in a better position to judge that than I.

At the mention of the king's safety, a sudden palpable tension entered the room. "Our beloved King John" was not just a formula with these men, but an expression of an honestly held emotion.

Here are the details, to the extent that we know them:

The robber, who turned out to be one Goodman Albert Chall, was apprehended on Sunday—yesterday—by my assistant, Lord Bontriomphe who is not without a certain primitive cleverness. In trying to escape along a rooftop, Goodman Chall leaped over a parapet and fell six storeys onto a paved walk.

Lord Bontriomphe reached him as he was expiring—it is nothing short of a miracle that he lived even that long—and held a brief colloquy with him which he subsequently quoted to me verbatim. I am sure you are familiar with Lord Bontriomphe's abilities along that line. I quote the conversation in full:

BONTRIOMPHE: Just lie still, I've called for an ambulance.

CHALL: That ain't no good. You know that, gov. Look at me; I'm all broken up. I can't feel nothin'.

BONTRIOMPHE: Is there anything you want me to do?

C: I got to tell you somethin'.

B: About the robberies? You don't have to—

C: No, no—it's somethin' else. I was kind of holdin' this as a trump, 'case I got caught. But I won't need it now. I won't need nothin' now. I want to get it said in case I—in case I don't make it. Which it looks like I won't.

B: What is it?

C: I would have told anyway. You can see that, can't you? I would have told anyway before June first. You know that?

B: Told what?

C: About them killin' His Majesty. I wouldn't have let them do that. You believe me, don't you? I would have told anyway. You know that.

B: Of course I do. I believe you. Tell me about it now.

C: I heard about it by accident. Oh Gawd, the pain is startin'. It hurts somethin' awful. I must be all busted up inside.

B: There'll be a healer here in a minute. Talk to me—it will keep your mind off the pain. What about them killing His Majesty?

C: I overheard them talkin'. It was at my ten percenter's. They didn't know as I was there. They're goin' to do it for His Majesty at the coronation. They's been plannin' it for a long time, is what it sounded like.

B: Who? Who are they?

C: Why—the Poles. I thought I said so. It's not so far, once you're started. The trick is wearin' of the right hat. You can fool anybody if they see the right hat. And . . . and . . . and it's pointed the wrong way. That's what will fool them, you see. It's pointed the wrong way!

And with these words Albert Chall, master thief, expired. We assume the last sentence or so to be a dying ramble, but as to the rest, we are not sure. We are, of course, doing what we can to ascertain the veracity of his story, but there is small hope of discovering anything beyond his dying words.

The identity of his "ten percenter" is being assiduously pursued. There is some chance of locating that person and interviewing him, and I will, of course, immediately inform you of the results of such an interview. To the best of our information Goodman Chall neither spoke nor understood Polish. If there is any further information we can give you, please inform us post haste.

> Long live His Majesty, John IV.
> In Haste,
> London

The Marquis put the last page of the letter down and looked around. "My lords?" he asked.

Duke Richard stood up, his face white. "Long live His Majesty, my brother John," he said softly.

"Amen," the Archbishop of Paris said firmly.

The six men in the room crossed themselves. "June first, that's the day of the coronation," Duke Richard said. "Barely three weeks away. What can we do?"

"I called you all here to help me decide what is to be done," Marquis Sherrinford told him. "Your Highness because, as the Duke of Normandy, you are responsible for the safety of everyone in the Duchy. Lord Darcy because, as Chief Investigator of the Court of Chivalry, as well as the man overseeing the security arrangements in Castle Cristobel during the coronation, you are, or will be, intimately involved in whatever decisions we make. Your Grace because your advice is valuable, and the assistance of the Church may prove invaluable. Master Sir Darryl Longuert because, as ranking member of the Sorcerers' Guild present, you will have to help us design and implement our, ah, magical defenses, if any.

"I, as the King's Equerry, am, of course, directly responsible for His Majesty's safety. And I can assure you that I take that responsibility very seriously."

"Do you think that this can *possibly* be true?" Duke Richard asked, sitting slowly back down in his chair. "It doesn't make sense!"

"His Highness is right," the Archbishop said. "A threat to His Majesty's life from King Casimir—or any other Pole— makes no apparent sense whatever. Nominally, we are enemies, but actually—I can't believe he'd be so stupid!"

"What do you say, Darcy?" Duke Richard asked. "How does it strike you?"

Lord Darcy paused. He was supposed to know such things, and his answer would be given weight.

For most of the twentieth century the kings of Poland had been interested in expansion. At first they had contented themselves by moving east, bringing one small Baltic state after another under Polish hegemony.

By the mid-thirties King Sigismund III had annexed or controlled most of the territory from Revel on the Baltic to Odessa on the Black Sea. But then the Russian states to the east had formed a loose coalition for the purpose of fielding a vast army against further Polish expansion. And since the Russian coalition included states deep into central Asia, their army could be vast indeed.

So King Casimir IX, Sigismund's son and heir, decided that Western discretion was the better part of Eastern valor, and cast his covetous gaze on the disorganized and fragmented Germanic states that formed a buffer between the Slavonic and Angevin Empires.

While the Poles were expanding to the east, their Angevin majesties had paid little attention. The Imperial Territories of New England and New France on the far side of the Atlantic had taken most of their attention, and were allowing the Angevin Empire to expand as fast as it could responsibly administer its new land and new people. The Russian states, like the rest of Asia, seemed half a world away.

But when the Poles turned their gaze west, they saw their way to the Mediterranean and to the North Sea both blocked by the Anglo-French Empire or its dependents. Not that the Germanic states were really dependent upon the Angevins for anything except stopping the Poles. In theory they owed fealty to the Angevin Emperor as part of the old Holy Roman Empire, but in actuality they had never paid a twelfth-bit of tribute to the Plantagenet kings, and never would. But they did know that, with the Angevin Empire on their west, they could tell King Casimir to go to hell; just as, with the Polish Empire on their east, they could remain as independent as they wished of Angevin influences. It was a balancing act they had become quite good at.

And besides, the German states produced good fighters. Their men served as mercenaries in the Angevin Legion, as well as half the other armies around the world. If Bavaria and Hanover and Hesse and Prussia and all the other little German states could ever stop feuding and get together, the combination would be quite fierce. Nobody would purposely do anything that might encourage such a thing.

But Casimir coveted clear water, which he could not reach. On land, the Germans stood in his way. At sea, the Baltic exit to the Atlantic was closed by the Scandinavian fleet, and the Slavonic navy's exit from the Black Sea was closed at the Sea of Marmara by the Roumelian fleet, both backed up, if necessary by the Angevin Imperial Navy.

Therefore, on land as on sea, King Casimir IX saw himself as ultimately blocked by the Plantagenets and their empire. His response was to create a powerful weapon and put it to work against the Angevins; a weapon which, he thought, would cause the undermining of an empire in the fullness of time. He might not live to see it, but his son Stanislaw, or certainly his grandson Sigismund, would.

This weapon was the *Serka*. A contraction of an expression meaning, roughly, "the King's right arm," the *Serka* was the Polish Secret Police. Owing allegiance only to King Casimir, the highly-trained, highly-dedicated agents of *Amt V*, the *Serka*'s External Division–West, were dedicated to the overthrow of the Plantagenet dynasty and the Angevin Empire.

But against all of this, which seemed to indicate that agents of Casimir IX could well be plotting the death of John IV, there was the overriding question as to why they would do such a thing. The death of John would not bring the wheels of Anglo-French government to a halt. As able as John was, there were other Plantagenets available to take the throne. If Parliament thought either of John's sons too young, or otherwise unsuitable, there was Duke Richard to act either as King or as

Regent. And beyond him, in male and female branch, the Plantagenet tree had many suitable leaves.

And, for any disruption that the death of John might accomplish, there was the counterweighing factor of the danger of discovery. If the death of a reigning Plantagenet could ever be brought directly to the door of the Polish king, it would mean immediate war; a war the Poles could not possibly win.

"I don't see it, Your Highness," Lord Darcy said. "I'm not saying that the dying words of that thief were lies, but that there is either more to the plot that he was unaware of, or he misunderstood what he heard. Plotting the death of Our Beloved Sovereign does not make sense in any way that I can see. Even for the Polish."

"What else could it be?" His Grace the Archbishop asked. "What else could it mean?"

Lord Darcy turned to Lord Peter. "What do you make of it?" he asked.

Marquis Sherrinford raised his hand. "I should explain," he said to the Archbishop, "that Lord Peter, while serving, quite ably, as my private secretary, is also the Lord Commander of His Majesty's Most Secret Service."

"Ah!" Archbishop Maximilian said, turning to Lord Peter. "You are the famous Q, are you? I knew that Grand Master Lord Petrus de Berquehomme was the Chief Sorcerer for the Most Secret Service, but he was most secretive about the identity of his, ah, boss."

"How did you know *that*, Your Grace?" Marquis Sherrinford asked sharply.

The Archbishop of Paris looked faintly embarrassed. "I, ah, was Lord de Berquehomme's confessor for a while when he was in Paris. But, of course, in that capacity I could never have mentioned it. I also, ah, helped develop the spells for the Pearls of Identity. Lord de Berquehomme asked for my assistance because of some theoretical work I had published on the Law of Simularity. It was quite a little problem. It made me feel rather adventurous, I must admit, to be even that close to the Most Secret Service. I trust that I was of help in some minor way."

"Indeed," Lord Peter said. "It is of utmost importance to the Service to have a means of identifying our agents that cannot be forged, cannot be duplicated, and cannot inadvertently give the agent away. You have performed a valuable service indeed. Lord de Berquehomme never told me of your connection with that particular problem."

"At my insistence, I assure you," the Archbishop said. "It was entirely too, ah, trumpery an occupation for an archbishop. Although I admit that I enjoyed the challenge."

"A pretty problem," Sir Darryl said. "I have often admired the, um, result. I'd like to discuss with you sometime how you handled the symbolic referants."

"Delighted," the Archbishop told the wizard. "With Lord Peter's permission, of course."

Lord Peter nodded. "Of course we have no secrets from the Wizard Laureate," he said. But he didn't sound too happy about it.

Sir Darryl laughed. "You're right, of course," he said, replying to Lord Peter's expression rather than his words. "The fewer who know, the less the chance of the wrong person finding out. Your Grace, I withdraw my request."

"Tell me," Duke Richard interrupted, "what is the meaning of the reference to a 'ten percenter'? It is a term I am unfamiliar with."

"It is thieves' argot, Your Highness," Lord Darcy explained. "A ten percenter is a receiver of stolen goods; so-called because he pays out a bit over a twelfth-bit for each sovereign's worth of illicit merchandise, or roughly ten percent of the value."

"I see," said Duke Richard. "So His Slavonic Majesty hires thieves to spy for him. Spying is such a foul business that I am surprised that even a good Angevin thief would stoop to it." He turned to Lord Peter with a sudden realization. "I'm sorry," he said. "I didn't mean to imply—"

"That's all right, Your Highness," Lord Peter said. "It is a common reaction. *Their* spies are dirty, filthy scum, not fit to wipe your boots on, while *our* spies are noble gentlemen doing dangerous work for the love of King and Country. Would that it were so, Your Highness, but I'm afraid that sometimes the desired image is at fault—in both directions."

"What do you think, Lord Peter, about this message?" Lord Darcy asked again.

Lord Peter paused. "I have been giving the matter careful thought for the past few hours, as you can imagine," he said. "And I must admit to the possibility that it is true. I have no evidence that it *is*, mind you. And that is surprising; seldom does anything happen of this magnitude about which we don't pick up at least a ripple. But it is quite possible. King Casimir has made some injudicious decisions in the past. And then there is always the distinct possibility that this is an operation of the *Serka* that the king knows nothing about.''

"You mean we might be facing a 'will no one rid me of this meddlesome priest' sort of syndrome, eh?" Archbishop Maximilian asked.

"Exactly, Your Grace," Lord Peter agreed. "It could well be that some *Serka* official has decided on his own that what his King *really* wants is the death of His Majesty, although he doesn't mention it."

"The question is, what are we to do about it?" Duke Richard asked. "My lord marquis, you are in charge of His Majesty's security. What precautions do you intend to take?"

"I think Lord Darcy and I will have to sit down and discuss possibilities, along with Coronel Lord Waybusch, who is in charge of Castle security," Marquis Sherrinford said. "It is a delicate question, Your Highness. We will have the delegations of over a hundred trade guilds, a few hundred various organizations, and some sixty sovereign and not-so-sovereign states arriving over the next week for the coronation. Including the heir apparent to the throne of His Most Slavonic Majesty, as well as the Polish foreign minister. Of course His Majesty's safety must be held of first importance."

"None of these people will get to see His Majesty except under carefully controlled conditions," Duke Richard said. "Sir Darryl, can we get some sensitives to stand at the doors to the throne room as these people come through? Grab them if they show murderous intent? Would murderous intent be detectible?"

The Wizard Laureate of England thought for a minute. "It's not that simple," he said. "Something can be done, but it won't be that clear-cut unless we're very lucky. You see—"

There was a loud knock at the door, startling the five men in the room. *Reality knocks,* Lord Darcy thought. *And we are not yet ready for reality.*

"Excuse me, my lords," Marquis Sherrinford said. "They wouldn't have allowed anyone to knock unless it were very important. I'd better see what it is."

"Yes, yes," the Archbishop said. "Go ahead."

Marquis Sherrinford opened the door a crack and peered around it. "Yes?"

"Beg pardon, Your Lordship," came a gruff voice from beyond. "But Coronel Lord Waybusch has sent me for Lord Darcy. He's to come at once. Is His Lordship in here?"

"Yes, I'm here, Serjeant Martin," Lord Darcy called, recognizing the Norman-French accent of the Coronel's aide. "What is it?"

Serjeant Martin stepped into the room and stood stiffly at attention. "Beg pardon, my lord," he said. "But it is murder. A foul murder, and also an impossible one."

Lord Darcy stood up. "Where?" he asked. "And who was killed?"

"In the bakery shop of Goodman Bonpierre in Between the Walls, my lord. Master Sorcerer Raimun DePlessis."

"DePlessis?" Sir Darryl rose to his feet involuntarily, as though about to do something. Then, realizing it was too late, he sat back down. "Well, well," he said. "A lovely man. How strange."

"What's that?" The Archbishop of Paris looked startled. "What about Master DePlessis?"

"He was the victim, Your Grace," Serjeant Martin said. "Stabbed through the heart with no weapon in sight, and no way in or out of the building."

"Incredible," the Archbishop said, crossing himself. "I had dinner with him last night. A fine healer. A brilliant theoretician."

"I'm on my way," Lord Darcy said. "Send someone for Master Sean O Lochlainn, and have him meet us there."

"It has already been done, my lord," Serjeant Martin said.

5

THE CONSTRUCTION OF CASTLE Cristobel was a process that had been ongoing since the thirteenth century. The original fortress had been expanded, modified, and rebuilt so many times in the past seven hundred years that, with the exception of the ancient and central Arthur Keep, only a careful perusal of the architectural documents could tell one what was built when.

The massive and well-protected Norman Gate had been designed as the main gate to the Castle. Protected by a wide moat, it faced a gentle slope and was the only gate accessible by carriage. Over the centuries a group of commoners providing services to the Castle had been allowed to build their houses on the slope outside the gate, and a town had grown up. In the sixteenth century the moat had been filled in and a new castle wall had been extended to the bottom of the slope, enclosing the town; which henceforth and thereafter was known only as "Between the Walls."

Now Lord Darcy followed Serjeant Martin through the footway in the Norman Gate and along a series of narrow, twisting streets in that ancient cluster of houses and shops. The rain seemed to have let up for the moment, but the overcast was still complete; and the slate-gray sky cast a feeling of

gloom over the shadowless streets. As they rounded one
corner, turning onto Paternoster Lane, Lord Darcy saw groups
of gossiping shopkeepers gathered in doorways up and down
the narrow street. *Nothing like a murder,* he thought wryly, *to
disrupt the workday.*

A small group of armsmen were clustered in one doorway,
which told Lord Darcy which shop he was headed for even
before he could read the baker's sign swinging above; and the
puffs of light blue smoke he noticed emanating from the
doorway when they approached told him that Master Sean
O Lochlainn had arrived before him and was already hard at
work on the forensic examination of the corpse and the murder
scene.

Coronel Lord Waybusch was standing to one side of the shop
door, looking worried. A stocky man in his early fifties, with a
head of thick, black hair and a wide black mustache, the
Coronel was wearing the gold-and-crimson dress uniform of
the Household Guard, which looked as though it had been
designed particularly to show off his ruggedly masculine good
looks. "Glad you're here, Darcy," he growled, sticking his
large right hand out to be shook. "Job of keeping order in this
damned carnival is going to be quite enough without having
any damned mysteries to solve. Putting you in charge of this, if
you don't mind. If His Majesty approves. Impossible crime;
right up your alley."

"I know none of the details, Coronel," Lord Darcy said.
"Could you fill me in?"

"Damned few details known," Coronel Lord Waybusch
said. "We'll know more, of course, as soon as Master Sean
finishes his preliminary examination. The chirurgeon has seen
the body already. Certified that the chap's dead. As if we
couldn't tell." He looked into the cloud of blue smoke that was
the interior of the shop, and then looked away. "Don't like to
disturb a wizard while he's doing his thing," he said. "Any
man who's an expert at his job should be left alone to do it
without outside interference. Most particularly wizards."

"A prudent philosophy," Lord Darcy agreed. He usually
liked to get a preliminary look at the scene of the crime and the
corpse as soon as possible; but as Master Sean seemed well
under way in his magical tasks, it would be best to wait until he
was done. Interfering with wizardry in progress sometimes had
unexpected and disconcerting effects for all concerned.

"The goodman over there," Coronel Lord Waybusch said, pointing to a quartet of rain-caped commoners standing together nervously in the company of two uniformed armsmen in the doorway of a shop down the street, "the elderly one with the apron, is Master Bonpierre, the baker. It's his shop, and he found the body. He can tell you what there is to be told until Master Sean is finished."

"Thank you, Coronel," Lord Darcy said. "I shall speak with him."

Lord Darcy walked over to the quartet of tradesmen across the street. "Master Bonpierre?" he asked.

The eldest of the four men stepped forward and doffed his oversized white cap. A skinny man with a prominent nose, he was swaddled from neck to knee under his rain cape in a white apron that seemed several sizes too large for him. "Your Lordship," he said. "That would be me. This goodman here is Master Chef Virgil DuCormier, and these are my two journeymen; Paval Skettle and Robert Pitt." He pointed in turn to a short, dark-haired man, who appeared to be in his mid-thirties, and two self-composed, intense men in their late twenties who stood quietly behind him.

Lord Darcy nodded. "I am Lord Darcy, and I shall be investigating the death. I need to ask you some questions," he told them. "I understand that the bakery is your shop and that you found the body. Is that right?"

"Yes," Master Bonpierre agreed hesitantly. "Leastwise, it *is* my shop. As to finding the body, well, we all found it together, as one might say."

"It was horrible!" Journeyman Pitt volunteered. Master Bonpierre turned around and silenced him with a glance. Murders were for masters to discuss, not mere journeymen.

"Tell me about it," Lord Darcy suggested.

Master Bonpierre tipped his head to one side thoughtfully, as though he was composing an epic poem and wanted to get every word right the first time. "It was like this," he said finally. "We arrive at the shop, the three of us, on the minute of two o'clock, by the sounding of the Stephain bell, as is usual. We meet Master DuCormier there, as was arranged, and I unlock the door. But the door, although unlocked, will not open. I am surprised."

"Two o'clock is your usual opening time?" Lord Darcy interrupted.

"For the shop, yes," Master Bonpierre said, looking slightly annoyed that the flow of his narrative had been broken. "I am, as I say, surprised. I think at first that it is sticking because of the weather—rain-swelled, you understand. But it has never done this before, and indeed this is not the case. I push at the door, but to no avail. It does not want to open. This is not usual."

"Why so late?" Lord Darcy asked.

Master Bonpierre sighed. "We do not have our ovens in the back of the shop," he explained. "They are, instead, in a separate bakery built up against the new wall. It is there that we go at four in the morning to make bread. It is there that our dozens are sold; to the Castle kitchens, to the military, to the inns. Then at two we open this shop for the trade, and the 'prentices bring over the stock, and we stay open till the stock is sold or till vespers. Whichever, as you might say, happens soonest."

"There's no oven in this shop?"

"Only a small one for special orders," Master Bonpierre said. "Birthday cakes and such. The large one was converted into a preservator last Michaelmas."

"Why were you meeting Master DuCormier outside the shop?" Lord Darcy asked. "Doesn't he work with you?"

"No," Master Bonpierre said.

"At present I am employed in the Castle kitchen," Master DuCormier said in a thick French accent, stepping forward. "I am a master chef of the cakes and pastries and *des confitures*— the sweetmeats. Also the table decorations I do. I have come especially from Paris for His Highness's coronation. I will be creating the reception cake."

"I see," Lord Darcy said. "And you came here. . . ?"

"To arrange for the vending of *des souvenirs gateaux*—the little cakes to commemorate the occasion."

"Very commendable," Lord Darcy said. "Thank you for clearing that up." He turned back to Master Bonpierre. "Now please go on with your narrative. What happened?"

"Yes, Your Lordship. At two o'clock we arrive at the shop. The door does not open. I push at it immensely, you understand, but it will not budge. Journeyman Skettle, who is a strong fellow, he pushes also upon it. To no avail. What are we to do? the 'prentices will be along at any moment with their panniers full of bread.

"I think of the rear window. . . ." Master Bonpierre paused for the brilliance of this to be appreciated. "It will admit a person. A small person."

"What of the front windows?" Lord Darcy asked.

"They are both barred, Your Lordship. It's a regulation on establishments selling comestibles. Mostly to prevent small children from climbing in at night and damaging themselves, or eating themselves sick."

"Is there no rear door?"

"There is, Your Lordship; but it opens only from the inside. It's double-barred at night, and there isn't even any keyhole."

"But the rear window?"

"It is high up off the ground, and it is only used for ventilation. It is hinged at the bottom, you understand, and opens no more than six inches at the top. In the normal course of events it cannot be opened far enough to allow entrance. But, as these are abnormal events, I have Journeyman Pitt take a brick and smash the glass out. Then we boost him through the window and ourselves go around to the front, so he can let us in."

"The bakery seems to adjoin the buildings on each side," Lord Darcy commented.

"Yes, it does," Master Bonpierre agreed. "There is an alleyway at the back that is accessed from a locked gate around the corner. We did not bother with that today, but asked Goodwife Brewler if we could go through her shop." He indicated the store next to the bakery, which appeared to sell silver, brass, and pewter kitchenware.

Lord Darcy turned to the tall, bony youth. "So you went through the window, Journeyman Pitt?"

Pitt rolled his cap into a ball and screwed up his face in concentration. "I did, Your Lordship," he affirmed. "And I went through to the front room and opened the door. It were the bar what were keeping it closed. I mean it were barred from the inside—like the back door."

"How could that happen?" Lord Darcy asked.

"It couldn't," Master Bonpierre stated. "No way. Not unless it was magicked."

Lord Darcy let that stand and turned back to the journeyman. "Why didn't you open the back door instead of the front?" he asked. "Your master was standing right there; he wouldn't have had to run back to the front."

Pitt scratched his head. "I didn't think of it," he said. "Master told me to open the front door, so open the front door I did."

"And then?"

"And then," Master Bonpierre took over again, and continued his thoughtful description, "I enter the shop. I join in wondering how the front door could have become barred; it is a mystery. Journeyman Skettle opens the shutters on the front windows while I light the lamps. Then the 'prentices arrive with their panniers full of good French bread. I take my rain cape off and go around the counter to prepare to receive the bread. And then . . ."

Master Bonpierre's description slowed to a halt. His eyes widened as, once again, they saw what they had seen an hour before. "And then—on the floor behind the counter—I see . . . him."

"Yes?" Lord Darcy said. "Take your time."

"He is lying there dead—on the floor behind the counter— this overly large man dressed in the robes of a master wizard. There is a surplus of blood on the floor past his head. The floor, you understand, leans that way. He is arranged in death, you know, lying there."

"You mean composed?" Lord Darcy asked. "As though he expected to die, or was ready for it?"

"No, no," Master Bonpierre said. "*Arranged*. As by the undertaker. His feet together. His arms crossed—so—over the great belly. His raiment pulled down and folded neatly about him. It was, somehow, more shocking than if he had just been lying there."

"I see what you mean," Lord Darcy said. "What then?"

"Then I send Journeyman Skettle out for the nearest armsman, I send the 'prentices back to the ovens with the panniers of bread; and we, the rest of us, go outside the shop to wait for him."

"You didn't touch anything in the shop?"

"No, no. Certainly not. Not after the body was found."

"Very thoughtful, thank you," Lord Darcy said. "You know we like to have the scene of a crime left as pristine as possible for our investigations."

Master Bonpierre shuddered slightly. "It was not fore-thought, you understand. It was simply lack of desire. We all wished to be outside the shop while that body was inside it."

"I understand," Lord Darcy said. He looked around at the others. "Tell me, did any of you recognize the corpse? Have any of you ever seen him before?"

There was a murmuring of negatives from the four bakers. None of them had ever seen the corpse in life, to the best of their recollection. And none of them ever wanted to see such a thing again, thank you.

"Thank you all very much for your assistance," Lord Darcy told them. "An armsman will be by sometime later to take full statements from each of you. Please do not let this upset you, it is merely our routine."

Lord Darcy walked through the kitchenware shop, nodding politely to Goodwife Brewler, who made a curtsy so deep that she must have thought that he was at least a royal duke in disguise. The back alley was just that, a back alley. It was narrow, paved, and swept clean. There appeared to be no entrance other than the back doors of the shops on both streets and the gate at the far end. A small table was against one wall, with several chairs around it; where, Lord Darcy guessed, some of the shopkeepers shared cups of caffe and a game of cards on a quiet afternoon.

The back of the baker's shop was as described. There was a door, which had no keyhole and was bolted from the inside, and a window about seven feet off the ground, which had recently had all the glass broken from its frame. On the ground to the left of the door, under the roof overhang, were a stack of old and well-used straw panniers, which had worn out in the baker's service. They were not doing too well in the almost-constant rain.

Lord Darcy contemplated hoisting himself up and peering through the broken window, but decided against it. Whatever there was to see, he could see much better from inside, when Master Sean was ready for him. He returned through the kitchenware shop to the street.

The tubby little forensic sorcerer emerged from the bakery shop about ten minutes later, his cabalistically-marked carpet-bag in hand. Putting it carefully down to the side of the door, he wiped both his hands carefully on a bleached white cotton handkerchief which he pulled from his sleeve. "You can go in now," he told Coronel Lord Waybusch. "I'm done for the nonce. Mind you, don't disturb anything. Be especially careful about the covered brass bowl on the tripod, it's still quite hot."

"I have no interest whatever in going in," Coronel Lord Waybusch said firmly. "I shall leave that to Lord Darcy here. No point in my mucking around when I have the services of two such experts as yourselves."

"Ah, Your Lordship," Master Sean said, turning to face Lord Darcy. "I didn't see you standing there. Would you like to see what there is to be seen?"

"I would indeed," Lord Darcy said. "I have been admirably patient, Master Sean, and kept out of the shop while you were busy. Now let us go in together and I shall look things over while you tell me what happened."

"As I've told you before, my lord, I am but a magician, not a miracle worker," Master Sean said. "I may be able to give you a few indications as to what took place, but don't expect a lot of detail. Forensic sorcery needs facts to work on; and when the facts aren't there, the greatest magic in the world cannot create them."

"All that I ask, my dear Master Sean, are the facts you *have* assembled and any logical surmises you can make from them," Lord Darcy said, peering into the doorway. "How long will it take for this smoke to clear?"

"Oh, yes," Master Sean said. "Sorry about that." He took a small silver wand from the leather pouch at his waist. "If you'd stand aside for an instant, my lord . . ." He stood in the doorway, legs planted firmly in a position of power, and felt the air in the room with his left hand as though there were an invisible handle somewhere just within his grasp. Then, with the wand in his right hand, he drew some small circles in the air and muttered a set of unintelligible phrases.

There was a low, prolonged crackling noise, which went on for about twenty seconds, and the room was clear of smoke.

"Excellent, Master Sean," Lord Darcy said.

"Elementary, my lord," Master Sean replied, a broad smile creasing his chubby face.

"Well, then," Lord Darcy said, rubbing his hands together, "let's see what there is to be seen." He stepped into the room and turned slowly around, observing and categorizing, getting the feel of this space that now enclosed a murdered man. "What are your findings, Master Sean?" he asked.

Master Sean stooped over to touch his tripod-supported bowl, and decided it was still too hot to put away. " 'Tis a shame," he said. "Lying there on that wooden floor is the mortal remains of Master Raimun DePlessis, a true gentleman, and one of the finest theoretical thaumaturgists of our time."

"A friend?" Lord Darcy asked sympathetically.

"A casual friend," Master Sean said. "But a friend all the same. We would meet at the occasional sorcerers' convention. We dined together, and sat and talked many times. We appeared together on a panel once. He was a healer, you know. Most of his theoretical work was on the healing art. He will be missed."

Lord Darcy patted Master Sean on the shoulder. "And his killer will be punished," he said. "We'd better put our minds to that part of it. What did you find?"

"Aye, my lord, you're right," Master Sean said. He took a small notepad from his cloak. "The victim was killed by an upward thrust to the heart by a blade of small cross-section. It penetrated between the third and fourth ribs, and was certainly fatal. Death occurred within a couple of minutes of the wound. There were no other indications of violence on the body or in the room."

Lord Darcy walked over to the counter and looked down at the large body lying behind it. Someone, presumably the murderer, had spent some time and effort straightening the body itself and its clothing, until it looked as if it was laid out for burial. Going around, Lord Darcy knelt down at the foot of the body to take a closer look. "Master DePlessis was a very large man," he said. "And he has left a very large corpse. There isn't much space here between the counter and the wall; whoever arranged the body must have been acting under a powerful compulsion. Were you able to get everything you need in this confined space?"

"Actually, my lord, I raised the body to the countertop— after I put the preservation spell on it, of course. I returned it when I was done so that you can see exactly how he was found. I never know what Your Lordship is going to find pertinent to an investigation."

"Very thoughtful of you, Master Sean," Lord Darcy said. "But I've seen everything I can down here. Help me move the body back to the countertop."

"That won't be necessary, my lord," Master Sean said. "Just stand away for a second."

Lord Darcy moved back and watched as, with a few gestures, Master Sean floated the body from its spot on the floor to the wooden top of the counter, which groaned slightly as the heavy corpse settled onto it.

"I didn't know you could do that so simply, Master Sean," Lord Darcy said. "I thought levitations were a more complex procedure."

"Oh, they are, my lord," Master Sean affirmed. "But when I did it the first time, I built in a tendency to repeat. The spell is worn out now, and it will take either another spell or two strong men to move Master DePlessis to his next resting place."

Lord Darcy examined the body. "Stabbed through the heart, you say?" He opened the sorcerer's cloak and saw that the puncture went through the gold-trimmed light blue sorcerer's gown, which was soaked with blood. The area where the corpse's head had been showed a small pool of blood, not quite congealed. Of course, it had stopped congealing when Master Sean had put the preservation spell on the body. No further biological action would take place until the spell was removed.

"Not too much blood," Lord Darcy commented. "Of course, if he died within a minute or two, then the heart didn't have much time to pump blood through the wound." Lord Darcy tried to move one of the crossed arms, but it resisted his pull and snapped back into place. "Hmm, rigor is setting in. How long ago would you say it happened?"

"Between three and three and a half hours before I performed the tests, my lord," Master Sean said. "Which was about a half hour ago. Let us say that Master DePlessis died between eleven-thirty and twelve o'clock."

"Good, let us say that," Lord Darcy agreed. "Here—what's this?" He pried open the corpse's hand and worked loose a folded piece of paper that had been concealed in the loosely-made, but now tight-as-iron fist. "Did you notice this?"

"Yes, my lord, but I left it for you," Master Sean replied. "I felt that it was more in your province than mine."

"You figured correctly, Master Sean. Thank you for your forbearance. Let's see." Lord Darcy unfolded the paper and held it up to the light of the nearest lamp. "A stiff, yellowish paper, about four by six inches. Torn from something on two sides, but neatly. Probably with a straightedge."

"Yes, Your Lordship, but what does it *say*?" Master Sean demanded.

"Ah, I can see that you really did exercise self-control in not removing this from Master DePlessis's hand before I got here," Lord Darcy commented. "Let me see. Broad-nibbed pen. Steel point. Printed rather than written. What a shame, handwriting is so much more suggestive of character. Our murderer gave us something here, but is it enough?"

"Is it from the murderer, then?"

"I believe so. Certainly."

"Then, my lord, what—"

"Here," Lord Darcy said. "Read it yourself."

Master Sean O Lochlainn took the yellowish paper rectangle and moved over to the window.

"It's a rhyme," he said. "A children's rhyme."

"It is a hellish message," Lord Darcy said, staring out the window at the gray sky. "It frightens me."

Master Sean read it to himself:

Ten little wizards sat down to dine
One wizard stuffed his face—and now there are nine.

6

"IT CAN BE UNDERSTOOD in several ways," the Archbishop of Paris said, thoughtfully rubbing the scrap of paper in his right hand between his thumb and forefinger. "As a pronouncement, as a challenge, as a threat, as a warning; even merely as a comment. A 'look how clever I am' sort of thing." He smoothed it out on the table and passed it back to Lord Darcy. "But at any rate, I think you're quite right, Darcy; whoever did that is dangerously insane. That, however, is my opinion as a worried human being, and a not particularly skilled, second-hand judge of character, not as a cleric and a sensitive. As a sensitive, I get nothing useful from that paper."

They were meeting at ten in the evening in the private study of Duke Richard's suite in the private quarter of the castle. A severely plain and functional room, uncluttered with any decoration save for a shield blazoned with the coat of arms of Normandy on the far wall and a recent portrait of His Majesty between the recessed windows on the near wall; it showed clearly that the Duke of Normandy wished to be thought of as a serious-minded man. As, indeed, he was.

Duke Richard, his lean, bearded face creased with worry, sat in a heavy, solid, unadorned Geoffrey II wooden chair behind its companion Geoffrey II table, which had been on that spot since it was placed there for the use of an old, stout, rheumatic Geoffrey II some three hundred years before. Matching chairs were drawn up around the table in front of him, holding the same assemblage that had gathered before in the Map Room, with the addition of Master Sean O Lochlainn and Coronel Lord Waybusch. The group formed what Marquis Sherrinford was pleased to call an "Extra-Ordinary Council for the King's Safety."

"Why 'ten little Wizards,'" Duke Richard wanted to know.

"Perhaps he just liked the rhyme, Your Highness," Lord Darcy suggested. "Or perhaps he has a grudge against nine other sorcerers. At any rate, the verse is taken from an old children's rhyme."

"Really?" Duke Richard asked, turning his somber gaze on Lord Darcy. "I don't think I know it."

"It's very English, Your Highness," Lord Darcy explained. "The original refers to 'ten little Skreymen.' The English firmly believe that people from the Isle of Skrey are—I suppose the best word is 'foolish.'"

Coronel Lord Waybusch nodded. "I remember," he said. "A nursery rhyme. Haven't thought of it for years. It went something like this:

"Ten little Skreymen bought a cask of Skreyish wine,
    One fell in, splash, and then there were nine.
Nine little Skreymen swinging on a Skreyish gate,
    One fell off, plop, and then there were eight."

"Ah, I see," Duke Richard said. "It's an enumeration to the vanishing point. Do you remember the rest of it, Coronel?"

"I think so, Your Highness, although it's been a long time." Coronel Lord Waybusch pursed his lips thoughtfully.

"Eight little Skreymen baking with a Skreyish oven,
    One shoveled coal in, crack, and then there were seven.
Seven little Skreymen fighting with their Skreyish sticks,
    One put a point on, ping, and then there were six.
Six little Skreymen . . .
    "Ah, let me see . . ."

The Coronel faltered, and Lord Peter Whiss picked up the recitation:

"Six little Skreymen setting out their Skreyish hive,
One called the queen names, buzz, and then there were five.
Five little Skreymen—"

"Enough, enough—I think we get the point," Duke Richard said, waving a hand at Lord Peter. "A sort of seriation of disaster. In this context one would suppose that it must be taken as an implicit threat. Thank you, Lord Peter."

"I don't suppose that we can conclude that the assailant of poor Master Raimun is an Englishman?" the Archbishop of Paris asked. "Not that it would help us very much if we could."

"On the basis of his knowing the rhyme, you mean, Your Grace?" Marquis Sherrinford asked. "I don't think so. I knew it myself, and I grew up in Brittany."

"Can we conclude that this killing is or is not related to the threat to His Majesty's life?" Duke Richard asked.

"I'm afraid not, Your Highness," Lord Darcy said. "We can conclude very little from the evidence we have so far."

"Beyond the fact," Sir Darryl said dryly, "that the killer, whoever he is, seems to have a well-developed dislike for sorcerers."

Duke Richard stood up and moved around to close the heavy drapes that framed the two windows. A royal duke did not usually close his own drapes; a push of the call button at his feet would have produced a servant in very few seconds. But it was something to do—and at that moment he needed something to do. He turned back to the group and gripped the back of his chair. "That's what I was afraid of," he said, staring at them somberly. "Let us review the precautions that are being taken to safeguard His Majesty's life. Please feel free to comment on another's remarks; this is not the time to stand on ceremony."

Marquis Sherrinford leaned forward. "I suppose I should begin," he said. "I have the responsibility of seeing to His Majesty's physical safety from moment to moment—at the best of times a difficult task. His Majesty is not the sort of man who can be managed, but we do our best. We are closing off the royal apartments to everyone who has no need to be there. Every person entering has to be personally known to the guard and, if not a member of the royal family, must know the day's password. I'm afraid they all think it's rather silly, particularly since we are not telling them what it is for, but I can't help that. The avoidance spells at all the doors are being strengthened."

"That is so," Archbishop Maximilian said. "One of the best lock-and-key men in the sorcery business is here for the coronation. He happens to be the Papal Envoy, His Eminence, Cardinal Sabatini. Privacy and avoidance spells are his avocation."

"And very good he is at it," Master Sean agreed. "With his spells on the doors, those with no business in the royal apartments won't even realize that they're passing the doors."

Sir Darryl nodded his agreement. "A pleasure to watch him work, Your Highness. Deft, sure touch. Simple, elegant spells. The better someone knows his subject, the easier he makes it look to outsiders. High technical skill indeed."

"Unfortunately," Marquis Sherrinford said, "we have no way to assess the technical skills of our adversary. We must do more."

Coronel Lord Waybusch coughed. "I have drawn up a plan," he said, "with the assistance of Lord Peter Whiss and Lord Darcy, and the advice of Sir Darryl Longuert, for the increased physical security and policing of the entire Castle Cristobel inner area." He pulled a rolled-up paper from his boot and unrolled it on the table. "Now you understand, Your Highness, that this, of itself, cannot capture the, ah, Polish agent. It can, however, make it damned difficult for him to wander about.

"This map of Castle Cristobel shows the revised plan. The Castle is, as you can see, actually made up of three 'castles,' interconnected and surrounded by a common great wall. The Arthur Keep, the oldest, contains the private quarter we are in, as well as the throne room, the ballroom, and most of the administrative offices. This has seven entrances, four of which can be closed off, and the other three guarded. We are also instituting a roving guard everywhere except the royal suites themselves.

"Now the throne room itself is an unlikely point of attack, as Lord Darcy and Sir Darryl agree, but we are not taking any chances. As you can see by the map, the throne room can be entered by four doors, one in each wall. There are the Gallery of Kings and the Gallery of Queens on the sides, and the Great Hall in front, through the Doors of State. To the rear, there is a small door that connects to a private corridor. To the left it goes to an inner stair up to the royal quarters, and to the right it leads into what is now the Lord Chamberlain's offices. Right across the corridor from the throne room is this door, which leads to a small antechamber and then to the ballroom.''

Everyone leaned over the map and examined it with interest. Here was a tangible thing to look at, to make them feel that something was being accomplished. *Everything's under control,* Lord Darcy said wryly to himself, *we have a map*.

"This area is being closed off completely," Coronel Lord Waybusch continued, indicating the corridor in back of the throne room. "The door to the Lord Chamberlain's office will be sealed."

"But His Majesty uses that passage to go to the throne room from his apartments," Marquis Sherrinford objected.

"Special triplex locks are being put into the doors from the throne room and the ballroom. The locks will only open to three keys, and the keys are tuned—is that the right word, Sir Darryl?—tuned to the individuals holding them."

"That's right," Sir Darryl said. "A spell of relevancy ties in the three, do you see? The person, the key, and the lock must all agree, or it won't work and the door won't open. A very time-consuming and expensive spell to put into operation, but very effective. Only the three people with tuned keys can open the locks, and no new keys can be created."

"Absolutely positive, Sir Darryl?" His Highness asked.

"Absolutely? No, Your Highness, not absolutely. Anything the mind of one man can create the mind of another man can unravel. But there are very few sorcerers who could do it—I can only think of six—and it would take even the best of them quite a long time."

"How long?" Marquis Sherrinford asked.

"Say half a day or longer," Sir Darryl replied.

"That's good enough," His Highness agreed. "And who gets these keys?"

"His Majesty the King, Her Majesty the Queen, and Marquis Sherrinford here," Coronel Lord Waybusch said.

"Go on," His Highness directed.

"Yes. Well, the Kings and Queens galleries are constantly guarded. Formerly there were three guards in the galleries at all times, now we have upped it to six. And these are all hand-picked men, with orders not to let anyone through who hasn't a daily pass, which will be given out at the Lord Chamberlain's office. And that means *anyone*, even Your Highness. Of course, your pass will be brought to you each morning."

"Me?" Duke Richard looked startled, "But—"

"That is to allow for impersonation, Your Highness," Lord Darcy interjected smoothly. After all, the guards can't be expected to know Your Highness's appearance well enough to be sure that you are really you, if you see what I mean."

Duke Richard nodded. "Very good thinking. If any guard fails to ask me for my pass, I will personally have him patrolling the moat every night for the next month. What else?"

"The Great Hall entrance to the throne room presents the most problems," Coronel Lord Waybusch said. "It can't be closed off. But it can be controlled. Luckily there is a guardroom to the right of the Doors of State. A company of guards will be based there from now on. Nobody will get in or out those doors who hasn't been personally checked by a captain of the guard. Presumably if they've earned their captain's fleurs-de-lis, they're intelligent enough to handle the job. Any who aren't will be removed."

The map kept trying to roll up as Coronel Lord Waybusch talked, so he reached into a pouch at his belt and pulled out a pair of gold parallelepipeds about an inch and a half square and three inches high, which he used to weight down its far corners.

"Now the second castle . . ." Coronel Lord Waybusch paused while Duke Richard reached curiously for one of the odd rectilinear objects and picked it up to examine it.

"They are traveling salt and pepper shakers, Your Highness," Coronel Lord Waybusch explained, looking faintly embarrassed. "Twisting the top reveals the holes. Gifts of my lady wife. She seems to have a horror of my being stuck in the field without condiments."

"I see," Duke Richard said, twisting the top of the one he was holding several times, and then replacing the object. "Very clever. Do go on."

"Now the second castle, the so-called White Chateau, is not properly a castle at all. Built, as it was, within the walls that existed at that time, it was never meant to be fortified. In case of attack, it would be abandoned and its residents evacuated to the Arthur Keep. It is where most of our honored guests are staying, or are going to stay, for the coronation. It can, and I am told it will, hold over two thousand people in comfort. The main building has over four hundred rooms, and the two els have over two hundred fifty each. There are thirty-two exits, in all directions."

"Hard to guard," Marquis Sherrinford said.

"True," Coronel Lord Waybusch agreed. "And also, luckily, unnecessary. As Lord Peter has pointed out, the White Chateau does not connect with the Arthur Castle directly, and His Majesty has no call to go to the White Chateau. We are placing increased guards about, but mainly to report anything of a suspicious nature that occurs.

"Now the third, Great Cristobel, is the most recent—which still makes it over four hundred years old—and is more like what I think of as a castle. Several great halls, a grainery, troop quarters downstairs, servants' quarters upstairs, and with only six entrances to the whole place. Easily guarded, easy to check who goes in and out, and also quite pointless. But we shall do it, nonetheless. Even Between the Walls shall have both roving and stationary guard points.

"The internal guardposts have been set up so that a roving guard will pass each stationary post at least every quarter hour of the night. Very mundane, very ordinary, but it's what gets the job done." Coronel Lord Waybusch took his gold shakers back, and the map rolled closed with a snap. He stuffed it back into his boot. "I don't say it's perfect," he said. "I'll be damned glad of suggestions or criticisms."

"We should eliminate burglary and reduce petty theft to the vanishing point," Marquis Sherrinford said, "but I don't know how much good this will do in protecting His Majesty."

"Nor do I," Coronel Lord Waybusch agreed. "When you have a better idea, let me know. There will be close to six thousand people here for the next few weeks; an unmatched forest for our lone tree to hide in. Particularly since we cannot, as yet, call it by name. Give me something more to go on, and I swear to you that I will find someplace to go."

"Now I return to where we began," Marquis Sherrinford said. "Perhaps the unfortunate death of Master Sorcerer Raimun DePlessis is somehow related to the threat to our sovereign. At any rate, we must keep that possibility in mind."

"I assure you we are, my lord marquis," Lord Darcy said.

"Just what do we know about the murder so far?" Duke

Richard asked. "Aside from the fact that the murderer is a rhymester?"

"Master Sean," Lord Darcy said, "if you would be good enough to give His Highness a forensic report, I'll add what I can to it when you're done."

Master Sean O Lochlainn pushed himself out of his chair at the left end of the table and stood, his hands holding the lapels of his blue-and-gold sorcerer's robe, facing the others. "Your Highness, Your Lordships," he said, "I won't bother you with the technical data unless you want it—the various spells I used, and such. All standard, I can assure you.

"Master Sorcerer Raimun DePlessis died between eleven-thirty and noon today. He was killed by a penetrating blow to the heart from a narrow-bladed weapon, which was not found. At the time of his death there was one other person in the room with him, whom we must assume was the murderer. He almost certainly knew his assailant, and despite the fact that the room was locked from the inside, with both doors and windows either barred from the inside or unopenable, neither black magic nor white was used to accomplish the crime. There was a pool of blood on the floor by the body, which was shown by simularity tests to be Master Raimun's own blood. Unfortunate, but as Lord Darcy said, it would have been too much to hope that the murderer, while stabbing Master Raimun, would accidently cut himself."

"Have you any explanation for the locked doors, Master Sean?" Marquis Sherrinford asked.

"I have not, my lord," Master Sean told him. "Except that it was not done by magic. And, that being so, it is in Lord Darcy's province to solve that problem, not mine."

"Is there anything else, Master Sean?" Duke Richard asked.

"There was one other thing of note, Your Highness, but I cannot honestly say that I know what it means."

"Yes?"

Master Sean paused to pick his words carefully. "I performed a hologramic spell on the room, to find traces of whoever was in the room during or since the crime." He turned to Sir Darryl and His Grace of Paris. "It was the double-fringe moiré test, using sandalwood, finely-divided charcoal, and myrrh; are you familiar with it, Sir Darryl? Your Grace?"

"I have used a variant of it for, ah, less serious purposes," Sir Darryl said. "A Wizard Laureate spends a large part of his time devising entertainments, and this lends itself to a certain impressive sort of divination. All quite good-hearted, I assure you. Do you know the method, Your Grace? It's quite showy."

"I've read of it in the literature," Archbishop Maximilian answered. "I'm sorry I missed a chance to see it done. I thought it required two sorcerers."

"Yes, that's right," Sir Darryl said, looking bemused.

"It is a lot easier with an assistant, but it can be done alone. You have to be careful to—well, I'll go into it later with Your Grace and Sir Darryl, if you like. In the meantime . . ."

Master Sean turned back to the others. "I don't want to color my facts with my suppositions," he said. "My facts are the result of good, reliable magic. My suppositions are just that—suppositions—and may be totally wrong."

"And what are these facts?" Duke Richard asked.

"The man who was in the room with Master Raimun when he was killed, the man we must suppose is the killer—showed up only slightly on the hologram. He did not make much of a psychic impression on the room—on his surroundings. That is the fact. It was as though he was only partially there. What that means, I cannot tell you."

"Perhaps the man was only there for a brief time," Marquis Sherrinford suggested.

"No, my lord," Master Sean said. "I am not making myself clear, but then it is not a clear concept to grasp hold of. This person was in that room for about half an hour. I know I have been saying 'man,' but I shouldn't have. There is no indication of the gender of the person. But in some way I cannot explain, it wasn't a whole person. The psychic afterimage of this person did not show up nearly as strongly, as clearly, as it should have."

"Come now, this is very interesting," Lord Darcy said. "If I were to ask you for your supposition, Master Sean—with the understanding that it may be totally inaccurate, but just to get a better feel of what you are trying to describe—what would you say? How would you categorize what you saw?"

"My lord, I am not a superstitious man," Master Sean said. "Being a sorcerer leaves little room for superstition. A superstitious magician is unable to manipulate symbols properly, and symbolism is a large part of magic. But with that said—my lord, if I had to characterize the impressions of the other person who was in that room with Master Raimun, I'd say it was a ghost!"

The Archbishop of Paris crossed himself. "Remember,

Master Sean, that there are supernatural happenings that are regarded by the Church as valid experiences. And there are supernatural beings that are regarded as real."

"Of course, Your Grace," Master Sean said. "I'd not be talking about any such. I've never had the experience myself of running across any of them, and I can't say that I'd care to; but a true supernatural being would probably show up even stronger on a hologram than would a mortal. It is the essence of life spirit that is detected, not physical bulk."

"I don't care whether Master Raimun was stabbed by a ghost or by a gazelle," Duke Richard said, slapping his hand down on the hardwood table. "What I want to know is whether it is related to the threat to His Majesty."

"As to that, I cannot say, Your Highness," Master Sean replied. "I wish I could. There was none of the characteristic residual miasma of evil one might expect in such a case; but then, in most cases evil is a matter of intent. It could be that a Polish agent would be so free of evil intent in his own mind, even while committing murder, that no evil intent would be projected."

"What do you think, Lord Darcy?" Duke Richard asked.

"I wish I could say," Lord Darcy replied. "I can't see any relationship at the moment, but we know so little about the threat, and so little about the murder, that I dare not even venture a guess. In either case we cannot relax our vigilance. I confess that I don't know which would be more worrying news: that we were involved with a single assassin who has killed Master Raimun as part of some obscure plot to get His Majesty, or that we have both a killer and an assassin on our hands simultaneously."

Duke Richard stood up, the impassive expression on his finely chiseled face almost concealing the deep worry beneath. "I have spoken to my brother about this," he said. "His Majesty bade me inform you that he knows that the safety of the realm could not be in better hands. I will now leave this to you. Please keep me informed. You have carte blanche on the goods, the treasury, and the personnel of the Duchy."

The others stood as His Royal Highness of Normandy left the room by the side door.

"Ha, hum," Coronel Lord Waybusch said as they all seated themselves. "Carte blanche, eh? Would that I could think of something useful to spend it on. Guards we have, as many as we can find places to put them. Beyond that I'll be damned if I know what we could or should do. You can't fight an enemy that isn't there. As far as the murder goes, that's in Lord Darcy's and Master Sean's capable hands; and I, for one, am damned happy to leave it there. If it can be solved, they will solve it. As far as the threat to His Majesty's life goes, that's all it is so far—a threat. With nothing tangible to sink our teeth into, there isn't much my people can do."

"We appreciate your confidence, Coronel," Lord Darcy said. "Master Sean and I will do our best to earn it."

The Archbishop nodded. "Even if it should turn out that poor Master Raimun's death has nothing to do with the plot against our King, we must not let it get lost. He was a good and worthy man; and even were he not, we must not allow any person to measure the worth of another's life by ending it."

"'For the death of any one diminishes us all,'" Lord Darcy quoted.

"Indeed," Archbishop Maximilian said. "Saint Simon spoke an eternal truth."

"It is the second time today that I have thought of that quote," Lord Darcy said.

Marquis Sherrinford coughed. "Let us not get too far afield in this discussion," he said. "We have two paramount duties before us; first, to protect the King, and second, to solve a dastardly murder. But no matter how dastardly the murder, the duty of protecting His Majesty must come first. Both because he is the King, and because he is alive. Our duty must be toward the living, when it comes in conflict with what we owe the dead."

"That is so," Lord Darcy agreed. "But we are not sure there is a conflict. It may be that it is to the interest of the living that we examine this violent and unexpected death. I have sworn an oath, as have we all, to defend and protect King John, and I intend to live up to that oath. But I have also a duty to investigate unnatural death. The fabric of society is not so tightly raveled that a cut thread does not threaten the pattern. And an unsolved murder is a cut thread which must be tied off."

"I did not mean to suggest otherwise, my lord," Marquis Sherrinford said. "Although I might not have put it so, ah, eloquently."

"What *are* we doing now?" Coronel Lord Waybusch asked.

"I mean, aside from myself and my men. What steps are we taking to find out how serious this threat to His Majesty is?"

Marquis Sherrinford turned to Lord Peter Whiss. "I think, Q, that you had better answer that."

"I would that I had a good answer," Lord Peter said. "This cursed rain will slow up both query and response. My couriers have gone out in all directions. I have been on the teleson all afternoon, but the extensive flooding has temporarily wiped out many of the teleson connections. You know the device will not work over water."

"Running water, Lord Peter," the Archbishop of Paris interrupted.

"I assure Your Grace that this water is running," Lord Peter said. "At the moment all I can tell you is that my agents have been—or are being—alerted; and that this must take top priority. The few reports I have been able to get are all negative. Which means to say that nobody knows anything. Nary a whisper. This is probably a good sign, since it is hard to believe that an operation of this importance would be mounted without word of it having gotten out."

"Perhaps nobody knows of it save those who are doing it," Marquis Sherrinford suggested. "We, surely, would not advertise such a project, were we to embark on it."

Lord Peter ran his hand through his hair. "Let us look at that, my lord," he said. "If we decided, for whatever reason, to assassinate the King of Poland, who would know?"

"Assuming you were to undertake such a morally repugnant act," His Grace of Paris said, "I would assume that as few people as possible would be told."

"Well," Lord Peter said, "if the idea originated in my department, certainly I would have to be told. And, I assume, that in any of the other intelligence services the same would apply. Then I, of course, after being convinced that it is a good idea, would still not take the responsibility for such an act on myself. I would discuss it with my immediate superior, the King's Equerry."

Marquis Sherrinford nodded. "You'd certainly better," he said.

"And would you approve it on your own, my lord?" Lord Peter asked.

"Not a chance," Marquis Sherrinford said. "I would disapprove it on my own; but if I thought it was a good idea, which I cannot imagine, I would still have to take it up with His Majesty."

"Exactly," Lord Peter said. "And His Majesty would discuss it with the Privy Council; and with the Lords Military, and probably the Lords of the Admiralty, and each of the councilors and lords would discuss it, in the utmost secrecy, with his staff and advisors, and the ripples would spread. And it would be overheard by servants, by innkeepers, by companions, by casual acquaintances. And it's much too exciting a secret not to be retold—in the utmost confidence, of course. And by the time it reaches that third level, five different Polish spies will have heard different parts of it, and relayed word back to their spy masters in Poland."

"What are you telling us?" Coronel Lord Waybusch asked. "That a Polish plot against King John is unlikely because you would have heard of it?"

Lord Peter smiled ruefully. "That is what I would like to be telling you, Coronel," he said. "My assumption would be that I should have heard of at least some fragment of the plan through my agents-in-place. But I can't be sure that it is so. Perhaps one crazy Slav is doing this without His Slavonic Majesty's knowledge—or perhaps five or six. Just enough to keep a secret."

"How would you find them, then?" Marquis Sherrinford asked.

"We will recognize them by the signs they leave," Lord Peter said. "Like searching forest trails for the spoor of some rare wild game. I and my agents will look outside the castle, outside the Duchy of Normandy, outside of France, and outside the Angevin Empire, in ever-widening circles; and Lord Darcy and his men will look inside. By their works we shall know them. Always assuming that they exist."

"And if not?" the Archbishop asked.

"If, as I sincerely pray, not, we then shall regard it as a training exercise. Right, Lord Darcy?"

Lord Darcy nodded. "It is difficult to look for something that you hope doesn't exist," he said. "I suppose we can all use the practice." He turned to Coronel Lord Waybusch. "With your permission, my lord coronel, I propose to go to the village of Tournadotte tomorrow, taking Master Sean with me. We shall probably only be gone overnight."

"You don't need my permission, my lord," Lord Waybusch

said. "But I cannot forbear commenting that it seems like a damn strange time to go visiting villages."

"There was a double murder in the village," Lord Darcy explained. "I don't know whether there is any connection, but the coincidence seems noteworthy to me."

"A bit farfetched, I'd say, my lord," Marquis Sherrinford said. "There must be a murder a day throughout the Angevin Empire, with no relation to any Polish plot. But I suppose you know your business."

"If you'll excuse my saying so, Your Lordship, much of what Lord Darcy does seems farfetched when he does it," Master Sean said. "But it somehow never turns out that way. He seems to have a talent for jumping from an unwarranted assumption to a foregone conclusion without touching any of the ground between. I'd listen to him."

"I stand—sit—corrected," Marquis Sherrinford replied, nodding to Master Sean. "When a sorcerer tells me to listen, I listen." He stood up. "Let us adjourn this meeting until such time as we have something more to tell each other. Your Grace, as we didn't have a prayer to start this meeting, perhaps it would be appropriate to end it with a benediction."

The Archbishop of Paris rose, and the others with him. "We are humble in Thy sight, oh Lord," the Archbishop said in a firm, conversational voice, as of one speaking to an old friend. "And we beseech Thee to give us to see the light, so that we may know the truth regarding this vile plot and may best defend our Glorious Sovereign John the Fourth against unseen enemies. Amen."

"Amen," the others in the room echoed.

7

CASTLE CRISTOBEL STATION, A regular stop on the Paris-Le
Havre line of the *Continental and Southern,* was about a
quarter mile outside the main gate of Castle Cristobel. While
the utility of high, thick stone walls as a defense was
dwindling, what with the introduction of cannon that could
hurl a thousand-pound projectile five miles, still no one in
authority could quite bring himself to authorize cutting holes in
the Castle wall big enough to drive a locomotive through.

At six-thirty in the morning Lord Darcy passed his suitcase
up to the driver of the Castle hackney and then, rain cape
buttoned up to the neck and clutching his traveling case, his
walking stick, and his rain hat—the wide-brimmed, flat-top
sort called a "Londoner" in France, but a "skimmer" in
London—he climbed into the waiting vehicle for the short trip
to the station. Master Sean, his plaid rain cloak gathered
around him with the hood drawn over his head, scrambled up
and, putting his symbol-decorated carpetbag on the floor
between them, settled into the seat opposite.

"Sorry to drag you out for such a short trip at this hour,
Edwards," Lord Darcy called up to the driver, who could be
seen adjusting his rain slicker through the open trap.

"A pleasure serving you, my lord," Edwards called back

down. "I'd have been going to meet the train anyway. What with His Highness's coronation creeping up on us, the guests are still arriving by the trainload. And a lot of *them* wouldn't walk the quarter mile to the Castle gate, even if it weren't raining. Which it is. Won't be too bad this morning, though. There's only one first-class car on the morning train on Tuesdays and Thursdays. *They* won't travel naught but first class." He slammed the trap down and guided his horse out through the covered carriage yard, through the main gate, and down the short road to the station.

"I believe we've just been complimented, Master Sean," Lord Darcy told his tubby traveling companion. "Goodman Edwards feels that we are not too good to travel second class. We must not disappoint him."

"It's all one with me, my lord," Master Sean said. "On a longer trip I like the leg room of first class, and having the use of a club car has certain advantages for one who'd like an occasional glass of good Norman beer to keep from drying out. But for a journey of under three hours, a second-class carriage is quite suitable."

"Ah, my old friend," Lord Darcy said, folding his hands around the gold handle of his walking stick and leaning forward, "there's more leg room in first class, to be sure, but there's more poetry in second class—and more honesty in third. Well, here we are." He pulled the Londoner squarely onto his head and, opening the hackney door, stepped out into the steady downpour. "Thank you, Edwards," he called up to the driver. "I'll take care of you when I get back."

"No need of that, my lord," Edwards said, touching his whip to his hood and ignoring the rivulets of rain washing down his face. "But thanks to ye all the same." He handed down Lord Darcy's leather traveling bag to him with a practiced flip, and Master Sean's right after. As soon as Master Sean had descended and slammed the door, Edwards moved the carriage off to the waiting area by the side of the building, where there were already waiting two other Castle hackneys and a fine private coach.

Lord Darcy and Master Sean entered the station, and Lord Darcy went to the window to purchase tickets to Tournadotte. The stationmaster himself was on duty, as it was too early for any of his clerks to arrive. He was a gaunt, clean-shaven, elderly man who had to stoop down slightly to get through doorways. The blue-and-gold uniform hung from his shoulders as though it were a giant's hand-me-down. "If ye'd like a little something to break yer fast, my lord," he told Lord Darcy, "ye and yer companion might as well settle into the restaurant for a spell. Yer train is going to be a bit late."

"I didn't think the restaurant would be open so early," Lord Darcy said. "Just how late is the train?"

"We've opened the restaurant early for the Le Havre-Paris Express, which is making a special stop here all this month on account of the coronation. It was due here over an hour ago, but the Good Lord only knows when it will arrive. The Eure and the Seine have both overflowed their banks west of here, and the whole valley is turning into a lake. It doesn't stop the trains, of course; the water's only a foot or two deep at the worst, and the roadbeds are all raised. But it does slow them down something awful. They have to keep an eye out for washouts, ye see.

"As to yer train, the local to Le Havre, Yer Lordship, it won't be much more than an hour late, as it's going in the other direction. But I can't speak for the express. It's bad business. Trains are supposed to run on time." And with that article of faith stated, he nodded dolefully to Lord Darcy and moved off.

Lord Darcy and Master Sean went into the small, deserted restaurant attached to the waiting room, and the young attendant brought them over a basket of newly baked rolls, a tub of fresh butter, and cups of steaming hot caffe with good, fresh Normandy cream. Lord Darcy leaned over and inhaled the steam rising from the caffe. "A truly magical elixir," he said. "The discovery of this wonderful bean alone makes the hardship and expense of the exploration of New France worthwhile. Some sorcerer should devote time to discovering the magic of a cup of caffe."

"There are things one should just accept on faith, my lord," Master Sean replied, breaking open a roll and applying butter liberally to the interior.

"I think some weather wizards are going to lose their jobs over this," Lord Darcy commented, indicating the rain streaming down outside the window.

"That's not fair, my lord," Master Sean replied. "They simply predict the weather, they don't cause it."

"That is so," Lord Darcy agreed. "But six or eight months ago, shortly after His Highness—the King's Uncle Edouard,

Prince of Gaul—passed on, when the Privy Council picked the date for the coronation of Duke Gwiliam, a senior official weather wizard predicted that the weather at this time would be suitable. I remember distinctly reading it in the *Court Gazette* at the time. 'Suitable' was the very expression. Heads will roll."

"Weather prediction is not an exact branch of magic," Master Sean said, defending his unknown colleague. "The equations are very difficult. And the further into the future a weather wizard tries to see, the murkier his answers become."

"Heads will roll," Lord Darcy reiterated, taking a large gulp of hot caffe. "The Privy Council are not a forgiving group." He buttered another roll.

An hour and fifteen minutes later the local to Le Havre finally pulled in and Lord Darcy and Master Sean boarded. The journey to Tournadotte, normally a trip of under three hours, took just over five hours. For the last hour the scenery outside resembled a vast lake, out of which were thrust small islands that had been hills, trees, farmhouses, and occasional bewildered cows and sheep. The water didn't seem to be much over a foot deep, but it covered most of the ground in this essentially flat valley.

The Tournadotte station was larger than Lord Darcy had remembered. The train, wheezing and spitting smoke, entered a large, glass-covered shed where six tracks came together before exiting in various directions. It was, Lord Darcy knew, the main nexus where the trains from the south intersected with the direct Paris line.

Prefect of Police Henri Vert himself, in a rather disheveled uniform, was waiting for them on the platform, at the head of three armsmen. "It's good to see you again, Lord Darcy, Master Sean," he said, enthusiastically shaking hands with each of them. "Good to see you. Glad I could be here to meet you. Almost didn't hear you were coming. The Castle just got through to my office an hour ago. Said they were trying all night. The teleson is very unreliable in this weather."

"It's a real pleasure to see you again, Prefect Henri," Lord Darcy said. "You're looking very fit."

"For one of my years, you mean, my lord?" Prefect Henri asked, twisting the ends of his mustache with a practiced gesture of thumb and forefinger. "Well, there's none of us getting any younger. Although I must say that you don't look any different than when we worked together twenty years ago.

A bit more distinguished, perhaps. And you, Master Sean, you're getting positively younger. It must be the influence of all that good magic you surround yourself with. I've heard it said that the practice of magic keeps one from growing old."

Master Sean laughed. "I think that means that it takes magical art to keep one from looking like he or she is growing old. But time catches up with all of us, with or without the Talent."

"We can't stay in Tournadotte long, unfortunately, Prefect Henri," Lord Darcy said. "Perhaps overnight at most. So the sooner we get to work on these murders, the sooner we can find time to sit down and talk."

"Ah," Prefect Henri said, "it was the murders that brought you, and the murders that you are anxious to arrive at. Well, I shall not detain you. I, also, am anxious." He waved his arm to one of the uniformed armsmen behind him and pointed to the luggage. "Jean, take our guests' bags into the boat. We shall be off."

"Boat?" Lord Darcy asked.

"It is the only way to get around," Prefect Henri said gaily. "A flat-bottomed scow that is used for hauling pigs across the Eure in dryer times. Now we have requisitioned it, and for the past three days it's been used for hauling armsmen about the town." He led the procession into the station proper and across to the main entrance.

"I didn't realize that the flooding was that bad," Lord Darcy said. "What about the townspeople? Are they being evacuated?"

"No need," Prefect Henri said as they exited the station. "The water is only a foot or so deep on the main street, unless you step into a hole. All the town's functions are, ah, functioning. Much of the town is on high land, or at least higher land. We have another two or three feet to go before the situation is serious here. Some other villages on lower-lying land have already been evacuated. His Highness Duke Richard has set up several evacuation centers throughout the Duchy, which are well-equipped with food, bedding, extra clothing, and all the necessities."

"Of course," Lord Darcy said. Duke Richard's skills as an administrator were well established. Normandy was in good hands during this damp crisis.

The rain had temporarily settled down to a fine mist, against which his wide-brim Londoner offered no protection, so Lord

Darcy folded it and put it between the straps of his traveling case. He followed Prefect Henri into the scow, which was a large, rectangular construct about twenty feet long and ten feet wide with a perfectly flat bottom and sloping sides. Large iron rings at the front and back showed that it must have normally been pulled back and forth across the Eure River by ropes when it was transporting pigs. Now it was being poled along through the main street of Tournadotte by two muscular armsmen standing at the rear.

"We will put you up at the inn, the *Gryphon d'Or,* where I, myself, am staying," Prefect Henri said. "I have made it my headquarters for the duration of the flooding emergency. It is also, as I wrote you, the scene of the crime."

"Always nice to have things close at hand," Lord Darcy agreed, watching the village shops passing as the scow was poled by them. The villagers seemed to be taking the involuntary turning of their village into a lake very well. The shop entrances were built a few stone steps above the street and, though their basements were probably flooded, they were mostly open for business. There were a few other small boats on the street, a few men on horseback, their mounts carefully picking their way along, and quite a few townsfolk determinedly pushing their way through the knee-deep water.

"It looks as though a little flooding is not, ah, damping the spirits of this village," Lord Darcy commented.

"Your Norman peasant is of a hardy breed, my lord, as you will remember from when you lived among us," Prefect Henri said. "The Norman stock is the backbone of the Empire." He stared belligerently at Lord Darcy, as though daring him to dispute the statement.

Lord Darcy laughed and patted the chief on the back. "I would not challenge an article of faith, Prefect Henri," he said. "And besides, you may well be right."

The *Gryphon d'Or* was five blocks from the station, three down main street and two to the right, in the direction of higher ground. The scow was landed about half a block from the inn and tied securely to a fence railing. A double row of planks had been placed over the sea of mud to the inn courtyard. Lord Darcy traversed them gingerly, right behind Prefect Henri, and Master Sean followed. Two armsmen brought up the rear, carrying the luggage.

The inn itself, a typical solid Gwiliamian structure, over two hundred years old and in the shape of a U, was above the floodline. The inner courtyard was fronted by the three-storey main building and flanked by two continuous lines of stables and outbuildings.

The owner of the inn, Goodman Lourdan, a stocky, angular, totally bald man in a white apron that covered him from neck to knees, was waiting for them in the courtyard and looking anxious. He came forward to meet them, and Prefect Henri performed the introductions. "Ah, Lord Darcy!" Goodman Lourdan said, "Master Sean O Lochlainn! It is an unbelievable honor and a pleasure to meet each of you." He grabbed Lord Darcy's hand and shook it firmly, then turned to Master Sean and did likewise. "Welcome to the *Gryphon d'Or*. I could only wish that we meet under more auspicious circumstances. I have admired both of you for many years. Professionally, that is, of course. I hope I haven't offended you. But you understand. Of course you understand. It must get tiresome. I will try not to ask you too many questions."

Goodman Lourdan led the way into the front hall of the inn, continuing to talk enthusiastically to his two new guests. Master Sean responded politely, but was clearly puzzled. Lord Darcy seemed to be secretly amused.

"I have followed your cases with interest for years, my lord," Goodman Lourdan told Lord Darcy. "You and, of course, Master Sean. The mysterious murder of Master Sorcerer Zwinge; the strange death of the Count de la Vexin; the impossible murder of Lord Arlen; the incredible disappearance of the barque *Lady Jeanne* in Portsmouth Harbour—Your Lordship and Master Sean did masterful work in solving them. Incredible. Have you ever thought of writing your memoirs, my lord? Here, Jonquil, take His Lordship's luggage up to his room. And Master Sean's. They have rooms fourteen and fifteen. See that the connecting door is unlocked. Hurry now! May I offer you a drink at the bar, my lord, or would you rather go up to your room and freshen up first?"

"Let us freshen up a bit first," Lord Darcy said. "Shake some of the grime and mud of travel off us. And then Master Sean and I will gladly meet you in the bar in, say, fifteen or twenty minutes. You and Prefect Henri will have to acquaint us with the details of this mysterious double murder which has happened in your inn."

"What a horrible thing," Goodman Lourdan said, frowning at the memory. "But if anyone can solve it, Your Lordship and

Master Sean are the pair, I've no doubt. It will be a pleasure to answer your questions—to watch you at work." The thought seemed to cheer him up, and a beaming Goodman Lourdan gave them their keys and waved them to the staircase.

The rooms were large and comfortable, with great king-sized canopied beds and oversized wardrobes and bureaus. Lord Darcy's room had an ornate Gwiliam II style writing desk, while Master Sean's had a chaise longue that any lady would have delighted lounging in. "Obviously, judging by the connecting door, designed for a husband and wife," Lord Darcy said.

"If you say so, my lord," Master Sean said, shaking his head. "But why a husband would choose not to sleep with his wife, or a wife with her husband, is beyond me."

"Sean, my old friend," Lord Darcy told him, "you have the romance of a bachelor in your heart."

Master Sean nodded. "Maybe you're right, my lord. And it may be that my being a romantic at heart is what has kept me a bachelor over the years." He went through the connecting door into his rooms and closed the door behind him.

Lord Darcy opened his suitcase on his bed and took out a fresh shirt. "You're supposed to be a magician," he called across to Master Sean, "not a philosopher. Now let's take ten minutes to freshen up, and then go down and let our landlord buy us drinks. I could use one."

Master Sean knocked on the connecting door ten minutes later. "Are you ready, my lord?" he called.

"Come in, Master Sean," Lord Darcy replied. "I'll be prepared to go downstairs in a second."

Master Sean opened the door just as Lord Darcy pulled his green dress tunic on. "I thought I'd better look the part," Lord Darcy explained. "Our landlord seems to have expectations of us."

"I wanted to ask you about that, my lord," Master Sean said, lowering his voice. "What is going on? Yon landlord seems like a nice enough fellow, but *what* is he prating about? He knows of our past cases better than I remember them myself. If I were of a suspicious nature, I would think that he was studying our methods so that he could commit a crime without getting caught. But then, why would he go to such lengths to inform us of his knowledge?"

Lord Darcy shook his head. "You have the wrong end of the stick, Master Sean," he said, chuckling. "Have you heard nothing of the new craze that is sweeping the Empire? Goodman Lourdan is a crime buff."

"A crime buff?" Master Sean sat on the hard-bottom chair by the door. "By all the saints, my lord, what sort of creature is that?"

"He studies the reports of criminal cases," Lord Darcy explained. "It started with that series of books: *Major Trials of the Angevin Empire*. Or so I understand. And then a popular series called, I believe, *True Tales of Criminals and Crime Detectors*, commenced publication."

"I, ah, have read a few of those myself, my lord," Master Sean admitted. "They were brought to my attention when a young gentleman came to interview me concerning a couple of our cases. I didn't give him any of what might be considered private information, you understand. But the way he presented it, he made it seem like a civic duty to explain these cases to him. I must say I was disappointed at the results."

"Really?" Lord Darcy asked. "In what way?"

"He sensationalized the cases, my lord. Shamelessly. I thought it would interest and educate the public to be made aware of the rigorous use of modern magical techniques in forensic sorcery today. It might even deter a few potential criminals if they saw how great their chances of being apprehended were. But instead of good, hard, well-grounded magic, he made forensic sorcery read like some sort of miracle." Master Sean chuckled. "Although I must say that he made your leaps of deduction also seem like miracles, an opinion I have sometimes shared."

"Be that as it may," Lord Darcy said, "the unintended result of the popularity of these series of books has been the writing of several other series on the same topics and the springing up of many small societies devoted to the study of crime."

"You mean, they try to solve crimes?" Master Sean asked, his voice rising in shocked surprise. "Without professional training? What a horrible thought! Why, one of these people at a crime scene could scramble the physical evidence, not to mention the psychical and magical traces, to the point where it would be worthless!"

"No, no, Master Sean," Lord Darcy reasssured him. "As you—and as they—well know, that would be against the law. These people discuss crimes that have already been solved; alternately from the point of view of the criminal and that of the detective. They write papers about how well the criminal committed the crime—disregarding the moral questions—and how well the detectives solved it. What they seem to have done is reduced murder and other capital offenses to the status of parlor games."

Master Sean looked doubtful. "Would that not tend to be destructive of the morality of those engaged in the practice, my lord?"

"It would seem not," Lord Darcy replied. "Except in some extreme cases, and then, as with other obsessions, it is the mania itself that becomes destructive, and not the object of that mania. The more serious of these people are developing what might be described as an 'esthetic of crime,' a questionable notion but, thank goodness, it is the esthetic of the observer, not the practitioner. If the mere study of crime were destructive of the soul, then you and I should be in mortal danger, would we not?"

"What you say is so, my lord," Master Sean affirmed. "But the idea still makes me nervous. Then our host is one of these 'buffs' who has studied our cases, do you think?"

"I would assume so," Lord Darcy said. "It seems, according to my informant, that two of these buffs' favorite criminologists are myself and my noble cousin the Marquis of London, with a running dispute as to which of us has the superior ability. You, my dear Master Sean, are the acknowledged champion forensic sorcerer in the Empire. Which, it is felt, gives me an unfair advantage in this putative competition. But then, the Marquis has Lord Bontriomphe as his eyes and legs, while I have to do with my own."

Master Sean sniffed. "I cannot bring myself to consider the solving of heinous crimes as a competition, my lord. The only competition is between us and the criminals, and it is too important for all of us detectives and forensic sorcerers to win every time."

"The people must be allowed their passions, Master Sean," Lord Darcy said. "As long as we don't share them, there is little harm done."

"That may be so," Master Sean agreed doubtfully.

"I shall be glad to discuss it with you further," Lord Darcy told him. "It is hard to be sure of one's objectivity on a subject that concerns one so personally. But right now let us go downstairs and have those drinks that our good host is awaiting on our arrival."

8

A HALF HOUR LATER Lord Darcy, with his second ouiskie and water in his hand, felt relaxed and largely recovered from the morning's trip. He sat at a round table in one corner of the spacious bar room with Master Sean and their host. Prefect Henri had excused himself to attend to police business, and they were awaiting his return before discussing the case at hand. Goodman Lourdan had soon realized that, for some unaccountable reason, Lord Darcy and Master Sean did not wish to discuss all their past cases in interminable detail, and was too polite to push the matter. So the conversation had mostly revolved around the interminable rain, the upcoming coronation, the difficulties in running an inn, and how fascinating it must be to be a detective.

But Goodman Lourdan was eager to describe the mystery that involved his own inn, and now, with Prefect Henri returning to the table, he would get his chance.

"I apologize for my absence," Prefect Henri said, dropping into the vacant chair. "Had to take care of some detail work regarding our current excess of water. Now, shall we get on with it?" He waved to the demoiselle at the bar and asked her for a ouiskie.

"We have all been waiting impatiently for your return,"

Lord Darcy said dryly, "so that we could discuss the murders with you present." He took a sip of his ouiskie. "No point in going over the same ground twice."

"Right," Prefect Henri agreed. "As you know, Goodman Lourdan found the bodies, so why doesn't he start."

"Just take it slowly, Goodman," Lord Darcy said, turning to the landlord, "and tell me and Master Sean everything that happened."

Goodman Lourdan closed his eyes and took a deep breath, marshaling his thoughts and memories. "It was a week ago tomorrow, Wednesday, that we found the bodies. The first thing I did, of course, knowing proper procedure as I do, was to call the armsman and order everyone to keep away from the scene. Not that there was any problem with that, I can assure you, Your Lordship, as far as the staff of the inn are concerned. You couldn't have driven them to the hill with sticks. They don't much like corpses. Local superstition, you know."

"And a sensible one it is," Lord Darcy commented. "What hill is that, Goodman Lourdan?"

"Right back there," Goodman Lourdan said, pointing through the window to his right. "It's off to the side of the inn proper, but part of our land. In the summer we have picnics on it—or we used to. I don't know how people will take to eating over the spot where a pair of corpses were found."

"And the bodies were found on the hill?"

"*In* the hill, more like it. They were buried. About two feet down."

"I see," Lord Darcy said. "Then exactly how did you come to dig them up?"

"Well, now, that's strange, how that happened." Goodman Lourdan got up and went over to the bar, poured himself and Master Sean each a fresh foaming glass of beer, then sat back down. He stared at Lord Darcy intently, and then Master Sean and Prefect Henri, and finally transferred his gaze back to Lord Darcy. He took a long sip of his beer. "It was the dogs," he said. "What they did in the nighttime."

"The dogs?" Lord Darcy asked patiently. This was clearly the high point of Goodman Lourdan's tale, and he wanted to tell it his way. Trying to hurry the story would only confuse matters, and the innkeeper might leave out an important point.

"We have three hounds," Goodman Lourdan explained, "which we let loose at night. Not dangerous animals, you see, just noisy. So they'll wake us up if anything is amiss."

"I see," Lord Darcy said. "So they barked that night."

"No—they didn't," Goodman Lourdan told him. "They didn't make a sound. It wasn't that. You see, they're trained not to bark at our staff or guests, only at tramps or people skulking around after dark."

Prefect Henri smiled. "I guess our killer didn't skulk," he said. "He carried two bodies out of the inn and buried them— but he didn't skulk."

"Well, after all, Prefect," Goodman Lourdan said defensively, "they're bright hounds, but they *are* hounds. If the killer behaved with self-assurance, and if he was first seen by them coming *out* of the inn, they'd probably leave him alone."

"Is that established, then?" Lord Darcy asked. "Did the killer come from the inn?"

"It's merely an assumption so far, my lord," Prefect Henri told him. "But it's the only logical one. One of the victims— the one we could identify—certainly came from the inn."

Lord Darcy nodded. "I see," he said. "Now, what about these nonbarking dogs?"

"Ah," Goodman Lourdan said. "Well, here's what happened, your lordship: The hounds, being hounds, will chase any wild game that crosses the property. They usually won't catch it, you see, and they won't chase it off our own land—or at least not far off—but they will chase it."

"Silently," Lord Darcy said.

"That's correct, your lordship. We can't have them waking guests for no cause. Well, on this Wednesday night, at about ten in the evening, our night bartender, Goodman Timothy Bainterre, happened to look out the window. That very window over in that corner, it was. And he saw a very strange sight. Very strange." Goodman Lourdan stared reflectively into his beer.

"Could you describe it for us, man?" Master Sean demanded. "What was it your bartender saw?"

"A rabbit!" Goodman Lourdan nodded, agreeing with himself. "He saw a rabbit. Standing, frozen, about halfway up the hill. The lights from the upstairs windows illuminated the scene. There was this rabbit, and surrounding him, our three hounds."

"Yes?" Lord Darcy said.

"They were, like, frozen in place, your lordship. The four of them. Goodman Bainterre called me over to see, and they were still there: this rabbit, frozen in fear, and three hounds surrounding it. But not attacking. The dogs were behaving as though the rabbit were protected by an invisible fence about three or four feet from him all around. They would run around the area, but not enter it. They would sort of snuffle up to it and then back away. It was very odd behavior."

"Indeed it was," Lord Darcy agreed, taking his pipe out and tamping some of his private blend carefully into the well-blackened bowl. "Come, now, continue; this commences to sound interesting."

"Well, Your Lordship, we put our rain capes on and took a pair of lanterns and went out to see what was happening, Goodman Bainterre and I. There was a sort of heavy mist in the air that night, but it wasn't what you'd call raining. We found, when we got out there, that we were having the same reaction as the dogs. We thought we'd pick up that poor, frightened rabbit and save it, but when we were there, we somehow didn't want to."

"But it wasn't the rabbit you were avoiding, it was the ground it was standing on," Master Sean interjected.

"That's correct. Although we didn't know it at the time, you see. Well, we couldn't bring ourselves to do anything, so we shooed the dogs away and went to bed. But the next morning we came back. The rabbit was long gone, but we still couldn't walk onto the patch of ground it had sat on. There was something . . . bewitched about that spot."

"And what did you do?" Lord Darcy asked, spinning the wheel on his flint lighter and applying the smoldering wick to the bowl of his pipe.

Goodman Lourdan shrugged. "What any right-thinking man would do in a case like that, Your Lordship. I called a priest."

"Of course," Lord Darcy agreed.

"Father Brunelle is not in town right now," Prefect Henri told Lord Darcy, "or I would have asked him to join us. He is seeing to flood victims farther down in the valley. But I'll tell you his story as I heard it."

"Very good, Prefect Henri," Lord Darcy said. "I'm sure you got all the information I would have. Please proceed."

"Well, Father Brunelle came over after morning mass— about ten o'clock, he thinks it was—"

"That's right," Goodman Lourdan interjected, "ten o' clock, right on the button."

"Thank you, Goodman Lourdan," Lord Darcy said.

Prefect Henri shifted in his seat. "Yes. Well, Father Brunelle examined the area and soon established to his own satisfaction that there wasn't anything unholy or supernatural about it, but that someone had placed an avoidance spell over the ground."

"As I thought," Master Sean said. "An interesting problem, casting such a spell over a patch of land with no natural boundaries. I assume that the spell turned out to be placed on the bodies, and they were buried on that spot."

"Well, now, not exactly, Master Sean," Prefect Henri said. "I will tell you the events as they happened, rather than just rush to the end, for fear of leaving out something of possible importance."

"Very good procedure, Prefect Henri," Lord Darcy told him. "I admire a man who knows how to give a report, it is a difficult skill."

"I understand that the Marquis of London's chief investigator, Lord Bontriomphe, is a master at that," Goodman Lourdan commented.

"I, ah, believe he is," Lord Darcy said, looking blandly at Master Sean, who successfully suppressed a smile.

"Well, the priest called in the town practitioner; a master wizard named Semmelsahn."

"Master Sir Pierre Semmelsahn?" Master Sean asked.

"That's the magician."

"A very good man," Master Sean commented. "A traveling lecturer at various colleges of thaumaturgy for many years. Could have had a seat at any of them, but said he didn't want to settle down. So he finally did settle down—and in the town of Tournadotte! Who would have supposed?"

"He's been here about four years now," Prefect Henri said. "Lives outside of town, actually. With his wife."

"Lucky thing for us too," Goodman Lourdan volunteered. "Hard to get a first-rate magician to live in a small, out-of-the-way town like this."

"I have him waiting outside," Prefect Henri said. "Knowing that Your Lordship likes to get his information first hand, I sent one of my armsmen for him."

"Well, bring him in, man," Lord Darcy said. "I eagerly await the story that he has to tell us."

Master Magician Sir Pierre Semmelsahn was a thin, well-groomed man with arresting blue eyes, a small mustache, and an engaging air of confidence. "Prefect Henri," he said, nodding his greeting. "Goodman Lourdan. Master Sean, good to see you again after all this time. And you must be Lord Darcy. It's a real pleasure to meet you, my lord."

"The pleasure is all mine, I assure you," Lord Darcy told the slender master magician. "Especially if you can add something to the already fascinating tale we have been hearing." He tapped the bowl of his pipe on the edge of the clay ashtray to knock out the dottle, and put the pipe back in his pocket. "Please sit down and talk to us. Tell all."

Sir Pierre fortified himself with a glass of cider, and took the empty seat to the right of Prefect Henri. "I don't usually deal with crimes," he said. "These days I seldom deal with any of the more exotic or esoteric realms of magic. Since I retired from teaching, I have become more of a workaday magician. Privacy spells, locks, preservation spells for our landlord's food and wine; that's the sort of work I concentrate on. But murder . . . I confess that I find myself attracted and repulsed at the same time. Who could do such a thing? And so methodically brutal."

"Tell his lordship and Master Sean about it, Sir Pierre," Prefect Henri said. "Give them the facts."

"The facts are simple enough, to the extent that I have been able to determine them," Sir Pierre said.

"Begin at the beginning," Lord Darcy instructed him, "and leave out no detail, however small. Precision in details is as important in criminal investigation as it is in magic."

"At the beginning," Sir Pierre agreed. "Little Jeanne Balzac, who is twelve years old and wants desperately to have a horse for her birthday, came running over to my house last Wednesday at ten minutes past ten—I keep track of such things—and told me that Father Brunelle was at the *Gryphon d'Or* and wanted me to come right away. Pausing only to pick up my tools"—he indicated the symbol-covered, well-worn leather bag at his feet—"I accompanied Demoiselle Balzac back to the inn. To this very room, as it happens. The good father was awaiting me, halfway through a tall mug of our landlord's best, and he explained what was happening and took me out to the scene.

"I looked the hill over, walked about it, and 'felt' it. . . ." Sir Pierre held his hands in front of his face and rubbed his fingers and thumbs together as though feeling the air. "Master Sean will know what I mean."

"Aye," Master Sean agreed.

"And I could sense no thaumaturgical disruption of the vegetable or mineral fabric of the hill. It was as it should be, except for a square patch about halfway up. There definitely was an avoidance spell at that precise spot. Marking the edges as best I could, I directed a couple of the inn's groundsmen to dig down along one edge of the patch."

"It was that well-delineated?" Master Sean asked.

"It was indeed."

"I thought it might be. Please continue."

Sir Pierre nodded to Master Sean and then picked up his narrative. "I ascertained that the . . . disturbance ended about a foot and a half down. The area below that was not protected. So I gathered a squad of men and we took that patch of avoidance right out of the ground. We dug a ditch on two sides and pushed a row of eight-foot oak one-by-fours right through. Then we lifted it up and walked off with it, eight men on a side. I could have merely neutralized the spell, you understand, but I wanted time to examine it first."

"Very clever," Lord Darcy commented.

"Where is it now?" Master Sean asked.

"The, ah, essentials of it are in the other room, awaiting your inspection, Master Sean," Sir Pierre assured him. "I'll get to that."

"Yes," Goodman Lourdan interjected, "tell them about the bodies!"

"I was about to. About a foot below the excavation we found two bodies stretched out side by side; one naked man and one woman clad only in a nightgown. They were in a surprisingly good state of preservation, having been in the ground for some weeks. I attribute that to the avoidance spell, which seems to have deterred the larger forms of necrophages."

"Did you recognize them?" Lord Darcy asked the landlord. "Did anybody know them?"

Goodman Lourdan nodded, his face assuming a doleful expression. "One of them, your lordship. The woman was Demoiselle 'Lisbeth Augerre. She worked here at the inn."

"And the man?"

"We are assuming that he was a guest," Prefect Henri said. "But we have no proof one way or the other."

"What tests or spells did you perform on the bodies?" Master Sean asked anxiously.

"None," Sir Pierre assured him, "save a preservation spell. They await your arrival, my dear Master Sean, in the same state as I found them."

"And Father Brunelle? Did the good father give the last rites, or invoke any of the power of the Church?"

Sir Pierre smiled. "I think he felt like invoking several, ah, powerful names—but he restrained himself."

"Excellent," Master Sean said. "Excellent!" He picked up his carpetbag. "Why don't I go and begin my magical examination, my lord, while you continue your questioning?"

"Of course," Lord Darcy agreed. "Unfair of me to keep you here when there's work to be done."

"Thank you, my lord. Sir Pierre, what sort of preservation spell did you put on the bodies?"

"Just a standard commercial spell," Sir Pierre told him. "More suited to meats and vegetables, perhaps, than bodies, but I fancy it has done its job."

"I'm certain it has," Master Sean agreed.

"I'll come with you and remove the spell," Sir Pierre offered. "Also the avoidance spell I left on the door to the room holding the bodies. That should save you a few seconds."

"Very kind of you," said Master Sean.

"Not at all," Sir Pierre told him. "I shall use it as an excuse to linger and watch you at work. It is always a pleasure to observe a true master, and as forensic sorcery is one of the disciplines that has always fascinated me, I shall be doubly lucky."

"How was that avoidance spell on the patch of ground worked?" Lord Darcy asked.

"Come," Sir Pierre said. "I'll show you."

Goodman Lourdan unlocked the door to a little corridor to the side of the bar and pulled it open. "Storage rooms and a couple of private dining rooms," he explained, leading the way in. He walked rapidly down the corridor and stopped about ten feet from the last door on the left. "That room in there," he said, waving at it. "I would prefer not to get any closer, thank you."

They all felt the same urge: to stay away from that room at all costs. Somehow they all knew that to enter that room, or even to look at the door too closely, was to invite sure and certain disaster.

"Now that," Master Sean said admiringly, "is what I call an avoidance spell!"

Sir Pierre approached the door and opened his wizard's bag. "This will just take a second," he said.

The others stood a bit farther back. It is never wise to interfere in the work of wizards, even in the simplest things.

Working with the deftness of long practice, Sir Pierre set a bronze brazier on a small tripod and put about a quarter of an inch of finely powdered charcoal on the bottom. He touched his wand to the brazier and muttered a few words, and the charcoal burst into flame. Then a prepared packet of precisely weighed and measured herbs and powders was tossed in on top, and sweet-smelling smoke wafted through the corridor. A softly murmured incantation of removal, and the work was done.

"Well done," Master Sean said. "The hand of the true master can be seen in even the small details."

Sir Pierre nodded his thanks to Master Sean. "Mind the brazier," he said, carefully placing it to the side of the door. "It'll take a minute to cool down."

Goodman Lourdan bustled ahead of them, pulling a large brass key from the bunch at his belt. "It seemed a mite unnecessary to keep the door locked, what with Sir Pierre's spell," he said, unlocking the door, "but the formalities must be observed. Right, Prefect Henri?"

Prefect Henri smiled good-naturedly. "It is citizens like yourself who ease our work, Goodman Lourdan," he said. "Honest, conscientious men who are willing to put themselves out for the good of the Empire."

Goodman Lourdan beamed. There's nothing that pleases a loyal citizen more than telling him that some minor inconvenience he has tolerated was for "the good of the Empire."

Sir Pierre led the way into the small dining room. The dining table had been pushed to the back of the room and was now covered with a white tablecloth. The shape of the tablecloth suggested what lay under it.

The sight of the cloth-covered bodies brought a somber look to the faces of the five men. Goodman Lourdan seemed fascinated by it for a long moment, then he shook his head. "If you'll excuse me, my lord, gentlemen, I really should get back to tending to my guests. If there's anything you need, just let me know." He nodded to each of them and backed out of the room.

"We should let you get to work, Master Sean," Lord Darcy said. "But I am curious about that avoidance spell on the hillside."

Sir Pierre pointed to a small serving table to the left of the door. "There it is," he said. "I don't know what to make of it, except that it's very clever. It seems sort of a convoluted way to go about such things."

On the table Lord Darcy saw what appeared to be a brown blanket which had been folded into a neat one foot by two feet rectangle. "That's the spell?" he asked.

"A receptical for the spell," Sir Pierre explained.

"May I examine it?"

"Be careful, my lord," Master Sean advised. "Such unattached spells can be dangerous."

"I'll watch myself," Lord Darcy told him. "Thank you for the warning." He cautiously touched the blanket, which felt like . . . a blanket; stiff with dried mud, of a thick weave, coarsely sewn around the edges. He unfolded one flap, which protested and shed dried mud as it opened. There was no sensation of any sort that suggested a spell. Even more cautiously he unfolded the blanket another fold.

A rolling wave of nausea enveloped him, accompanied by an unreasoned fear. He suddenly knew that he could no longer be in this room with this blanket. It was an object of disgust and loathing, not to be touched. Lord Darcy dropped the blanket and retreated hastily across the floor.

"So that's it," he said, using a powerful act of will not to go running out the door. "The spell is imbedded in one side of the blanket. That's a new one. Would one of you master magicians close that for me? I find that I don't want to go near it."

Sir Pierre retrieved the blanket and refolded it, placing it back on the small side table. "Is it not interesting, Lord Darcy?" he asked. "I, also, have never seen anything quite like it."

"Very impressive," Lord Darcy said. "I apologize for my overreaction, but I was not expecting anything that strong."

"Your reaction was quite moderate, my lord," Sir Pierre told him. "Most people who are not sorcerers are unable to remain in the same room with that spell-in-a-blanket when it is unfolded. Notice that Prefect Henri is nowhere to be seen. He left rapidly when you lifted the fold."

"A very clever notion," Master Sean said. "Very clever indeed. I shall examine the workings of that spell with much interest."

"I fail to see the purpose of it," Sir Pierre said, "although it is indeed cleverly done. It would be more effective to put the spell directly on the objects you don't want disturbed. This seems an indirect and dangerously roundabout way of achieving that end. As evidenced by the fact that we have, indeed, dug up the bodies this was meant to conceal."

Lord Darcy felt in his pocket for his pipe, and then, reflecting that the tobacco fumes might muddle some of the signs Master Sean was looking for, left it in place. "True," he said, "but that was largely fortuitous. This would seem to be an ingenious method for allowing someone who does not possess the Talent to use the spell."

"My thought exactly, my lord," Master Sean said.

"I see," Sir Pierre said thoughtfully. "I didn't think of that. Sort of a variant of the preservator box."

Lord Darcy agreed. The preservator box, which kept food placed within it fresh, had a general preservation spell placed over the whole box, and thus eliminated the need to place a spell on each separate item of food. "Except in this case," he said, "it was an avoidance spell. Clever adaptation of an existing idea. It also shows careful advance preparation on the part of the murderer."

"And that he had the aid of a master sorcerer," Master Sean added. "Yon blanket is not the work of a journeyman."

"How big is it when it's unfolded?" Lord Darcy asked.

"About six feet long by four feet wide," Sir Pierre told him.

"Very interesting," Lord Darcy said thoughtfully. He took his pipe out of his pocket. "I shall leave you two to your forensic labors now, and anxiously await your conclusions in the barroom."

"Very good, my lord," Master Sean said. "Now, Sir Pierre, about the preservation spell you put on the bodies. I trust you used the Elmsley Count rather than a Jordan . . ."

Lord Darcy left the two master sorcerers to their work. He found Prefect Henri settled at the corner table in the barroom, and joined him. "I should like to speak to the staff," Lord Darcy told Goodman Lourdan when he came over, "one at a time, if it's convenient."

"I'll send them in," Goodman Lourdan said. "Can I get your lordship a drink? Or you, Chief?"

"Caffe would be acceptable, if you can manage it," Lord Darcy told him.

"A pot of caffe and a pitcher of cream coming right up," Goodman Lourdan said. "And yourself, Chief?"

"Make it a big pot," Prefect Henri said.

Lord Darcy busied himself lighting his pipe, and then turned to Prefect Henri. "Tell me about Demoiselle 'Lisbeth Augerre," he said. "Who was she, what did she do, who were her friends, what sort of man would she be with, and why did she get herself killed?"

"And I thought you were going to ask me something difficult," Prefect Henri said. He took a packet of scribbled-on white cards from his pocket and leafed through them. "Here we are," he said. "Demoiselle 'Lisbeth Augerre. Daughter of Goodman Jourald Augerre, a teamster and drayman. Twenty years old. Worked at the inn for the last four years. Good grades at school—she went to the parish grade school—but quit at sixteen, as soon as she could. Well-liked by the rest of the staff, although the men thought her a bit standoffish."

"The virginal type?" Lord Darcy asked.

Prefect Henri looked up from his notes. "The truth is, my lord, that the girl had an innate fondness for older men, and men of . . . quality. And she was, let us say, sexually promiscuous."

"Are you saying that Demoiselle 'Lisbeth was, in life, a prostitute?" Lord Darcy asked. "If so, then say it, Prefect."

"But that would be inaccurate," Prefect Henri protested. "The demoiselle did not, as far as we know, ever put a price on her affections. It is just that she was honestly attracted to mature, important men. She liked working at the *Gryphon d'Or* because it attracted such of the nobility as pass through Tournadotte. She spent her days making beds and her nights making memorable the stay of such unattached males as she deemed important enough to interest her."

"A, ah, noble attitude," Lord Darcy said. "When was she missed from the inn?"

"About a month ago," Prefect Henri said. "It was not like

her not to show up for work, but nobody took it seriously amiss for about a week. There were, you see, so many possible explanations. Then the armsmen were notified, and a missing commoner report was filled out."

"And now we know where she's been," Lord Darcy said. "And the man?"

Prefect Henri shrugged. "A naked, middle-aged man in good physical shape, with a trimmed mustache and a spade beard. No such man has been reported missing. We can't even begin to look for someone answering a description that fits about twenty percent of the male population of the Duchy of Normandy."

"Could he have been a guest of the inn?"

"If so he was going from no place to no place, and nobody missed him when he failed to arrive."

"An apt image," Lord Darcy said. "Did the demoiselle have any suitors? Was there anyone who might have suffered an attack of raging jealousy watching the demoiselle in action?"

"I think not, from what I could discover," Prefect Henri replied.

"I also think not," Lord Darcy said. "Any explanation that does not account for that spell-binding blanket is no explanation at all."

Goodman Lourdan returned to the table bearing a large pot of caffe, and the bar girl brought a pitcher of cream and a pair of fine china cups. "I'll begin sending the staff in now, Your Lordship," Goodman Lourdan said. "Will Your Lordship mind if I remain and listen? I'll stay as quiet as a mouse."

"No, that's fine," Lord Darcy said. "Sit yourself down, goodman." He turned back to Prefect Henri. "Well, let's hope that Master Sean comes up with something to aid in the identification. It's hard to establish motive—or much of anything else—until you find out who the corpse is."

For the next two hours Lord Darcy talked to the staff of the inn, from the assistant bottle washer to the chief housekeeper. None of them said anything of the faintest interest or use, until finally even Goodman Lourdan began to show his boredom with the procedure. "Your Lordship certainly is thorough," the innkeeper said.

"Detection is mostly a process of elimination," Lord Darcy told him. "Not as thrilling a process as the novelists make it out to be. But then, they can leave out the dull parts, while you and I, Goodman Lourdan, must sit through them."

There were a series of crashes from the main room, as though doors were being slammed and a heavy object or two was being dropped, then the sound of boot-clad feet stomping across the room toward the barroom door. It swung open to reveal a noble youth in riding dress. The youth removed his wide-brimmed hat and held it across his chest. "Lord Darcy?" he asked.

"Yes?" Lord Darcy felt a quickening of excitement, as his trained mind analyzed and deduced so fast that it seemed like a premonition when he heard the youth say:

"I am the Chevalier Raoul d'Espergnan, my lord. A King's Courier. I have been dispatched by the direction of Lord Peter Whiss to request your immediate return to Castle Cristobel. There has been another murder."

9

TWO HOURS LATER, AT half past eleven that evening, Lord Darcy closed his examination of the murders at the *Gryphon d'Or*. As incomplete as it was, it would have to be wrapped up and abandoned for the time being. The summons from Lord Peter was, by extension, a summons from His Majesty, and could not—must not—be put off. As the Chevalier d'Espergnan had no knowledge to convey of the murder he was reporting, Lord Darcy and Master Sean, by common consent, declined to speculate on the event. They would soon know all there was to know, and would be striving to discover the rest.

The Oostend-Paris Express, due through Tournadotte four hours before, had not yet arrived at the station, but was now expected momentarily, which saved Lord Darcy and Master Sean the necessity of slogging through the flooded valley on horseback, as the young chevalier had done to reach them. The train might take all night to reach Castle Cristobel, but with any luck they could get some sleep while it was pushing its way through the great lake that the Norman coastal valley had become.

Master Sean had completed the bulk of his forensic examination by that time, and he left the few remaining tests in the capable hands of Sir Pierre, who was eagerly anticipating the new experience. He spent half an hour giving Sir Pierre detailed instructions and a few special substances from his symbol-covered carpetbag, before he was satisfied.

Prefect Henri accompanied them on their watery way back to the station. The barge was affixed with lanterns at the four corners, and Lord Darcy thought they must make an odd sight indeed as they poled their silent way along the deserted streets. "I was looking forward to sitting and talking with the two of you over a pint of ale on the morrow," Prefect Henri said. "But we'll have to put it off. It's always life's pleasures that we have to put off. Life's tragedies have a way of insinuating themselves into your daily activities until they cannot be ignored. About these murders—"

"Give me a day or so to reflect," Lord Darcy said, "and to talk over Master Sean's findings with him. I shall get word to you."

"Do you have any suggestions of a direction in which we should point our investigation?" Prefect Henri asked. "Any little hint will help. I have to keep on it, and I'd like to feel that I'm making progress instead of just motions."

"There are several indications," Lord Darcy said. "The answer certainly lies in the identity of the guests of the inn from about four weeks ago. One may have been the murderer, and another was certainly the victim. I had intended to get a copy of the inn's register for the period. Would you please do that for me and send it along as soon as possible? Include whatever particulars the staff can remember about each guest. Then try to track them down in both directions; where they came from and where they went. See if you can establish links between any two or more of them. A difficult task, after so long a time, but do what you can. I'd be especially interested in any guests who planned to go on to Castle Cristobel."

"You think that a guest committed this crime?"

"Not necessarily, but I think, as you, that the victim was a guest. But even that notion presents problems. Why did nobody miss him when he failed to show up wherever he was headed? But then, perhaps he was missed and, because of this cursed weather, we haven't heard of it yet. We must find out. I will inform the Court of Chivalry that we are assuming this case, so you will get what help you need—if this rain ever stops, so people can get through."

"Then you believe that this case is important?" Prefect Henri asked.

"All murders are important," Lord Darcy replied, "but this one—or these two—may be of special importance to the Empire. Yes, I believe so."

An hour later the Oostend-Paris Express came chugging and sloshing to a stop along the platform and Lord Darcy and Master Sean boarded the first-class carriage. All the sleeping compartments were filled, but they managed to get a day compartment to themselves. Lord Darcy stretched himself out across one of the two facing seats. "I'm going to try to get some sleep," he told Master Sean, who was settling into the other seat. He closed his eyes.

When he woke up, light was streaming through the window. Master Sean was still sitting in the same position across from him, reading a book. Lord Darcy stretched and pushed himself to a sitting position. Out the window, as far as the eye could see, was water. Except for one lone elm tree a couple of hundred yards away, they might have been in the middle of an ocean. The sky was slate gray, and the diffused light cast no shadows. The train was not moving.

"What time is it?" Lord Darcy asked. "Where are we? The view reminds one suspiciously of what one imagines of the River Styx."

"Good morning, my lord," Master Sean said, looking up from his book. "It is about eight o'clock. I have no idea precisely where we are, but I don't think we're dead. The dining car is serving breakfast, and I understand that the dead don't eat. Did you sleep well?"

"I seem to have," Lord Darcy said, "although I think I have a stiff neck. Good morning, Master Sean. I trust you got a little sleep yourself."

"Aye, sufficient," Master Sean acknowledged.

"We should have been in hours ago," Lord Darcy said, staring out the window. "What happened?"

"Mud slide," Master Sean told him. "Ahead of the train. They're digging it out now. We're only a half hour from Castle Cristobel, I understand, but it will be two or three hours before we can proceed. I inquired about the possibility of our proceeding on foot, in case you felt the necessity, and was informed that much of the way has certainly turned to quicksand. It is, as they say, inadvisable."

"Well, then," Lord Darcy said, "let me go wash up, and then let's see what delights the dining car has to offer two hungry travelers."

The *Continental and Southern* subscribed to the theory that a well-fed traveler is a happy traveler. An hour after they first sat down, Lord Darcy and Master Sean faced each other across the remains of eggs, smoked ham, wheat and barley cakes, and assorted jams and condiments, while the porter refilled their caffe cups for the third time. "I do believe I'm beginning to wake up," Lord Darcy commented, stretching and reaching into his pocket for his pipe and pouch.

"Aye, my lord," Master Sean said. "I feel the same—but I'm not altogether sure that I can rise from this chair. I may have overeaten slightly."

"Unless you were planning to go for a swim," Lord Darcy said, "we might as well sit here and drink our caffe. You can describe for me the results of your thaumaturgical investigations yesterday."

"I haven't much to tell you, my lord. The most suggestive results are highly uncertain, due to the length of time since the murders and the method of disposal of the bodies; and the most certain results are uninformative."

"Whatever crumbs you have for me," Lord Darcy said, "I shall gratefully accept."

Master Sean reached into his symbol-decorated carpetbag and pulled out a large notebook. "With the aid of Sir Pierre Semmelsahn—who, incidentally, is a very good man—I performed the basic forensic examination upon the two bodies. The male was in his mid-forties, below average height, sound of wind, and in good health at the time of his death. He was strangled with a fine wire, which was left tied around his neck. Simularity tests on the wire and such other pieces as we could find around the inn proved negative. Sir Pierre is going to continue hunting for samples to test."

"The killer brought it with him," Lord Darcy said. "But I wish I knew why." He struck a match and touched it to the rim of his pipe, sucking at it thoughtfully. "This crime was planned, in great detail, somewhere else, and then accomplished at the *Gryphon d'Or.* And if I knew why, Master Sean, I'd probably know who."

Master Sean looked up at Lord Darcy and then back down to his notebook. "The female, Demoiselle Augerre, was twenty, comely in life, dressed in a cotton nightdress with lace ornamentations. She and the male had had intercourse within two hours of their deaths—which took place within moments of each other.

"The dirt under the male victim's fingernails shows a strong correlation to the inn, but not to any specific room."

"It would be too much to hope," Lord Darcy said. "If we knew which room the victim came from, we could probably identify him. But that was a month ago, and who remembers one guest of average appearance in a busy inn a month later? How much trouble would the killer have had getting into the room, assuming that's what happened?"

"The *Gryphon d'Or* has the usual privacy spells on the locks on its rooms," Master Sean said. "Commercial jobs, but well and conscientiously done. A master sorcerer could have gotten through such a locked and protected door in about three minutes without a key. A clever journeyman could have done it in ten minutes or so with a key, and perhaps an hour without. A layman would have had to break down the door, which surely someone would have noticed."

"Picture a layman with a spell-in-a-bottle, prepared in advance by some master sorcerer," Lord Darcy suggested. "What then, Master Sean?"

Master Sean started to shake his head a strong negative, but then he paused and looked thoughtful. After a minute of frozen silence, he slowly nodded his head. "It *could* be done," he said. "It could indeed. Mind, it wouldn't be easy, my lord. It would take a real master to prepare the concoction, and the layman would have to have some training in handling the symbolic equipment—a brazier and such. And there are spells to be said. But it *could* be done."

"I think it was done, Master Sean," Lord Darcy told the tubby magician. "There is no other reasonable explanation. The gentleman—I think we can assume he was a gentleman— whose body we examined today was in his room with Demoiselle Augerre. They were, or had been, engaged in, ah, amorous dalliance. Surely the door was locked. Nobody likes being interrupted at such delicate moments. What puzzles me is the rabbit."

"Rabbit, my lord?"

"Yes. The rabbit that started all this. The one that paused right over that infernally clever blanket, thus puzzling three hounds and revealing what otherwise might have been a perfect crime."

"That's no problem, my lord. It's a question of balance."

Lord Darcy looked quizzically at his companion. "What sort of balance, Master Sean?"

"A balance of fears, my lord. There was this poor rabbit, bounding desperately away from three hungry dogs. Now, just as a man in a similar situation would leap into a roaring river current to escape a pursuing tiger, so the rabbit leaped into the area of repulsion when faced by a greater fear from behind. The dogs, who were only after a little sport and a little dinner, did not have nearly enough incentive to overcome the spell in pursuit of the rabbit. So there the little creature sat, frozen in fear, until the dogs gave up and went away. It's surprising that the rabbit didn't die of fright."

Lord Darcy nodded. "Thank you, Master Sean," he said. "You have solved one minor but vexing problem for me. Now I can concentrate on the more human aspects of this affair."

The waiter came by and refilled their cups. "We'll be moving in about ten minutes, my lord," he said.

Master Sean poured some of the rich, thick, yellow Norman cream into his caffe. "I have a feeling the problem that lies ahead of us will be fully as vexing as the one behind," he said. "You're going to have your hands full for the next little while, my lord."

"And yours, if anything, even fuller," Lord Darcy replied. "And I have a feeling that these cases are going to prove to be intimately and intricately related."

"I have learned to trust your feelings, my lord," Master Sean told him.

10

GOODMAN DOMREME STOOD AT nervous ease before the long table, his large, well-callused hands clasped behind his back, his work-lined face creased in worry. Behind the table sat the eight men who, besides His Majesty himself and Father Gibbin, Goodman Domreme's confessor, the goodman stood most in awe of in the whole Empire.

"Just tell your story slowly and clearly," instructed Marquis Sherrinford, who sat fourth from the left, on Duke Richard's left hand. "You will be doing His Majesty a great service in aiding in this investigation, Goodman Domreme. Don't be nervous."

Which, of course, made poor Goodman Domreme even more nervous. "I'll try, Your Lordship," he said. "Yesterday afternoon I went into the ballroom—"

"No, no," Marquis Sherrinford interrupted. "Start at the beginning. We want to hear the whole thing."

Goodman Domreme looked puzzled. "But, Your Lordship, that is the beginning. Isn't it?"

"Tell us your name and job," Marquis Sherrinford said, "and what you've been doing in the ballroom, and the precautions you've taken, and then what happened yesterday. A connected narrative, my good man. We don't know what bit of information Lord Darcy will find useful, so we need it all. Take your time."

Lord Darcy and Master Sean sat patiently, waiting for the story to be unfolded. They had been hurried to this meeting— this conference, this investigation-by-committee—upon their arrival at the Castle a half hour before, and had as yet not found out a thing about yesterday's murder. Marquis Sherrinford preferred going to the source. He didn't, so he said, want to take a chance of misleading Lord Darcy with a secondhand narrative. Usually a good idea, but in this case perhaps a bit time-consuming.

Goodman Domreme stood there and thought it out. Just as it had never bothered him that there were people who knew things he didn't, it had never occurred to him that other people didn't know everything he did. And *these* other people, he would have thought, knew everything. There was Richard, Duke of Normandy, who must possess all secular knowledge; and next to him on his right, the Archbishop of Paris, who surely possessed all heavenly knowledge; and on his right, Coronel Lord Waybusch, in charge of the guards, whose job was knowing everything; and on his right Master Sir Darryl Longuert, Wizard Laureate of England, who certainly knew everything magical. To the Duke's left were Marquis Sherrinford, the King's Equerry; and then Lord Darcy, Chief Investigator for the Empire, who everybody knew could read your mind. Next to him was Lord Peter Whiss, who, rumor claimed, could tell when you were lying. And at the end of the table, in his wizard's blue robes, was Master Sean O Lochlainn, who, it was said, could make corpses talk.

Goodman Domreme took his time. If he knew something these gentlemen did not, it was up to him to remedy that. And he didn't want to make a mistake. "My name is Isadore Domreme," he said thoughtfully. "I was born of poor but honest parents in the village of—"

"Start with six days ago," Marquis Sherrinford interrupted again, sounding annoyed. "Start with the ballroom six days ago."

Goodman Domreme nodded slowly. "Six days ago, Your Lordships," he said, "I was instructed to refinish the floor in the grand ballroom. We had been waiting for dryer weather to do it, on account of the shellac dries so slowly in damp weather, but Goodman Druthers, who is in charge of castle maintenance, decided as we weren't going to get any dry weather before His Highness's coronation, so we were to go ahead and do the job now.

"So we cleared out the furniture and stripped and cleaned the floor. We used a standard stripping spell, as was supplied by Goodman Peppier, the journeyman sorcerer who has a contract with the castle maintenance department for such things, and a lot of ammonia and water. It took two days to strip, clean, and dry the floor. Used a spell to help with the drying, too, Your Lordships."

"Go on," Marquis Sherrinford encouraged the man.

"Yes, Your Lordship. Three days ago—Tuesday, it were— we put down the new layer of shellac. All the doors were locked at that time, to prevent anyone accidentally walking on the new shellac and ruining the finish. Goodman Druthers decided to let the floor dry naturally. He said if we used magic to dry the shellac faster, it might bubble. Begging your pardon, Sir Darryl, Master Sean."

"No pardon necessary," Master Wizard Sir Darryl Longuert, Sorcerer Laureate of England, said mildly. "It might, you know. It might bubble. No denying that."

"And then, yesterday?" Marquis Sherrinford prompted.

Goodman Domreme looked hurt. That's what *he'd* wanted to talk about all the time. "Yesterday," he said, "I unlocked the service door to take a look at the floor—see how much more drying time it needed. I," he said proudly, "was put in charge of the drying."

"Yes?"

Goodman Domreme's eyes got large with remembering. "There was a gentleman," he said. "Right in the middle of the floor. He was lying there. Dead."

Lord Darcy closed his eyes and visualized the ballroom. It was a rectangle, about a hundred feet wide and a hundred twenty feet long. There were a row of columns running the length on each side, about fifteen feet from the wall and fifteen feet apart. A balcony ran all around the room; wide enough at the front to hold a small orchestra, it was no more than three feet wide for the rest of its circumference. There were a number of doors leading into the ballroom. Lord Darcy didn't know about doors off the balcony. He would find out.

The service door must be one of the two small doors opposite each other in the side walls toward the back. In addition to this there were two large doors in the front wall, the grand entrance and the grand exit, and two large doors at the middle and toward the back of each side wall which led to refreshment rooms and lavatories. The back of the room had, as Lord Darcy remembered, only the one small door, which led, through a small anteroom, to the private corridor across from the throne room. And only Their Majesties and the Marquis Sherrinford had keys to that. But still, it was not exactly a locked-room mystery. Not yet, anyway.

"Describe the salient facts about the body, Goodman Domreme," Marquis Sherrinford said.

"How's that?"

"Tell us about the corpse. The way you found it. Anything you noticed at the time."

"Ah, yes, Your Lordship. There were a few things as I noticed. As I told Goodman Druthers, as I told the armsman when he came to investigate, there were some odd features to the happening. Not that but what finding a dead corpse in the middle of the ballroom floor was pretty odd to my way of thinking, Your Lordships."

"Do go on."

"I went around the body, being careful to stay near the wall, where the shellac was already dry, so as I could get a glimpse of the gentleman's face. It was not someone with whom I was acquainted personally. But I could see that he was—had been—one of the gentry. First thing as I noticed was that he'd had his throat slit. A pool of blood there was on the floor all under the head and shoulders. And blood all around the body for maybe a yard or two in every direction, looking like it had been sprayed. And with the shellac still wet. No way to get it out without sanding down to the bare wood, which is going to be a pretty job. Next thing I noticed was that there was no weapon by the body—no knife or razor or anything like that. Which was odd, you see."

"Why was it odd?" Lord Darcy asked, speaking for the first time.

Goodman Domreme had the look of a man who is taking an oral exam and is not going to be caught by a trick question. "Well, Your Lordship, it means he didn't commit suicide. And, as he wasn't murdered—at least not by mortal hands—"

"Mortal hands?" Coronel Lord Waybusch interrupted, looking startled. "Just what do you mean, Goodman, 'not by mortal hands'?"

"Would you explain that, Goodman Domreme, if you please?" Marquis Sherrinford asked. "What made you think that he wasn't murdered?"

"It was the shellac," Goodman Domreme explained, twisting his fingers together behind his back. "It was still damp, so it took footprints. And there weren't any footprints in the room except the dead man's own!"

A half hour later Lord Darcy and Master Sean stood on the balcony overlooking the ballroom and stared down at the scene of the crime. Goodman Domreme was circuiting the perimeter, lighting the gas lamps, and each new light brought the scene below into clearer and more terrible view. The corpse was still in place, sprawled in death into a posture impossible in life; a preservation spell keeping it, and all else in the area, as it had been found. Dried blood could be seen in a large fan around the body, where it had spurted out of the still-living throat. And a pool of blood had gathered under the head and shoulders. A trail of two-by-four-foot cardboard rectangles led from the service door to one side of the body, put down at Marquis Sherrinford's instruction so that any markings in the newly shellacked floor would not be disturbed.

Duke Richard had gone about his duties, but the other five members of the committee were ranged behind Lord Darcy and Master Sean O Lochlainn. They awaited Master Sean's assurance that the murder was one they could understand. It *could* have been done by magic—a magician wielding a spell could cause a knife to float on air and, unsupported, to jab and thrust—and slice. *That* they could understand. *That* Master Sean could find traces of with his forensic arts. That could be guarded against by the proper counterspells supplied by a master sorcerer.

But if magic—white or black—was not employed in the murder, why then the thing became incomprehensible. And no man was safe in his bed.

Marquis Sherrinford approached the edge of the balcony and glared at the corpse, as though the death were a personal affront. "It was my decision not to move the body, my lord," he said. "None of us wanted to take the chance of disturbing some clue—some bit of dust, or etheric vibration—which you or Master Sean might pick up."

The victim had been identified as Master Paul Elovitz, Chief

Magical Officer for the Teleson Group. He was a portly man in his late fifties, who enjoyed his work, his young wife from a recent marriage, and his two (now grown) children. He would no sooner commit suicide than he would declare war on Spain. He had come as a representative of the Communications Guild, as well as a Master Sorcerer, to attend the coronation. Those few of his friends, and business acquaintances currently at the castle agreed that he was a happy, harmless man who had never knowingly given offense to anyone.

Lord Darcy turned to Marquis Sherrinford. "The body has not been examined?" he asked.

"The body has not been touched," Marquis Sherrinford told him. "The same, ah, dreadful question is on all of our minds, but we agreed that it was more important for you and Master Sean to see the corpse *in situ* than for us to indulge our morbid curiosity."

"Well, then," Lord Darcy said, "if you will excuse us, my lord, Master Sean and I shall go down and examine it."

There were two entrances to the balcony. The one they had come up led through a dressing room area for the orchestra, which was itself kept locked, and the only two keys in the charge of the seneschal and the concertmaster. Subject to Master Sean's affirming that the affinity spells on the locks had not been disturbed, that made the use of that entrance highly unlikely. The second entrance was from a small door in the ballroom itself, the one right across from the service door.

Lord Darcy and Master Sean went around through the orchestra area and out the interior hall, until they reached the service door to the ballroom. There Lord Darcy paused to survey the room from this new angle, and then, carefully staying on the cardboard path, he and Master Sean went out to examine the body.

"It looks like we've got our locked-room mystery," Lord Darcy told Master Sean.

"So it would appear, my lord," Master Sean agreed. He was holding his hands out in front of him and rubbing the air between his fingers, palping it for any feel of the miasma of evil that would surround the body if black magic had been used in his murder.

There were, indeed, but one set of tracks—the victim's own—in the damp shellac. They came from the left-hand side door and terminated at the victim's body, which lay about twenty feet into the room. "That's curious," Lord Darcy said. "Notice the definition on those tracks, Master Sean. The flat of the foot and the toe are well defined, but the heel is hardly in evidence. I would say he was running, except that the footprints are so close together. Hardly more than a two-foot separation from one print to the next. It's a strange sort of hesitant running."

"And what would you say was the cause of that?" Master Sean asked, kneeling down to get a better look at the nearest footprint.

"I don't know. If something were pushing him back while he was trying to run, that would explain it. But what that something could be, I can't say—and it didn't leave footprints. But I have a feeling that when we figure out what it was, we will be a long way toward knowing what happened here."

The floor was still tacky, as Lord Darcy verified by pressing the side of his hand against it. He knelt down by the body and looked it over carefully. After a few moments Master Sean joined him. "What do you think?" Lord Darcy asked.

"I think he's dead," Master Sean replied. "Look at his face, my lord; it is an expression of terror frozen at the moment of death. I think Master Paul was in mortal terror of someone—or some thing—and it chased him in here and killed him. Could it have been sheer terror that caused him to run with that hesitant step?"

"I don't think so," Lord Darcy replied. "But it was something." He looked up at the balcony. "Is Goodman Domreme still up there?" he called. "Good! Please get some more of this cardboard and bring it out here."

Lord Darcy stood up and stared musingly at the body until Goodman Domreme arrived with the cardboard. The goodman did not seem disposed to remain, and Lord Darcy did not insist. "Just one thing before you go, Goodman," Lord Darcy said. "Tell me how long you think before the floor will be completely dry."

Goodman Domreme knelt and poked at the floor by the door, and then repeated the gesture farther out on the cardboard, keeping his eyes carefully averted from the still figure on the floor. "I should say another two days or so, Your Lordship," he said.

"Thank you, Goodman Domreme. You have been a great help."

Goodman Domreme bowed and scurried out of the room. Lord Darcy and Master Sean spread the cardboard about until the floor all around the corpse was covered for three or four feet in every direction. "Give me some help with this, Master Sean," Lord Darcy said, indicating the corpse, "and I'll get out of your way as quickly as possible."

"You're not in my way, my lord," Master Sean insisted, as he efficiently helped Lord Darcy roll the body over onto its back on the cardboard.

"Well," Lord Darcy said, "will you look at this!"

He reached down to the collar of the dead man's tunic. There, pinned to the fabric with a long, straight pin, was a rectangle of stiff paper.

"What did you find, my lord?" Marquis Sherrinford called from the balcony, where he was still interestedly watching the procedure.

"It wouldn't happen to be a wee bit of doggerel verse?" Master Sean asked.

"It is a piece of paper pinned to the dead man's tunic, my lord," Lord Darcy called to the Marquis. "On it are printed the following words:

Nine little wizards snickered at fate
One wizard laughed aloud—and then there were eight!

Lord Darcy twisted the stiff paper between his fingers and took it over to the nearest gas lamp to improve his light. "Not the same paper as the first one, my lord," he called, "but I'd judge that it was the same pen. Broad steel nib. Probably the same ink. And the same hand—although that's harder to tell. I'll have Master Sean check the two notes for simularity."

There was a long silence after this, finally broken by Marquis Sherrinford. "I shall go speak to His Highness," he called down. "He must know about this at once. Please report to me when you have anything to add."

"Of course, my lord marquis," Lord Darcy assured him. "But it will be at least a day before I have anything to report, unless the killer made some stupid blunder. Which, given the present indications, seems unlikely."

The group of balcony watchers trooped out behind Marquis Sherrinford, leaving Lord Darcy and Master Sean alone to perform their miracles of magic and deduction.

Lord Darcy carefully searched the body, removing everything found in vest pocket, watch pocket, sleeve pocket, belt purse, and outer tunic pockets and laying each item precisely on one of the squares of cardboard. Master Paul had been a conservative man, judging by his dress, unwilling to adopt the newfangled notion of putting pockets in trowsers. He was possessed of a fine rabbit-skin wallet and card case, which held his sorcerer's license, signed by the Bishop of Ulster, and a quantity of parchment business cards.

"Magicians seem to have an affinity for parchment," Lord Darcy remarked, examining the wallet and setting it aside.

"The people expect it of us," Master Sean explained. "And as symbolism is very important in magical invocation, and the best symbol for an object is the object itself, the symbolic value of the commonplace is never overlooked by a prudent wizard. A commercial sorcerer such as Master Paul here probably performed many small magical feats for his company's clients and customers. He would find having a parchment business card very useful for transferences, removals, affinities, and the like. He probably also has three fountain pens, with blue, red, and green ink. Possibly a fourth with brown."

Lord Darcy uncapped the three fountain pens from the stack of Master Paul's belongings one at a time, and scribbled briefly with each on the back of a business parchment. "No brown," he said shortly. "But you're right on the others. Are you saying that this Master Paul Elovitz reduced wizardry to the level of tomfoolery? Is that the usual course of business magic?"

"Not at all, my lord," Master Sean said. "You misunderstand. Most magicians get a great deal of pleasure from being able to entertain their friends and neighbors—and business acquaintances—with small examples of their skill. Just as a poet might write a sonnet to amuse a friend."

"I stand corrected, my friend," Lord Darcy replied. "I spoke without proper reflection. After all, is that not in a sense what occupies Master Sir Darryl Longuert much of the time? The Wizard Laureate to the Court of King John IV, one of the ablest practical magicians of our time, so I understand, spends most of his time thinking up party tricks."

"Ah, yes, my lord," Master Sean said, chuckling, "but they are memorable party tricks."

Lord Darcy nodded. "Let's see what else we have here," he

said. "A pipe, a tobacco pouch, a tiny brass bowl, a flint and steel, a small, symbol-decorated leather pouch—I take this to be a sort of miniature sorcerer's tool bag, Master Sean, what do you think?"

Master Sean took the pouch and carefully opened it. "Not protected," he said. "No spell on it. I suppose he never let it leave his person. Let me see: a nutmeg, a vial of hmmm, a toad's stone, cinnabar, powdered ah, so, hmmm. . . . Yes, my lord, judging by the contents, it is a small sorcerer's bag. Not by any means complete, but indeed enough to amuse one's friends."

Lord Darcy stared critically at the pouch. "Go over that at your leisure, Master Sean," he said, "and make sure that everything is as it should be. If you find anything suggestive of a different interpretation on the use of that pouch, let me know."

"Aye, my lord," Master Sean said, closing the pouch and placing it inside of his own wizard's carpetbag. "Have you anything in mind that I am to look for?"

"Frankly, Master Sean, I have not. Still, we must look." Lord Darcy leaned over and closely examined the body for some time, from head to foot, pausing to minutely study the wound in the throat with a pocket magnifying glass. "A very sharp, fine cut," he commented, "possibly with a razor. Unusually wide. Notice, Master Sean, it is almost literally from ear to ear. And placed high up on the neck, right under the chin. See—it's above Master Paul's rather prominent Adam's apple. An unlikely place for a knife wound."

"What do you make of that, my lord?"

"At the moment I am merely collecting data," Lord Darcy said. "No hypothesis springs to mind. But I am sure, my dear friend Master Sean, that once I have heard your report, all will be made clear." He stood up and looked around. "I have a problem, Master Sean. Perhaps you could help me."

"My lord?"

"I would like to look over this floor. Very carefully. Inch by inch. But to do so, I would have to either cover it all with cardboard mats, and therefore not be able to see it, or creep about the uncovered floor on my hands and knees, thereby destroying the evidence, if any, as quickly as I uncovered it."

"An interesting problem, my lord. "How can I help?"

"It occurs to me, Master Sean, that you possess the skill to levitate objects. I, for the purpose of this discussion, wish to become an object."

"Aha!" Master Sean said, his ruddy face breaking into a large smile. "I understand, my lord. An interesting idea. Let us make the experiment."

"The strain wouldn't be too taxing, would it, Master Sean?" Lord Darcy asked. "I shall probably require about half an hour's worth of floor study. Of course, we don't have to do it all at once."

"No problem at all, my lord, I assure you. If you wish to do it all at once, that's fine. It is not, you understand, exactly my own strength that is being used to support you in the levitation."

"I don't understand," Lord Darcy admitted. "For any man who doesn't have the Talent to study magic is as frustrating an undertaking as for a completely tone-deaf man to study the clavier. The gratification that a Talented person gets from seeing that the spells and incantations *work* provides instant reinforcement for all that mathematics and symbolic logic that they teach in the mantic arts courses. But for the rest of us, except for a rare dedicated soul like Sir Thomas Leseaux, it will forever remain a mystery." Lord Darcy spoke of a mutual friend, now living in London, who had been involved in an important case some years earlier.

"Ah yes, my lord. Sir Thomas may not have the Talent, but he has a talent for subjective algebra and symbological theory that has advanced the magical arts as much as any Talented practitioner." Master Sean stood up and removed a bronze brazier and tripod and a few other small objects from his magical carpetbag. "Give me a few moments to prepare my spells, my lord, and I'll be ready to levitate you the length and breadth of this ballroom for as long as you require."

"Very good, Master Sean," Lord Darcy said. "Let me go get a small lantern while you are preparing, and I, in my turn, will be ready to go exploring."

Lord Darcy went off to borrow a small bull's-eye lantern from the Castle arms room, and when he returned, he found Master Sean swinging a silver thurible through a wide arc over the body and muttering the last of a complex spell in Aramaic. The bronze brazier set on a tripod by the corpse was giving off a pungent, sweet smell.

"I didn't realize all this was necessary, Master Sean," Lord

Darcy said, indicating the brazier and the thurible. "I thought you simply lifted yourself off the ground."

"Oh, I do, my lord," Master Sean replied, setting the thurible aside and picking up his gold-capped black wand. "But lifting *you* off the ground is a different proposition. Besides, I have to protect the body from any possible slippage of the spell. I haven't examined it yet."

"Of course," Lord Darcy said. "Well, let's get to it. After I've gone over the floor, I'll leave you to your examination of the body. We seem to be examining a lot of bodies this week."

Following Master Sean's instructions, Lord Darcy lay down on his stomach on the cardboard. Master Sean leaned over and daubed a thick salve smelling of cloves and musk on Lord Darcy's wrists, ankles, and forehead. Then he stood up, and taking his wand, waved it in a series of magical passes over Lord Darcy's prone form.

Lord Darcy felt himself rising into the air until he was about a foot off the cardboard. "You can propel yourself by thinking of where you want to go," Master Sean told him. "Picture it in your mind. I'll stand here and keep you levitated until you're done. Is the, ah, altitude about right, my lord?"

"I think so, yes," Lord Darcy said. He uncovered the bull's-eye on the small lantern and thought *Front door on the left* as clearly as he could.

He began to move. Slowly he glided across the floor toward the front door on the left. His speed picked up. He was going to hit the door! *Stop!* he thought.

Lord Darcy came to a jerking stop about a foot away from the door. "This requires a little concentration," he called to Master Sean.

"That is so, my lord," Master Sean agreed. "Let me know if you need anything."

Lord Darcy turned to look at Master Sean. He was standing a short distance from the corpse, his feet planted firmly on the cardboard, approximately three feet apart, his arms outstretched over his head, with the wand in his right hand pointing toward the sky—or, in this case, the ceiling.

"Are you comfortable, Master Sean?" Lord Darcy asked. "That looks like a difficult position to hold."

"Only mildly uncomfortable, my lord," Master Sean told him. "Apprentice magicians learn to hold postures like this for hours at a time. Just go on with your investigation. I'll be all right."

"Very good," Lord Darcy agreed. He slowly moved his horizontal body around the ballroom, examining the floor carefully with the aid of the bull's-eye lantern and his magnifying glass. The areas around the various doors received his most concentrated attention. After about twenty minutes he declared himself done and directed his prone form to move over the cardboard.

"You can put me down now, Master Sean," he said.

Master Sean waved his wand thrice in the air, and Lord Darcy was deposited back on the cardboard as gently as a soap bubble. "I hope the experience was interesting and helpful, my lord," Master Sean said.

"Interesting, certainly," Lord Darcy replied. "I have never had an experience like that before. The feeling of flying is quite remarkable, even when you're only a foot off the floor. As for being useful, I think it well might have been. It might indeed."

"You found something?"

"An indication only. And at the moment I'm not quite sure what it is an indication of. But it is something." Lord Darcy squatted down beside the body and squinted across the floor. "Yes. I think I can just make it out from here. As I thought, the marks are in a direct line between the body and the door on the left."

Master Sean knelt beside him and peered at the newly shellacked light wood floor. The bright gaslight from the rows of lamps on all sides made flickering highlights on the glossy finish. It was hard to see anything that you were not staring directly down at. And Master Sean was not sure exactly where to stare. "What marks, my lord?" he asked.

"Two very slight, thin lines, no more than a sixteenth of an inch wide, if that. One is about eight feet from the body in the direction of the door, about three inches long; and the other about ten feet farther on and about eight inches long. The marks are very distinct if they happen to catch your eye, and practically invisible if they don't. They are on the left-hand side of Master Paul's footprints, about two feet away."

Master Sean spread his arms out and gestured with his wand. Slowly he rose into the air and rotated forward until he was parallel to the ground. Tucking his robes back so they would not drag, he lowered himself to a foot off the floor and then floated over to where Lord Darcy indicated the first mark was. He examined it for a minute and then moved on to the other mark. "What could have caused them, my lord?" he asked, floating back to the cardboard and righting himself, to settle down effortlessly on his feet.

Lord Darcy shook his head. "I have only a vague and unsettling idea," he said. "But they are clearly there since the floor was shellacked. And the only other thing introduced into this room since then is this corpse, whose course of entry they parallel. So I feel that somehow they are related. But at the moment I know not how."

"I will run simularity tests on the marks, my lord," Master Sean said, staring doubtfully at the shiny floor, "if I can think of anything to which they might be similar."

"Test them for signs of blood, Master Sean," Lord Darcy suggested seriously. "Specifically, Master Paul's blood. And oil—test them for oil."

"Oil, my lord?"

"Yes. Oil or grease. Just the slightest trace, probably. Won't hurt to try."

"Certainly, my lord," Master Sean agreed, clearly baffled at the suggestion.

"I will leave you now to perform your magic on the corpse and surroundings," Lord Darcy said. "Fully confident that you will come from here in an hour with the name and location of the murderer ensorceled from the thin air and writ large on a scrap of wizard-gray parchment."

Master Sean sighed and opened his symbol-encrusted carpetbag. "I would that it were that simple, my lord," he said. "But I trust that I shall come out of here with my meager findings, and you will make that logical leap that is beyond the magic arts and discover the murderer's name among the dry words of my report."

Lord Darcy laughed. "Each of us stands here convinced that the other is a miracle worker," he said. "While the truth is that you are merely a magician, and I a logician. But in truth it is the combination—the team—that does it. For I fully confess that I would be lost without my Master Sean."

"Thank you, my lord," Master Sean said, a faint flush crossing his already ruddy face. "But you'd better leave now, so I can go about my job."

Two hours later Lord Darcy and Master Sean were closeted with Marquis Sherrinford in his inner chamber; a small, plain room with a leather couch, a small table, and four chairs, behind Marquis Sherrinford's regular office, which in turn was behind the room occupied by Lord Peter. Too small for working, it was a space for retreating to when the press of the day was overwhelming, or when Marquis Sherrinford's recurring headaches got too bad for him to handle. At the moment it was merely the one place where they would not be disturbed.

"And what," Marquis Sherrinford asked, waving them to seats, "have you managed to discover regarding the death of poor Master Paul? What magical agency followed him into the ballroom and cut his throat?"

"None, my lord," Master Sean replied. He lowered himself firmly into one of the brocaded chairs. "As far as I could tell through the most sensitive tests at my command, whatever killed Master Paul Elovitz, it was not done by the exercise of magical powers."

Marquis Sherrinford looked at Master Sean and then at Lord Darcy, and then shook his head. "As if we didn't have enough on our minds," he said, "now we have to search for a murderer who kills by a mysterious method beyond magic. I feel put-upon, gentlemen, by a cruel and unyielding fate. But, by God, we're going to give it a run for its money. There's got to be some way to attack this problem that will give results."

"I don't think it's quite that bad, my lord," Lord Darcy said. "Because Master Paul's demise is mysterious, and yet unmagical, is no reason to suppose that it is beyond magic, nor yet beyond solution."

"You think you know how this was done?" Marquis Sherrinford asked.

"I have several hypotheses, my lord. I would rather keep them to myself until I have a chance to test them, but I think I will be able to adequately explain the method used to kill Master Paul, innovative as it was. It's the motive that concerns me. In this case the method will not take us to the killer. The motive may. The motive obviously has determined the method. And I think we'd better concentrate on finding it out, because I don't think our killer will stop at two."

"I'm not sure I understand what you mean about the motive determining the method," Marquis Sherrinford said.

"It's simply this," Lord Darcy explained. "We have here an

impossible crime. Now, clearly it is not really impossible—it was committed, and therefore it is possible. But it *appears* impossible. Was it supposed to? Let us look at the crime of murder—planned murder—from the point of view of the killer. He sets out to commit a murder. He desires two ends: the demise of his victim, and his own safety. That is, he wants someone else dead, and he doesn't want to get caught."

"That much is clear," Marquis Sherrinford agreed.

"But in the normal circumstance there is no reason why he should make the crime look impossible. And, indeed, if it takes a second longer or presents a particle more risk, then there are strong reasons why he should not."

"Then why has this murderer done so?" Marquis Sherrinford asked.

"Why?" Lord Darcy leaned back in his chair and stared thoughtfully at the wall for a second. "There are two possibilities. First: it was an accidental or secondary effect of the killing. That is; the murderer set out to kill, and because of unplanned circumstances, the crime looks impossible. For example, the murderer shoots his victim in a room with one door and then flees from the room. The victim lives long enough to lock the door behind him, perhaps not realizing how badly he is wounded and in fear that the murderer will return. Then he dies. Leaving a perfect locked-room mystery by accident."

"And what is the other possibility, my lord?" Master Sean asked.

"That the murderer sets out to commit an impossible-seeming crime for some reason incidental to the murder itself. Perhaps he feels a need to baffle the investigators that is as strong as his need to kill. Perhaps the creation of the 'impossible' crime serves to shield some aspect of the murder that would otherwise be evident, and point suspicion at the killer."

"What could that be, my lord?" Master Sean asked.

"I don't know, Master Sean, but if that is the case, I intend to find out."

"What of the killings in that inn—the *Gryphon d'Or*—could they be connected with all of this?"

"I'm afraid they are," Lord Darcy said, "but I could well be wrong about that. At this stage it would be guesswork, and I refuse to guess. It is destructive of the logical facilities."

"I understand that one of the victims was a local girl,"

Marquis Sherrinford said, "and the other is as yet unidentified. Could it be another sorcerer?"

"Possible, of course," Lord Darcy said, "but that I doubt."

"Why?"

Master Sean chuckled. "No bit of verse," he said.

Lord Darcy smiled and nodded. "That's right," he admitted. "It may turn out to be the same killer, but I don't think he started killing wizards until he arrived here. That's another thing to consider—why here? Although there is probably a fair concentration of Sorcerers' Guild members presently in attendance for the coronation."

Marquis Sherrinford looked at a paper on his table. "Three hundred fifty-six," he said, "as far as we can determine. There are three hundred fifty-six wizards of one sort or another present at Castle Cristobel at this time, ranging in importance from Archbishop Maximilian to twenty-seven journeymen who are employed in the castle or are accompanying various masters. There are a few more expected to arrive but not present yet, such as His Grace the Archbishop of London, Grand Master Sir John Tomasoni, and Crown Prince Stanislaw of Poland. There are also a few sorcerers' apprentices that I didn't include in the enumeration."

"Crown Prince Stanislaw?" Master Sean asked. "I didn't know he had the Talent."

"I don't know to what degree," Marquis Sherrinford replied. "He is a master in the Polish guild, but I have a feeling that it's more of an honorary title. But, of course, he must possess some Talent or the guild could never accept him at all."

"That's so, my lord," Master Sean agreed. "Even the Polish Sorcerers' Guild wouldn't allow a non-Talented person membership just because he is royalty."

"How many Master Sorcerers are here, my lord?" Lord Darcy asked. "I don't think our murderer is going to settle for journeymen."

Marquis Sherrinford nodded. "I feel that myself," he said. "There are about sixty-five masters presently in residence. Why would anyone have a grudge against sorcerers? They are a helpful, useful group, which seldom offends any man. Also you would think that they would be a bad group to go up against. Why, a sorcerer could fry your blood if he didn't like you. Isn't that right, Master Sean?"

Master Sean considered the question seriously. "He could,

my lord," he replied. "Or, at least, most sorcerers could. But that doesn't make them immune from murder. First of all, to hold a sorcerer's license is to have been tested and certified by the Church as to both your abilities and intentions. Any man—or woman—who could even hold the intention of destroying another man merely because of dislike, would certainly not get or hold a license. As you well know, the license has to be renewed every five years, so the sensitives of the *advocatus manticii* have opportunity to observe any character changes that might make a sorcerer unstable. Such things do happen, but they are guarded against."

"What is done in a case like that?" Marquis Sherrinford asked.

"The sorcerer in question is warned, and advised to seek professional help. A specific healer, trained to handle such matters, may be recommended. His Grace of Paris can answer that better than I."

"What of a sorcerer that has gone around the bend, so to speak—who somehow is practicing bad magic, or using it illicitly before he is noticed? Does that ever happen?"

"Black magic, you mean? It would almost have to be, since magic is a matter of intent. White magic cannot be used to attack, but only to defend. Black magic can be used to attack, but in the process it gradually destroys the user. And, of course, any sorcerer caught and convicted of using black magic is deprived of his powers."

"Couldn't some magician continue to use magic even after his Church license has been pulled?" Marquis Sherrinford asked. "And then he'd have even less incentive to refrain from using black magic."

"You misunderstand, my lord," Master Sean said firmly. "A magician convicted by a court of his peers of using black magic is thrummed by a Committee of Executers—sorcerers sufficiently powerful to overcome him on the psychic level. The Talent is removed from him. He can never perform magic again. This is not done lightly, I can assure you. For one who has the Talent, being deprived of it is like depriving a sighted man of his eyes. Or so I am told."

Marquis Sherrinford nodded, obviously impressed by Master Sean's sincerity and conviction. "We, ah, blind men will have to take your word for the severity of this punishment," he said. "So magic—*white* magic—can only be used in self-defense. Is that right?"

"Self, loved ones, or a meaningful goal," Master Sean replied. "Defense of the Empire for a loyal subject, for example."

"But remember, my lord," Lord Darcy interrupted, "that that means attack or defend in the symbolic sense. There are times when a physical attack is, symbolically, a defense."

"True," Master Sean agreed. "The situation is complex, and the mathematics used to explain it—"

"Simplify it for me, Master Sean," Marquis Sherrinford said. "What I want to know is how a nonmagician can be murdering Master Sorcerers with impunity. Most people would be afraid to raise their hand to a sorcerer, for fear they'd be turned into toads."

Master Sean shook his head. "Not anyone who knows the first thing about magic. First—any spell takes preparation, and if a magician is taken off guard or unprepared, he is no more able to defend himself than the next man. Probably less, as swordplay and fisticuffs are not on the curriculum of most university magic programs. Second—there are many specialties within sorcery, most of them entirely unrelated to anything requiring a knowledge of self-defense—even magical self-defense. Master Raimun DePlessis was a healer and professor of theoretical thaumaturgy at the University of Drogheda. Master Paul Elovitz was the Chief Magical Officer of the Royal Angevin Teleson Society, and probably didn't even remember the incantation for warding off a simple staff attack. Neither of them presented much of a problem to a dedicated killer."

"Do you suppose he picked them for that reason?" Marquis Sherrinford asked. "Maybe the killer has a grudge against wizards in general and is attacking the weakest, or the least dangerous."

"I don't think so, my lord," Lord Darcy said. "That rhyme of his makes me think that he has specific targets in mind. Whether they are all here or not is another consideration. There might be three or four of them here for the coronation, and then one in, say, Paris, and another in—"

"So you think the 'Ten Little Wizards' rhyme really is a countdown?"

"Undoubtedly, my lord."

"Then there'll be more killing?"

"Unless we catch him—almost certainly."

Marquis Sherrinford sighed and pressed his palms against his temples. "And what of the threat to His Majesty?" he asked. "Some unknown person may be stalking through this castle at this moment, planning an attack on His Majesty, and we are powerless to stop him until he makes the attempt. And some other unknown person—or possibly the same one—is stalking through the castle intent on murdering some harmless, socially useful person, just because he or she happens to be a Master Sorcerer. And I have a headache!"

Harbleury appeared in the doorway as if Marquis Sherrinford's words were an incantation for producing Harbleurys. "It's time for your medicine, my lord," he said, bringing over a silver salver holding a glass of pink liquid.

"Is this something new, my lord?" Lord Darcy asked as Marquis Sherrinford downed the concoction in three gulps.

"Indeed," Marquis Sherrinford said. "That fellow Count d'Alberra recommended it. Compounded from tree bark, I believe."

"Is he helping you, do you think?"

Marquis Sherrinford thought about it for a minute. "May well be," he said. "Hard to tell in such a short time. Strange sort of healer—you just talk to him and he listens. Then sometimes he talks. But he never tells you to *do* anything—he just talks. No laying on of hands at all—I mean, he isn't a proper healer—but if this talking business works, well then, I'm all for it. 'Be not the first by whom the new is tried,' as that poet fellow said, 'Nor yet the last to lay the old aside.'"

"Well, if it works—" Lord Darcy said.

"Aye, my lord," Master Sean agreed. But he looked doubtful.

11

TWO DAYS PASSED IN which nothing of import happened. Lord Darcy interviewed as many master magicians as he could find at the Castle who had known either Master Sorcerer Raimun DePlessis or Master Sorcerer Paul Elovitz. All agreed that neither man had an enemy in the world. None could think of any reason why either would be killed. Lord Darcy had expected no less.

The body of Master Paul was removed to the Castle's morgue. The ballroom floor finally having dried, Marquis Sherrinford's permission was earnestly sought to begin sanding out the bloodstains. His Lordship turned the question over to Lord Darcy. After much thought and consultation with Master Sean, and one more trip to the ballroom, he gave his consent, withholding it only on the two mysterious scratches, which he had covered to preserve them.

The rain moved to the east, but the floodwaters, fed by the eastern streams, did not subside, and the Castle was nearly cut off from the outside world. This did not matter, as most of the guests had arrived, and the Castle's larders would feed many regiments for many months; which, after all, is the function of a castle.

Two trains a day arrived at Cristobel Station, on no fixed

schedule: one from the east and one from the west. The water was still not deep enough to endanger the locomotives' boilers over most of the run, but there was the constant danger of the track washing out, and a tremendous amount of extra fuel was needed to pull the cars through a three-foot lake.

The Dowager Duchess of Cumberland was waiting in the drawing room of Lord Darcy's suite when he returned in the evening of the third day. His man Ciardi intercepted him in the hall, murmured "Her Grace!" disapprovingly, and pointed to the open door. Then, with a sniff, he retreated back toward the kitchen. A simple man with a complex view of propriety, Ciardi thought it fine that Lord Darcy and Mary of Cumberland had been carrying on an *affaire de coeur* for the past decade. But it was, to his mind, wrong that *she*, on occasion, came to Lord Darcy. The baron should visit the duchess, and not the duchess the baron. Etiquette was quite firm on this.

Mary of Cumberland stood up when Lord Darcy entered the room. Tall for a woman, she was pleasingly slender, and had startlingly dark blue eyes. Her light brown hair was touched with gray, but if that was a sign of age, it was the only one she showed. Without the gray she would have looked on the young side of thirty, but she was far too vain to dye her hair. "My dear!" she said, stretching out her hands to Lord Darcy. "You see, I've come."

He took her hands silently and pulled her to him. They embraced, and he felt her warm, yielding body press firmly against his. "Yes," he murmured into her ear, "and after two months, you know how glad I am to see you. But I shall always wonder."

"Wonder what, my dear?"

"Whether it was me or murder that brought you here?"

She pushed him away. "Really, my lord!" she said sternly. "You think—" Then she broke out laughing. "I did not hear of the murder until yesterday," she said. "And then I was already in Rouen. I came with Edwin in the Ducal train. Since his wife's approaching accouchement prevents her from traveling, he was glad of even my company."

Her stepson Edwin, the present Duke of Cumberland, was a mere six months younger than his stepmother. But in many ways he had been born old, and he never pretended to understand the young and beautiful woman who had come so late into his father's life. But she had so obviously loved his father, and the age difference had not mattered to them. She had made her husband happy until his favorite mare stumbled and cut short his life in its prime—at the age of sixty-eight.

So the Dowager Duchess of Cumberland, a widow before she was thirty, held court at Carlyle House and was known for her brilliance and the company she kept. And her stepson married well, and took care of the estates, and hunted, and was perversely proud of this stepmother he didn't understand.

And Mary of Cumberland did good works, and no longer thought about men. For the first year the grief of her loss kept such thoughts from her. And after that, when the passage of time had healed the hurt, she came to realize just what she had lost. For she found that, after her husband, no other man interested her. They were all dull.

Until she met the Chief Investigator of the Duchy of Normandy, the Baron Darcy.

"You are the only man I have known," she murmured into his ear one night shortly after they met, "since my husband died, who did not bore me."

"A rare compliment," he had replied.

And their relationship had been a good one over the years because they respected each other, they cared for each other, and neither of them ever bored the other. And Mary of Cumberland, who had helped Lord Darcy in a couple of his cases when she happened to be present, had discovered within her the thrill of the hunt. She enjoyed the intellectual challenge of chasing murderers, and hoped one day to catch one.

"I thought your stepson was going to remain with his wife," Lord Darcy said, "until after the child was born."

"He wanted to," Her Grace told him, "but she chased him away. He is not a good man to have around when one is giving birth; he takes it all so personally. After all, it's not as though she doesn't know how—she has done a perfectly fine job of it three times already. And Edwin keeps fainting. It's strange— he's perfectly good with brood mares, I understand. But watching his own wife give birth gets him extremely upset."

"So he decided to attend his royal cousin's coronation rather than his wife's parturition?"

"She insisted," Mary of Cumberland reiterated. "And, as it gave me a perfectly good excuse for visiting you, I volunteered to go along. After all, the poor man shouldn't be left alone at a time like this."

"True," Lord Darcy admitted. "Husbands are notoriously bad at birthing."

"And so here I am," Her Grace said, "and it seems I won't be able to spend any time with you after all."

"None at all?" Lord Darcy asked.

"Surely not," Mary of Cumberland said, mock-seriously. "With you running around solving a murder, you'll be much too busy to pay any attention to me."

"If it was just the one murder," Lord Darcy told her, "I might be able to spare you a moment. But with four so far—"

"Four!" Mary put her hand on her mouth and her eyes narrowed. "You're joking!" she said, studying his face. "No, you're not joking. What has been going on here?"

"That is a very good question," Lord Darcy said. "I'm glad you're here, Mary. I need a cool, intelligent person to talk to about his."

Her Grace shook her head so that the tight rings of curls—the latest London fashion—bounced from side to side. "That's not so, my lord," she said. "What you need is someone you trust to bounce thoughts and ideas off while you pace back and forth in the bedroom. What you need is a wall. I am honored, my lord, to be that wall, but let's not build up that function to more than it is."

Lord Darcy laughed. "You may be right, Mary," he said. "But it takes a cool, intelligent, perceptive person to see that. And one with a lot of empathy to be able to do it properly."

"Well," she said, taking his hand, "let's go into the bedroom and start bouncing."

The next morning Lord Darcy woke early, showered, and then went in to breakfast, leaving Mary sleeping comfortably in the bedroom. He read through yesterday's Paris *Courier*, which had finally made it to the Castle, and sipped his caffe.

As he was starting his second cup, Mary stumbled into the room and dropped into the chair opposite him. "You let me sleep!" she said accusingly.

"It was an act of mercy," he told her.

"Certainly it was," she said. She turned to the kitchen door and yelled, "Maggy! Bring me a cup and a crescent roll!"

"Yes, Your Grace," came the muffled reply of Lord Darcy's cook through the door.

"I have something for you," Mary told Lord Darcy. "In the

excitement of last night I didn't get around to it; but if you'd left this morning without seeing it, you never would have forgiven me."

"It sounds portentous," Lord Darcy said. "What is it?"

Her Grace of Cumberland shook her head. "If I had forgotten to give it to you, it would have been portentous. As I didn't, it will merely be interesting." She handed him an envelope. "Henri Vert—the little man who's the police prefect for Normandy—gave this to me when our train stopped at the Tournadotte station. He was down there looking for someone reliable to take it on to you. I convinced him I was reliable, although at first he had his doubts."

Lord Darcy smiled. "You are reliable, my dear," he told her. "And it's but one of your minor good qualities."

"Why thank you," she said, passing him the envelope.

Lord Darcy ripped it open. There was a brief note and several pages of hand-printed data. "Dear Lord Darcy," the note said:

> I have assembled some of the information you wanted, and am sending it to you while the trains are still running. Here is Sir Pierre Semmelsahn's report on the tests that Master Sean wanted him to complete, and a list of all the guests of the inn for the time period in question. Sir Pierre has determined that the murders took place on the night of April 15th, which was a Tuesday. He says that Master Sean will agree with the result, since he suggested the method.
>
> The people on the list are those who were at the inn that night. Unfortunately, due to the weather, it is impossible to get any current information about any of them at this time. Where the records indicated their intended destinations, it is on the list.
>
> I hope this is helpful to you. We are interring the corpses temporarily in a crypt in the village church, as burial is impossible at the moment anyway. The spell of preservation is being maintained for the near future.

> Your friend,
> Chief Henri

"I'd better get busy on this," Lord Darcy said, rising and finishing his caffe.

"What are you going to do?" Mary of Cumberland asked.

"Check on these names. I imagine a good percentage of them were on their way to Castle Cristobel when they stopped at the *Gryphon d'Or*, and are here now." He ran his finger down the list. "Some of the names I already recognize. Master Sorcerer Raimun DePlessis was murdered in a bakery. Count d'Alberra is curing headaches. The Chevalier Raoul d'Espergnan is a King's Courier. They'll all have to be questioned."

"Is there anything else?" Mary of Cumberland asked.

"I should also give the sorcerer's report to Master Sean, to see if there's anything of value in it. All these wizards write in a sort of Latinate shorthand that's very hard for a layman to interpret."

"What can I do?" Mary asked.

Lord Darcy considered. "Help me locate whichever of the people on the list are at the Castle. As soon as we have found some of them, the former guests of the inn, you can help question them. Particularly all the women on the list," he told her. "They will talk more easily with you than with me or anyone else I could send."

"Very few of the King's investigators can send duchesses to do their bidding," she told him.

"Very few duchesses are as talented as Your Grace," Lord Darcy responded.

"Yes," she said, "that's true."

12

MARQUIS SHERRINFORD OPENED HIS eyes and sat up on the leather couch. He felt curiously refreshed. What had they been talking about? It was such a strange experience, discussing one's own youth. How could it possibly be therapeutic?

"And how is your headache now?" came the solicitous voice of the Count d'Alberra from somewhere behind him.

He shook his head slowly from side to side, testing for that needleprick feeling of sensitivity that usually presaged one of his attacks. There was no result. He felt somehow light-headed, but there was no trace of pain, or threat of pain impending. "Gone!" he said, sounding faintly surprised.

Marquis Sherrinford had gone to see Count d'Alberra for a scheduled hour of treatment, knowing that one of his headaches was about to begin. It was a sensation, as he described it to the Count, of hollowness in the head combined with pinpricks. Count d'Alberra said that he had been waiting for this moment. "If my treatment is to work, which I cannot guarantee," he had told Marquis Sherrinford, "it will commence at the start of one of your attacks of head pain. Once we have treated it from that point, subsequent treatments will be of greater ease and more assurance."

"You want to talk to me while I'm getting a headache?" Marquis Sherrinford had asked incredulously.

"Actually, I want you to do most of the talking, although I shall assuredly do a little," Count d'Alberra had told him. "And why is this so much stranger than the Laying On of Hands, which you, I feel positive, do have faith in?"

Marquis Sherrinford had thought about that for a moment. "I don't know—it just is."

But here it was, one hour after he had entered Count d'Alberra's little office, and he had no headache, no trace of a headache, or threat of an impending headache. Although one was certainly building when he had come in.

"I think, Count, that you have here a convert," Marquis Sherrinford said, pushing himself to his feet. He shook his head cautiously, but it was fine. "I will have to admit that whatever you did, it worked."

"You did it mostly," Count d'Alberra replied, getting up from the leather easy chair he had been reclining in and moving to the desk. "To be honest with you, I am not altogether clear how it does work, although I am developing a theory based on my case histories. But I am, of course, delighted that you find relief through my quaint techniques. Now you had best be on your way. You must have a busy schedule, with the coronation impending as it is, and I have another patient waiting."

"Yes, of course, Count. Thank you again. I'll see you tomorrow?"

"Yes. Usual time. And, my lord, please do not hesitate to come to me at any hour of the day or night should you feel a headache impending. Now that we know the technique works, it is entirely unnecessary for you to suffer any more of those debilitating episodes."

Count d'Alberra opened the office door and bowed Marquis Sherrinford out. There was a short, passive-looking man sitting on the wooden bench in the hall. He was slumping down on the bench and staring at the opposite wall, totally devoid of motion. It was as though he were turned off and waiting for someone to turn him back on. "Sorry to have kept you waiting, Goodman Bowers," the Count said, turning to him and smiling. "Please come in."

Marquis Sherrinford crossed the courtyard from the Stephainite Monastery feeling more cheerful than he had in some time. He had not allowed the headaches to get him down, or interfere with his work—outwardly. But only he had known the inward cost of maintaining a placid disposition and rendering equitable judgments while suffering from what, as he had described it to Count d'Alberra, "felt like a vise was being steadily tightened on the sides of my head, and then periodically struck with a hammer."

But now, just knowing that there was the possibility of control over the periodic pounding in his head sweetened the whole day and made everything seem possible.

Lord Peter was waiting for him when he entered the throne room. "There is mail, my lord," he said.

"Good, good," Marquis Sherrinford said, taking his cloak off and hanging it on a cloak rack behind the throne before he sat down. "I'd better get it cleared up right away. The Ancient and Honorable Society of Guild Halls' Celebratory Ball is tonight, and I must go, and there is much detail work that remains to be done. The guild masters are much more serious about such things than the nobility. The Castle staff is working like mad to get the ballroom and all ready on time. Harbleury here has charge of the arrangements. The guild masters dote on his every word. Anything new here, Harbleury?"

"The Polish delegation has arrived, my lord," Harbleury told him. "They were greeted by His Royal Highness of Normandy and His Grace of Paris."

"That's good," Marquis Sherrinford said. "I hope they can dance."

"They refused to exit from their private car on the train until they were assured they would be properly greeted," Harbleury told him. "Coronel Lord Waybusch was quite concerned. If we hadn't been able to round up His Highness and His Grace, they'd be on the train yet."

"Who came—the son, as promised? Or did they send a substitute at the last minute?"

"It was His Royal Majesty, Stanislaw, King of Courlandt and heir to the throne of Poland, along with thirty of his closest aides and confidants," Lord Peter told him.

"We make our royal sons princes, so they make theirs kings," Marquis Sherrinford commented. "It's a strange sort of regal oneupsmanship. Courlandt was merely a dukedom until 1923, then it suddenly became a kingdom. So Stanislaw is a king. And I doubt whether His Majesty has ever been in his kingdom of Courlandt in his life."

"We'll have to arrange for an audience for King Stanislaw here in the throne room tomorrow," Harbleury commented. "King meets king."

Marquis Sherrinford looked around the great room, equal in size to the ballroom that sat opposite it across the inner corridor; the pair like the two rectangular wings of an architect's butterfly. But the ballroom was for gaiety, while the throne room was for ponderous matters of state. It was designed to impress the sixteenth century barons who had come to pay homage here, and little had been changed in the decor since.

The walls were hung with the banners and pennants of battles long since won and the arms and armor of warriors long since dead. The room was dominated by the throne of the Plantagenets, from which John IV leaned down and greeted emissaries and accepted tribute and passed judgment as had his ancestors for these past eight hundred years.

"I'll inform His Majesty," Marquis Sherrinford said. "I leave it to you to see that they're kept happy while they're here."

"The suite of rooms we have reserved for them is barely large enough," Harbleury said. "Although they'll never notice the overcrowding, if what I've heard of their living conditions is accurate."

"Now, now," Marquis Sherrinford said. "Let's not have any anti-Polish sentiment. It's hard to like them; I think their suspicion of everything rubs off. But we must try. Although if it turns out that they *are* engaged in a plot to assassinate Our Most Sovereign Majesty . . ."

Harbleury and Lord Peter stared at Marquis Sherrinford with serious expressions. "My lord," Lord Peter said, "there is a letter from His Lordship of London." He held out an envelope. "It contains new detail about the apparent plot, although still not enough to do anything about it. Just more tantalizing detail."

"What? Let me see that!" Marquis Sherrinford almost snatched the stiff envelope out of Lord Peter's hand. "Send for Lord Darcy!" he said, pulling the folded letter from the envelope.

"I have taken the liberty of doing so already," Harbleury told him. "And also Coronel Lord Waybusch."

Marquis Sherrinford unfolded the letter and put on his spectacles. He read:

> To His Lordship, the Right Honorable the Marquis Sherrinford.
>
> From His Lordship the Marquis of London.
>
> On Tuesday, the 3rd of May, in the Year of Our Lord 1988.
>
> Greetings Noble Cousin.
>
> I trust this letter will further your efforts to guard and protect His Majesty.
>
> The "ten percenter" of the deceased Goodman Albert Chall was one Goodman (?) Ambrose Zekka of dubious antecedents. He was not to be found at his residence, and apparently disappeared with most of his belongings shortly after the sudden demise of Goodman Chall.
>
> A search of his chambers, and such of his belongings as he did not see fit to take along, came up with an assortment of ephemera which, taken singly, disclose nothing, but looked at together are strongly suggestive of certain possibilities.
>
> To Wit:
>
> One well-worn pair of shoes.
>
> One worn leather strap, seventy-two inches long, with a brass buckle.
>
> Fragments of glass.
>
> A small fragment of three-mouse paper with the words "Cannot" on one line and "His Maj—" on the line below written in Polish.
>
> A large fragment of what appears to be a house plan, of which I include an exact copy. I do not send the original for fear that this letter will go astray.
>
> Particles of mustache wax.
>
> A large piece of oiled cloth, about four feet square when opened out, which seems to have once had an avoidance spell on it, and still carries the residue. Which explains why the person who had the apartment missed it when he moved. It was not until the third time the apartment was searched that my

investigators found it—and then they had Master
Sorcerer Lord John Quetzal, the city's chief forensic
sorcerer, along.

Lord John Quetzal performed a series of tests
involving the dust in the room, the psychic pictures
left behind, and suchlike wizardry, and was able to
form sense-pictures of two persons who regularly
used the rooms. One was a shortish man with a dark
beard—probably pointed—and a "sense of great
control." But probably without the Talent. The other
is an enigma. Lord John describes someone who
"was there and yet was not there," and could get
nothing else about him—or her.

The leather strap was from a piece of luggage.
Since it was probably replaced, look for an old piece
of leather luggage with one new strap.

The broken glass was the left lens from a pair of
spectacles. On testing the degree of correction of the
lens, it was determined that it had none. Therefore
either the man who wore the spectacles has one good
eye, or the spectacles were part of a costume. I
assume the latter.

As to the paper fragment, it is tempting to guess,
but unhelpful. But it does support Goodman Chall's
curious contention. Unfortunately.

This information has been developed through the
efforts of my chief assistant, Lord Bontriomphe, and
several of our most able and most trusted plain-
clothes armsmen; Goodmen S. Panser, O. Cather,
and J. Keems. I shall not attempt to further identify
who did what, but all have proven noteworthy and
loyal servants of His Majesty.

Strangely enough, as far as we can determine,
Goodman Albert Chall did not speak Polish.

I trust this proves useful.

> God Save His Majesty.
> London

When Marquis Sherrinford looked up from the letter, Lord
Darcy and Coronel Lord Waybusch were standing beside him.
He silently handed the letter over for Lord Darcy to read and

stared at him impatiently as he did so. "What have we got here?" he asked when Lord Darcy had finished.

Lord Darcy passed the letter on to the Coronel. "Very interesting," he said. "Very interesting indeed."

"I'm glad you think so," Marquis Sherrinford said. "I can't make anything out of it. But it's not my job, I suppose. If you say it's interesting—"

"Dammit, Darcy, *what's* very interesting?" Coronel Lord Waybusch snapped. "I can't see that that gets us any forrader at all. What in heaven is three-mouse paper?"

"It's the watermark," Lord Darcy explained. "Blazon of the d'Enver family, who own the paper mill. Three mice with their tails tied together. It's a good grade of paper sold by the quire for correspondence. Unfortunately it's too common to try to trace the sale."

"I see," Marquis Sherrinford said. "And the words mean nothing by themselves, although as de London said, they are suggestive."

"Too damn suggestive," Coronel Lord Waybusch said, refolding the letter and handing it back to the Marquis, who passed it on to Harbleury. "Polish. The damn Poles have just moved into their rooms, did you know? Three dozen of them. Wouldn't get off the train until they were greeted proper by His Highness. Damn insulting about it, they were. Now they want their own guards, and their own damn cook for good measure. As if good, solid Norman food isn't good enough for them."

"It's just as well," Marquis Sherrinford said. "Let them guard His Courlandtish Majesty. We wouldn't want anything to happen to him, now would we?"

"I just don't like the idea of thirty of them wandering around the Castle when we've got word that some damn Pole is trying to kill His Majesty."

"The threat to His Majesty may be of Polish origin," Lord Darcy said, "but it would seem to come here from London. I doubt whether any of the Polish delegation here even know about it."

"I agree with Lord Darcy," Lord Peter said. "And between us, I have a way to check that."

"What sort of way?" Marquis Sherrinford asked. "Have you placed a magical spy-eye in their suite?"

"No," Lord Peter said. "That would be most unhospitable.

And besides, their sorcerer would be sure to spot it right away. What we have is a secret agent—a man of ours—right in the Polish delegation."

"Really?" Marquis Sherrinford looked surprised. "You mean one of them is really one of us? How, ah, fascinating. Who is it?"

"I'd rather not say," Lord Peter replied. "His safety depends upon *nobody* knowing his identity. And while I trust the discretion of you four gentlemen implicitly, it isn't my own life I would be putting at risk. When and if the time comes that he must reveal himself, you will know."

"Whoever he is, does he know of the threat against His Majesty?" Marquis Sherrinford asked.

"I haven't been able to get word to him," Lord Peter said. "So, unless he knows of it from the inside, so to speak, he doesn't know. And if he had discovered the plot, I must assume he would have gotten word to me."

"Is he reliable?" Coronel Lord Waybusch asked.

"Absolutely," Lord Peter answered. "If you ever meet him, I'll tell you his story and you will see why. On the other hand I must point out that, as he is attached to the delegation of Crown Prince Stanislaw, there is every chance that if such a plot existed, he would not know of it."

"Why is that, my lord?" Marquis Sherrinford asked.

"The Poles seem to run their government by factions," Lord Peter told him. "Crown Prince Stanislaw and his faction are in favor of a lessening of tensions between Poland and the Angevin Empire. Feel it doesn't do either side any good. Not that this is in any way a liberal faction, my lords. I'm sure that Crown Prince Stanislaw believes in the ultimate destiny of Poland to take over Europe and thence the world as much as does his father and his son Sigismund. But Stanislaw believes that the Angevin Empire should be left alone, and we will quietly wither away all on our own."

"Wither, is it?" Coronel Lord Waybusch asked. "We'll see who does the withering!"

"And this is the liberal view?" Marquis Sherrinford asked.

"Such as it is. The King, of course, believes in the total destruction of the Angevin Empire by fair means or foul, as does his grandson, Crown Prince Sigismund. And they both believe implicitly in the *Serka* as the means of accomplishing this. Crown Prince Stanislaw's views are not supported by his father or by his son. And it seems likely that the *Serka* would not feel impelled to notify Stanislaw of its most secret doings while his father is yet alive."

"Nonetheless," Marquis Sherrinford said, "get word to your man if you can. See if he can nose out anything."

"I shall, my lord," Lord Peter agreed.

"My lords, unless I am mistaken, there is some cause for concern here," Harbleury said. "And it may affect the current discussion." He was standing by the desk, to one side of the group, with the Marquis of London's letter in his hand. He had unrolled one of the accompanying documents on the desk and was staring at it as he spoke.

Lord Darcy turned around and leaned over to look at the paper. "What is it, Harbleury?" he asked.

"This map that was in de London's letter," Harbleury said, pointing to the document in question. "It seems to be of the interior of Castle Cristobel. Most of it is rather sketchy, but look—here's the ballroom, and the throne room, this is the armory, and this is the royal chambers."

"I think you're right," Marquis Sherrinford said, peering down at the pencil drawing.

"He is right," Lord Darcy said.

"There is some similarity," Coronel Lord Waybusch said, staring closely at the paper and tracing some of it out with his finger. "But look here—if this is the ballroom, then what is all this? A whole lot of rooms where the courtyard should be? That's not right."

"That would be the second floor," Lord Darcy said. "Whoever copied it placed them side by side. And look at this suite of rooms marked off by X's. It would seem to have some special significance. Which rooms are they?"

Harbleury straightened up and turned to them. "That is the Villefrance suite," he said. "It has been assigned to the Polish delegation."

"Well, I'll be a monkey's cousin!" Coronel Lord Waybusch said. "How do you like that?"

"Our mysteries are coming together, my lords," Lord Darcy said. "Have you noticed?"

"How's that?" Coronel Lord Waybusch asked.

"We have three mysteries," Lord Darcy said. "One: someone is, or may be, trying to kill His Majesty. Two: someone is murdering Master Sorcerers and leaving verses of a nursery rhyme. Three: someone murdered two people in an inn in Tournadotte."

"That is so," Marquis Sherrinford said. "But I'm still not convinced that the slaying in the *Gryphon d'Or* was more than a murder and robbery."

"It's possible," Lord Darcy admitted, "but highly unlikely. Considering the advance preparation that went into it, whatever was stolen must have been of immense value."

"How are they coming together?" Lord Peter asked.

Lord Darcy took the Marquis de London's letter from Harbleury and opened it. "Consider this," he said. "Do you remember Master Sean's description of the murderer of Master DePlessis?"

"He had no description, Lord Darcy," Coronel Lord Waybusch said. "He said he couldn't see the fellow clearly with his magic, or some such. Said the fellow was like a ghost."

"He said the impression was of someone who wasn't completely there," Marquis Sherrinford said thoughtfully.

Lord Darcy tapped the letter. "'The other is an enigma,'" he read from it. "'Lord John describes someone who "was there, and yet was not there."'"

"That's right!" Lord Peter said. "I knew there was something tugging at my memory when I read that."

"There can't be that many ghosts running around the Angevin countryside," Lord Darcy said. "I suggest that this is either the same ghost or a ghostly relative. That is—that the two findings are intimately connected. Precisely what Lord John and Master Sean are psychically seeing—or almost not seeing—we will have to find out."

"Gwiliam of Occam would certainly have agreed with you, my lord," Marquis Sherrinford said.

"I agree myself," Coronel Lord Waybusch said. "It isn't hanging evidence, but I wouldn't give odds against it."

"And what of the other two mysteries?" Lord Peter asked. "How do you tie them together with this letter?"

"As to the Polish connection, there's the scrap of paper and this map," Lord Darcy said. "Although it still doesn't verify the existence of a plot against His Majesty, it makes it hard to ignore the possibility. Considering the connection to the murders in the *Gryphon d'Or,* I would say that the square of oiled cloth was probably used to wrap the blanket that covered the corpses buried in the hill. It would defy logic that two such similar highly unusual objects were not somehow connected."

"So you would have it," Marquis Sherrinford said, "that we have here a Polish madman who, having killed two people in an inn at Tournadotte for reasons of his own, has now come to Castle Cristobel and, possessed of the secret of invisibility, is murdering Master Sorcerers. And this man is planning to assassinate our liege sovereign."

"That is one possible interpretation," Lord Darcy admitted. "No less possible than any of the others. Let us face it, my lords, whatever the correct solution turns out to be, it is going to be no stranger than that. We are looking at a situation sideways and with insufficient information. I assure you, my lords, that to whoever is responsible for this, it makes perfect sense."

"This cannot go on!" Marquis Sherrinford said, slapping his hand on the desk. "I cannot go in to His Majesty twice a day and tell him that his life is still in danger and we have done no more about it."

"We are doing all that can be done, my lord marquis," Lord Peter said. "I have every hope that we will apprehend this man. Success, when it does come, will come all at once, remember that."

"That may be so, Lord Peter," Marquis Sherrinford said. "But remember this—so will failure. All at once."

13

THE AGENT KNOWN AS Pyat entered the ballroom as early as possible, before many others had arrived. The guests were announced as they entered, and Pyat had no desire for anyone to look too closely as the name that was not his own was called out. There could be someone who would recognize the imposture. Or fail to recognize the impostor. There was no way to guard against the possibility of random discovery; one must simply be ready to brazen it out or to flee.

He walked among these Angevins feeling a sense of unreality, and a sense of power; like a fox in a hen suit wandering around the barnyard. He knew something they didn't know, something they couldn't even suspect; and it was a matter of power, of life or death.

He bowed to the ladies and nodded to the gentlemen, and wandered about the room, pausing for refreshment, speaking briefly to a brilliantly attired nobleman who had met him in his assumed identity. His manners were, perhaps, a bit overdone, a trifle foreign, but that served to make him more interesting.

And all the while something inside of him wanted to scream out "Look at me, you fools!"

It was the danger of his work. Since each moment was fraught with the possibility of discovery, there was no respite.

His costume was a disguise, his conversation was an act, everything about him was other than it seemed. It created in him the simultaneous dimorphic emotions of being a hunted animal and a demigod. It kept him alert.

He took a ouiskie-and-splash from a passing footman. What could be more Angevin than a ouiskie-and-splash? He walked about, admiring the beautiful women in their extravagantly lovely gowns. The men, he noted with disgust, also were extravagantly garbed. The court dress of today in the Angevin Empire was the fashionable dress of the seventeenth century, and the century had been a time of silk jackets with slashed sleeves, and puffed-out pants that ended at the knees above bright stockings and pointed shoes. These nobles and masters, the leaders of the Angevin Empire, looked like bright popinjays as they minced about the ballroom floor. He probably looked much like a popinjay himself in his acquired court costume. Lucky it fitted him as well as it did, since small differences would loom large in these tight things. *A decadent land,* he thought, looking about him, *and ripe for the plucking.*

The man who was his weapon approached him from across the room. "I feel it building inside of me," the man said. "You told me I would find release. Through you I would find release."

Pyat nodded briskly. "Release shall be yours," he said in an undertone. "It is all arranged as I promised. Go over to that corner and await me. I shall join you presently and tell you what to do."

"You are sure?" the man asked. "This must be." He was so intent, and yet so matter-of-fact about it, that even Pyat, who had created what he was, found it a bit unnerving.

"I have not failed you yet," Pyat reminded him. "But the time is not yet right. Just a bit longer. Perhaps an hour, perhaps two. Be patient. Enjoy the anticipation."

"The anticipation," the man said, savoring the idea as though it were a physical thing.

"You remember what I told you? The exercises? The preparation?"

"Yes. I remember."

"Good. Go, then, and prepare. That corner of the room over there. There are chairs. Close your eyes. Recite the words. Practice the exercises. Breath deeply. I will fetch you when it is time."

"I go," the man said, and turned and walked away.

Pyat looked around. Nobody had noted their conversation that was good.

His chosen target had not yet come in. Any of six would have done, but he chose this one for esthetic reasons. It, somehow, felt right. A powerful man would suffer an unseemly death. It was almost poetic. Poetic—what a strange thought, considering. He chuckled and joined in the conversation of the group he was standing next to. They were discussing crime novels. "Reading them is unhealthy," he told the group. "Could lead to committing crimes." It was all he could do not to break out laughing.

14

LORD DARCY AND MARY of Cumberland arrived late at the ball. They walked down the long hall leading to the ballroom together, she on his arm. The rows of mirrors on either side of the hall showed endless images of a handsome seventeenth century nobleman escorting his beautiful seventeenth century lady through an arras-draped stone-walled castle corridor. Even the guards of the Household Regiment in their traditional dress uniforms, unchanged for over three hundred years, added to the effect as they snapped to attention at the noble couple's passage. *We are dancing through time,* Lord Darcy thought idly, *and have just stepped back three centuries. Turn, turn, come together—*

"It isn't fair, you know," Mary of Cumberland told him, breaking into his musing as they approached the entrance line at the ballroom door. "If anyone notes our entrance, they'll say, 'Isn't that just like a woman, taking hours to dress.' When the truth is that *I've* been waiting for *you.*"

"Absolutely true, Your Grace," Lord Darcy admitted. "But I'm saved from having to admit it by the fact that officially we're not together. And besides, anyone who sees you in that gown will think that it was well worth the wait."

Mary of Cumberland smiled at the slender, sharp-featured

man beside her and adjusted the bodice of her red silk gown.
"The rules that society chooses to live by have always struck
me as especially fascinating," she said. "There are things one
can do but not talk about, and there are things one can talk
about but not do. There are things—not apparently gender-
related—that men can do, but not women, and there are things
that women can do, but not men. We live in an invisible maze,
and we have all learned where to turn and when, so as to find
our way through."

"Some of the rules are good, Mary, and many are necessary," Lord Darcy said mildly.

"You misunderstood me, my dear," Mary of Cumberland
told him. "As in magic, where there are absolutely essential
words to say and gestures to make or the spell won't work; so
in society there are absolutely essential words to say and
gestures to make or we won't understand each other or trust
each other, and it will all come tumbling down around us. The
problem is that the rules of society, unlike magic, have never
been formalized mathematically, and we don't know which
words are essential to the spell and which are just silly words."

"I see, Your Grace," Lord Darcy said, nodding. "I never
thought of it that way, but now that you've pointed it out, it
makes a lot of sense." This duchess, who was but did not work
at being a journeyman sorcerer, still had unsuspected corners in
her mind like the unseen facets of a prized gem that added to its
sparkle. And the lady did sparkle.

She went in through the main doors before him, to be
announced and join the throng, since they were neither married
nor formally engaged. But they could, without approbation,
spend the entire evening together once they were inside. Mary
of Cumberland, as usual, was right: when you thought about it,
it was strange.

Lord Darcy allowed several people to go in ahead of him,
and then went through the large doors. He presented his card to
the red-faced footman, who passed it to the ornately attired
majordomo, who tapped with his staff thrice on the floor and
bellowed, "His Lordship the Baron Darcy," as Lord Darcy
walked into the room.

The last time he had entered here, there had been a body on
the floor, and blood splattered in a great snowflake around it.
All had been removed—not a trace remained. There was, Lord
Darcy noted, a red carpet covering the outermost quarter of the
floor. That must be the result of his instructions to save the

strange marks on the floor. A thousand square feet of carpeting laid down to conceal two marks an eighth of an inch wide by no more than a foot long. And the freshly shellacked floor shone brightly where it wasn't covered with carpet. The household staff must have resorted to magic, Lord Darcy reflected, to get the new patches dry so fast.

The receiving line was short and averaged fifty pounds overweight. There was the Lord Mayor of London, by tradition the honorary head of the Honorable Society of Guilds of London, with a great red-and-gold sash around his neck bearing the arms of the City of London; his charming round-faced wife, and several people whose names Lord Darcy didn't catch above the babble of introductions. He shook hands with them all and wandered into the ballroom.

"My lord, good to see you here."

Lord Darcy turned around at the words. It was Goodman Harbleury, looking even more gnomelike in his lacy silken court costume.

"You surprise me, Harbleury," Lord Darcy said. "I had imagined these sorts of functions would bore you."

Harbleury chuckled and bobbed his head up and down. "You mean, what am I doing here when I don't have to come? You're right, of course. In many ways I have an enviable position. Having risen from a lowborn commoner to a position of power and trust, even though, at my own wish, still untitled, I have the best of both worlds. I can choose to go where I like, but am not forced by convention to attend boring entertainments and other occasions of nobility."

"I wouldn't have phrased it quite that way," Lord Darcy said, "but I suppose I meant something like that. Unless you have a secret passion for seventeenth century pageantry, or ballroom dancing, I would think that by now you had attended enough of these functions to find them totally uninteresting, and as you are not obliged to attend—"

"Ah, my lord, but in this case I am obliged," Harbleury explained. "On two counts. One, His Majesty and Marquis Sherrinford will both be here, and either of them might need me at any time. I would rather be on hand. Two, I am the, er, designer of this affair, and I feel impelled to see at first hand how it turns out."

"The designer?"

"Yes, my lord. The Lord Mayor of London, who, as head of the Honorable Society, was responsible for this ball, was not sure of the proper form to follow. After all, this is the first investiture of a Prince of Gaul in sixty-three years."

"Ah!" Lord Darcy said. "Light begins to dawn. So he appealed to you, as a protocol expert."

"That is so, my lord."

"And you—"

"Made it up, my lord. There wasn't anybody I could find who remembered what the Guild Halls' Ball was like sixty-three years ago, and the newspapers of the day were exceedingly ungenerous in their descriptions of the event. They told in great detail who was there and what they wore, but not what they did, or how. So I made it up."

Lord Darcy looked around him. The great arms-bearing shields of the one hundred fourteen guilds that comprised the Honorable Society lined three of the walls, arranged in sequential order from the date of the founding of the guild, leaning forward in their holders as if to keep watch on their members. It would have been an ominous look, but for the frivolous designs of many of the arms. There were the Honorable Bakers, 1487, for instance, with two sacks of flour rampant on a field of eggs. Or the Honorable Furriers, 1614, with a red hand *coupé* holding a string of mink pelts. Or the Honorable Fishmongers, 1627, with three dead herring on a white plate. All motifs, Lord Darcy was sure, that the designers of the arms and the founders of the guilds took very seriously. The colors were gay, and the effect of all of these taken together was almost overwhelming, for those few who thought to look up.

The side doors were open, and the rooms beyond were lined with tables covered with yards of white linen and strewn with a great variety of delicate foodstuffs, with the room on the left being reserved for liquid refreshment. "It looks like a larger version of the sort of entertainment the various guilds throw for themselves every year," said Lord Darcy, who had been to dozens. "A sort of formal dress but informal dinner-dance."

"You have no idea how difficult it was to talk the Lord Mayor and his guild-hall minions into that," Harbleury told him. "They wanted to get all-over fancy. Outdo the peerage at their own game. They would have looked silly, and I told them so. But they didn't believe me."

"How did you convince them?"

Harbleury smiled a crooked smile. "I talked about their heritage," he said. "And the strength of the guilds, and their place in the Empire, and the unending tradition of Angevin freedoms which were their strength and their joy."

"What does that mean?" Lord Darcy asked.

"Damned if I know," Harbleury admitted. "But it sounded exactly the right note, and we are going to have a pleasant evening out of what could have been a disaster."

Lord Darcy took Harbleury's hand and shook it firmly. "It is a pleasure to know such a master of the fine-sounding phrase," he said. "Whenever I need some talking-out done, I now know the man to do it. Very good job, Harbleury."

"Thank you, my lord," Harbleury said, looking modestly down. "I do much the same for his lordship and His Majesty on occasion, so I was not without practice."

Lord Darcy parted with Harbleury and almost immediately ran into his master, the Marquis Sherrinford, who was in earnest conversation with a short, dapper man with a spade beard. "Ah, Lord Darcy!" Marquis Sherrinford called out. "Stop for a second. Someone here I want you to meet."

Lord Darcy paused, greeted Marquis Sherrinford, and was introduced to his companion, the Count d'Alberra. "Ah, yes," Lord Darcy said, shaking hands with the short count. "You are the gentleman who is curing my lord marquis's headaches." Lord Darcy noted that although small in stature, the count was powerfully built, with massive shoulders and a barrel chest. He was also one of those men who regards shaking hands as a contest, and he squeezed Lord Darcy's hand unmercifully for a long moment before letting go.

"Thank you for the compliment, my lord," Count d'Alberra said. "But my friend here, the Marquis Sherrinford, is actually healing himself. I am pleased and delighted that my method is enabling him to do so. It is my hope that someday many of those ills that cannot be reached by conventional magic, that are today beyond the scope of either the healer or the chirurgeon, will be reached by the techniques I am developing."

"I know nothing of your methods, Count d'Alberra, I'm sorry to say. Is there any way you could describe them so that I could get some idea of what you do?"

"He talks to you," Marquis Sherrinford said. "And he makes you talk. All about your childhood."

"Childhood?"

"It is my belief," Count d'Alberra explained, "that the body is controlled by the mind. And that many illnesses that cannot be cured externally, by the Laying On of Hands, can be treated by the body's own defenses, activated by the mind. The problem is one of how to get these defenses turned on—how to get the mind to work."

"I see," Lord Darcy said politely. "And you do this by discussing your patient's childhood?"

"It works, my lord," Marquis Sherrinford said. "At least in my case it has. However strange the theory behind it—excuse me, Count—it does work."

"I cannot argue with success," Lord Darcy said.

"The childhood seems to be the key," Count d'Alberra said. "I was surprised myself to discover this."

The triple rap of the majordomo's staff sounded, and he bellowed, "His Majesty, the Crown Prince Stanislaw of Poland, King of Courlandt, Duke of Krakau, Knight-Commander of the Most Holy Order of the Bloody Sheep. Her Highness, the Crown Princess Yetta."

"Ah, His Polish Majesty and wife are here," Marquis Sherrinford said. "I'd better go over and greet him. Would either of you like to make the acquaintance of the future King of Poland?"

"I'd be fascinated to, my lord marquis," Lord Darcy replied.

"You'll excuse me," Count d'Alberra said, "but I can't stand the Polish!" And he bowed to the Marquis and Lord Darcy, turned on his heels and walked away.

"Well!" Marquis Sherrinford said. "You'd think a healer would have his emotions under better control. I mean, none of us *love* the Polish. Come along with me, Lord Darcy, and meet His Majesty. Who knows, someday you may have dealings with him."

"That's so, my lord," Lord Darcy said, and followed the Marquis across the ballroom floor.

Crown Prince Stanislaw was a short, muscular man, somewhere around fifty years old, with a round head and close-cropped, graying blond hair. "It is a pleasure, Lord Darcy, to meet you," he said with a heavy German accent, reminding Lord Darcy that High German was the language of the Polish court. "Your fame of detection has crossed even into Warsaw. Perhaps someday we will call upon your many talents, eh? Would you do that? Would you help the Poles?"

"It would be an honor, Your Majesty," Lord Darcy said, bowing.

"Dat is good," Crown Prince Stanislaw said. "Whatever is between our countries, people is still people, ja?"

"That's so, Your Majesty," Lord Darcy agreed.

"I go now," the Crown Prince said, "and dance with my wife. That will help convince these Angevin people that I am no monster, ja?" And with that he nodded to Marquis Sherrinford and Lord Darcy, and holding his arm for the statuesque, blond Princess Yetta, he stalked off to the dance floor.

Mary of Cumberland, Lord Darcy judged, had been alone long enough, so he bid the Marquis Sherrinford adieu and went to find her amid the throng. When he did, it turned out she was not alone, but one of two women in the midst of a gaggle of admiring men. Which was, he decided, as it should be. The other was a small, dark-haired woman with an intent, intelligent expression who Lord Darcy could not remember ever seeing before. The gaggle was about eight men deep, standing around, drinks in hand, trying to look casual. A tall, heavyset, broad-shouldered man with a ruddy complexion and an overly elaborate dress uniform was holding forth about something as Lord Darcy approached.

"Come join us, my lord," the Duchess said, catching sight of Lord Darcy as he approached. "Lord Darcy, may I introduce Lady Marta de Verre, and this is Lord Brummel, General Lord Halifax, Sir Felix Chaimberment, Master Sorcerer Dandro Bittman, Major von Jonn of the New England Legion, and I believe you know Master Sorcerer Darryl Longuert. The Major is telling us all what life is like on the New England frontier. It's absolutely fascinating."

"I imagine it must be, Your Grace," Lord Darcy said, joining the group after bowing slightly to each person as they were introduced. "The New England territory has always fascinated me."

The stentorian bellow of the majordomo suddenly silenced the hall. "His Most Serene Majesty, John the Fourth," the majordomo announced, "by the Grace of God King of England, Ireland, Scotland, and France; Emperor of the Romans and Germans; Premier Chief of the Moqtessumid Clan; Son of the Sun; Count of Anjou and Maine; Donator of the Sovereign Order of Saint John of Jerusalem; Sovereign of the Most Ancient Order of the Round Table, of the Order of the Leopard, of the Order of the Lily, of the Order of the Three Crowns, and of the Order of Saint Andrew; Lord and Protector

of the Western Continents of New England and New France;
Defender of the Faith. *God save the King!*"

"God save the King!" three hundred voices echoed.

"Her Most Gracious and Noble Majesty Marie," the
majordomo went on, "Queen Consort of John the Fourth,
Princess of Roumania, Duchess of Sark and Guernsey, and
Lady Commander of His Majesty's Winchester Guards. All
Stand."

Any who were not already standing rose as the King and
Queen entered the ballroom. By tradition they were an hour
late in arriving, and by tradition the ball proper would shortly
begin.

"Major von Jonn," Mary of Cumberland said, picking up
the thread where it had been dropped, "my lords, Lady Marta,
may I present Lord Darcy, the Chief Investigator for the Court
of Chivalry."

"A pleasure," von Jonn said, coming to an exaggerated
posture of attention and bowing stiffly in a distinctly Germanic
military greeting. "A true and distinct pleasure, it is. I have
heard of your exploits, my lord, and have been desirous of
meeting you for some time. Particularly since I returned from
the northern continent of the New World. I was planning to
look you up in London after the coronation."

"And why is that, Major?" Lord Darcy asked.

Mary of Cumberland was staring at Lord Darcy and
mouthing the words "on the list!" behind the Major's back.
Lord Darcy caught her eye and nodded slightly to show that he
knew. He had memorized the list of names forwarded by Chief
Henri, and Major von Jonn was among them. As was Lady
Marta's name, and Sir Darryl Longuert. Her Grace of Cumberland had indeed been busy in the few minutes she had been at
the ball.

"I have always admired criminal investigation," the Major
explained. "It strikes me as something that is important to
do—that is worth doing for itself. I have been thinking of
trying to go into that field, if it can be determined that I have
the ability. If you assume any sort of structured society,
whether this one or one drastically different, it must have laws
to define and protect itself. And the men who enforce those
laws are the men who hold the society together."

"Well, you have the philosophy, if not the ability," Lord
Darcy said, chuckling.

Master Dandro, a plump little sorcerer in his mid-forties,
with protruding teeth and a slight chin, raised a protesting

finger. "It is the Church that holds society together," he pronounced. "Religion and magic—faith and practice—the two cornerstones of Angevin society. And the Crown, of course, is the key block in the arch, if I may be permitted to extend my metaphor."

The Duchess of Cumberland smiled at the little sorcerer. "Really, Master Dandro," she said. "That's certainly an orthodox view."

Master Dandro turned to her and smiled a rabbity smile. "Orthodoxy is my only doxy," he said. He bowed slightly, chuckling at his own wit, and swiveled to face Master Sir Darryl Longuert. "I must congratulate you on your ascension to the laureateship, Sir Darryl," he said. "Who would have thought— But then, you always did have the knack for being at the right place at the right time."

"That must have been it," Sir Darryl agreed mildly.

"The last time we met—was it two years ago?—such a thing was furthest from your mind, as I recall. You remember, Sir Darryl; it was at the thrumming."

"Thrumming?" Lady Marta asked. "Is that an event?"

"In some places," Lord Darcy said.

"It is a sorcerer's term," Sir Darryl explained. "It's our expression for the ceremony of removing a sorcerer's, ah, powers. It is done very rarely, and then only for extreme cause."

"I know of what you speak," Lord Darcy told him.

"It's the aristocracy that holds society together," said Lord Brummel, an old man with too much white hair and a high rasping voice. He looked around for approval, and not getting it, went "hah, hum," and stared at the floor.

"Isn't that what you were doing out there in the wilderness?" Lord Darcy asked Major von Jonn. "Enforcing the rules of society in a place where they're still new?"

Major von Jonn shook his head. "The Twelve Nations, which is what the confederation of tribes around the northeast coast calls itself, has a civilization as old and as, ah, civilized as our own. We merely have superior guns and superior magic. Were it the other way around, they would have their colonies here, and call them 'New Seneca' or 'East Iroquois.'"

"An interesting observation," interjected a short, haughty-looking noble in a bright green court costume, who had just walked over and was standing to the left of Mary of Cumberland. He lifted his chin and peered through his quizzing-glass at the Major. "You think the savage aborigines of New England to be our cultural equals? I understand they paint their skins red and white and scalp their enemies."

"Some do," Major von Jonn agreed. "And in the principality of Hesse, where I come from, we cut the heads off thieves and hang them on pike staves in the village square. But we don't paint ourselves red and white. Therein must lie the civilizing difference."

"But they are immoral heathens, sir!" the nobleman snapped, looking annoyed.

"Not according to His Holiness, Pope Charles the Fourth," Major von Jonn reminded him. "The Papal Inquisition of the New Lands determined that the natives have a well-defined religion, whose moral boundaries are acceptable to Christianity. Heathens, yes; immoral, no."

Lord Darcy nodded. In the middle of the last century the Papal Inquiry had been set in motion over the question of the morality of the native religions of New England—the northern continent of the New World—and New France, the southern. After twenty years of study it had decided that, while certainly heathen—that is, un-Christian—most of the religions of the New World were clearly morally sound. The study was mostly of the quality of the magic practiced by the various peoples and religions. While in some cases—notably the war gods of the southern continent and up through the Duchy of Mechicoe— the reek of ancient evil was so strong that sensitives could not approach within a hundred yards of those temples; in most cases the rituals were as untainted with black magic as anything a Christian sorcerer or priest could ask for. And, of course, one of the tenets of modern religion was that the use of white magic was God's gift to mankind, just as black magic came from the Devil. Therefore it must follow that if a religion could use white magic, it must be at least moral, even if misled in matters of faith.

Of course, this did not mean that, as it became possible, the natives would not be converted to the True Faith, it just meant that there wasn't a dreadful hurry about it.

"Well!" said the nobleman, twirling his quizzing-glass at the end of its ribbon and glaring at the Major. "If you choose to make no distinction between the habits of a bunch of savages and the behavior of civilized men, so be it, sir."

"Major von Jonn, may I present Baron Hepplethong," the Duchess of Cumberland said smoothly.

"Ah!" Major von Jonn said. "A pleasure, Baron. That's a

British name, isn't it? From the Pict, I believe. It was only a few hundred years ago when your ancestors were painting themselves blue, wasn't it?"

"Humph!" Baron Hepplethong said, and turned away.

"That man is a fool," Lady Marta said, her dark eyes staring at Baron Hepplethong's retreating back. "Most men are fools, but he carries it to unnatural extremes. I have the misfortune to be distantly related to him. He believes in the natural superiority of the white race, the noble class, and the male sex. He also feels that people who wear green are morally superior to those who wear red or brown. I do not jest."

"We all are subject to the prejudices of our class and our time, my dear Lady Marta," Master Darryl said firmly. "Some of us more than others. You must learn to suffer fools, there are so many of them."

"I try, Master Darryl," Lady Marta said, turning back to him with a rustle of her skirts. "And I find that an occasional outburst helps."

"Why, so it does," Master Darryl admitted.

"An interesting theory you have," Lord Darcy told the Major. "Is it that you hold with the nobility of the savage, or the savagery of European civilization?"

Major von Jonn thought it over for a second. "Yes," he said finally. "I hold that there is no difference ethically, morally, or spiritually between us; only materially, the last and weakest of the four."

"No difference, Major?" Master Sorcerer Dandro Bittman asked. "Surely—"

"I apologize, Master Dandro," Major von Jonn said, bowing slightly to the sorcerer. "I did not mean no *distinction*. Several of their practices are quite different from ours in all of these ways. I meant no qualitative difference. Neither is superior to the other, given the basic differences between the two cultures."

"Yours is a minority opinion, Major, as I suppose you know," Lord Darcy told him. "But it is one which should be heard more often. It is a question that deserves to be debated and discussed, and not simply have the answers assumed by those in authority."

"So I have often said, my lord," Major von Jonn said.

"I don't suppose that your outspoken notions regarding the native New Englanders had anything to do with your return home or your desire to get into another line of work?" Lord Darcy asked.

"Actually not," Major von Jonn told him. "I have returned because I completed my five-year tour. I now have a six-month leave before I get reassigned. As to my change in interest—I cannot say that being a career soldier has ever truly appealed to me. It was the best route for advancement and education open to a young commoner from Hesse, so I took it. As I gained the education, I discovered that I disliked the career."

"Fascinating discussion, fascinating," Master Dandro said to the group at large. "But I must leave now. A matter of importance to discuss with His Majesty. You'll excuse me, I'm sure." And, smiling and bowing, he backed away from the group and into the surrounding throng.

"Why would His Majesty want to see Master Dandro Bittman?" Lady Marta asked.

"I fear that his description of the coming event might not tally with His Majesty's," Sir Darryl said. "When Master Dandro lies dying he will excuse himself, saying that there's a small matter he wants to take up with the Lord."

"A strange little man," Mary of Cumberland said.

"But a fine sorcerer for all of that," Sir Darryl told her. "His mind is rigid and not receptive to new ideas. But the ideas he holds are, ah, orthodox."

"Soldiering is a noble calling, young man," General Lord Halifax said. Looking like a brightly plumaged bird of prey, the tall, skinny general leaned forward and tapped the major on the shoulder. His two rows of medals clanked together on his chest. "It's soldiering that has built this empire, and that keeps it together. You young chaps from the principalities would have little chance for advancement at all were it not for the profession of soldiering that is open to you all. It's the hand that feeds you, young man, don't bite it!"

"I'm not, sir. Not at all," Major von Jonn protested. "As history has shown too clearly, any country that ceases to pay attention to soldiering soon ceases to exist. So it has been, and so it shall be into the foreseeable future. But personally, I've put in my ten years and I think it's time for a change. And it could be that some would say that those of us from the provinces should have other opportunity for advancement besides the chance to die for our country."

"Sir!" General Lord Halifax snorted.

Major von Jonn raised his hand. "Not I, General, I assure you."

From the front of the room the ballmaster, who was the president of the Honorable Guild of Glassblowers, and therefore had mighty lungs and a powerful voice, announced the commencement of the first dance. It was to be a cotillon, with His Majesty and Her Majesty leading.

The talk died down to a murmur and the assembled mass moved aside, and the King and Queen of England and France, Emperor and Empress of the Angevin Empire, took their place in the center of the ballroom. Flanking them were their sons, the Prince of Britain and the Duke of Lancaster (soon to be Prince of Gaul) and their wives. And then, in order of precedence, the aristocracy of the Angevin Empire and the leaders of its most powerful guilds.

Lord Darcy noticed that Richard, Duke of Normandy, was not there. When he took his place with Mary of Cumberland on the dance floor, he understood why. On the three sides of the overhead balcony not used by the orchestra, spaced evenly around the room, were a squad of men. They were in the uniform of the Household Guard, and indeed they were of the guard, but they were a picked group. Lord Darcy recognized the figure of Richard of Normandy in guard's officer's uniform at one end of the balcony, and Coronel Lord Waybusch at the other.

Mary of Cumberland saw where Lord Darcy was looking and looked up. "Guards?" she asked. "What good can they do from up there?"

"Archers," Lord Darcy told her. "Trained, practiced long-bowmen. The English archer has been defending the Empire for eight hundred years, and he's still at it. A bow is still the best weapon for a medium distance in an enclosed space. More accurate and much quieter than a handgun. It must be Duke Richard's idea. He is determined that nothing is going to happen to his brother."

Lord Darcy looked grave, and Mary of Cumberland squeezed his arm. She knew what he was thinking. "So are we all," she said.

The music started, and King John and Queen Marie, and the three hundred people around them, began the stately cotillon. Lord Darcy put his arm around the Duchess of Cumberland's waist and held her perhaps a bit more firmly than was called for. "Let's dance," he whispered.

15

BY TRADITION THEIR MAJESTIES came late to social gatherings and left early. They came late because everyone wanted to be there to see them arrive. They left early because, by tradition, no one could leave a party until after the royal couple had departed. They stayed for two and a half hours at the Guild Hall Ball, which made it a success. The orchestra played "God for Arthur, England, France, Scotland, and Wales," which was always sung with the name of the current king, so everyone mouthed "God for Jo-hn, England, France . . ." and so on, and on the last note King John and Queen Marie left the ballroom through the private door at the back. The Queen, escorted by two ladies-in-waiting, went to her chambers. The King and Marquis Sherrinford went into the throne room.

About ten minutes later Harbleury found Lord Darcy talking to the Dowager Duchess of Cumberland, Father Phillip, and Archbishop Maximilian of Paris, and tapped him on the shoulder. "If Your Lordship will excuse me," Harbleury said to him softly, "His Lordship the Marquis Sherrinford would like to speak with you for a moment."

"Of course," Lord Darcy said. He excused himself from the others and followed Harbleury to the private door, where the Marquis awaited him.

Marquis Sherrinford silently led Lord Darcy through the anteroom, across the corridor, and unlocked and opened the rear door to the throne room. "The doors are self-closing," he explained. "And since the only keys are attuned to myself and Their Majesties, I can't send for you, I must bring you. Which makes what I am about to show you all the more remarkable."

"What's that, Your Lordship?" Lord Darcy asked.

"You'd better see for yourself," Marquis Sherrinford replied, leading the way through the curtains behind the throne and around to the throne itself.

The lighting was dim, the only illumination coming from the flickering flames in a pair of gas wall brackets on opposite sides of the great room, which were set barely strong enough to assure that they wouldn't blow out. This was probably the normal night lighting for the room; if the King or Marquis Sherrinford needed to enter, servitors would bring up the lights.

The only people visible in the room beside Lord Darcy himself, and Marquis Sherrinford, and Harbleury—who were behind him—was a shadowy figure who sat silent on the great throne and a solitary man standing in the middle of the floor, facing the other way.

Lord Darcy took two steps forward, and then recognized the man standing in front of him by the characteristic Plantagenet shape of his head and shoulders. He dropped to one knee. "Sire."

The Emperor of the Anglo-French, Sovereign of New England and New France, turned around. Even in the dim light Lord Darcy could see that this night the cares of Empire hung heavy on his shoulders.

"My Lord Darcy," His Majesty said, taking two steps forward. "We meet from time to time, you and I, over the bodies of other men. Figuratively, since you are my Chief Investigator. And now, for the first time, literally." His Majesty waved his hand toward the throne.

Lord Darcy stood and glanced toward the throne and the mysterious, silent figure on it. He was prevented from turning to face it by his monarch's presence. One did not turn one's back on the King.

"Let us ignore protocol," said King John, realizing the problem. "For the moment I am merely the Duke of Navarre, and you have a body to examine. Go to it, my lord."

The Duke of Navarre was one of King John's favorite incognitos, a fiction that would prove useful now. Lord Darcy could work while the Duke of Navarre peered over his shoulder. The Duke of Navarre, after all, was not the King.

Lord Darcy turned to look at the shadowy figure on the throne. "I assume," he said, "that this was not an attempt on His Majesty's life."

"His Majesty and I entered the throne room together," Marquis Sherrinford said. "The, ah, person on the throne was thus when we entered. No one else, save for Harbleury, came in or went out."

"That's clear, then," Lord Darcy said. He took the two steps up to the dais and studied the figure on the throne. It was a small, plump man, slumped over and with his eyes open, staring. Even in the dim light there was no question as to whether he was dead or what had killed him. A long, wooden pike shaft protruded from the man's chest, and it appeared to have been driven straight through his body, transfixing him to the throne.

Lord Darcy bent over the body. "I will need a chirurgeon," he said, "and Master Sean O Lochlainn, if someone would send for him. Also, I need more light."

"Harbleury," Marquis Sherrinford said, "please find Master Sean and Sir Moses Benander and bring them here. And then Lord Peter. You will say nothing of this."

"Of course, my lord," Harbleury said, and retreated from the room by the rear door.

The "Duke of Navarre" had found the light pole used for the gaslights and was slowly going around the throne room turning on and lighting the wall fixtures. *It must be the Duke of Navarre,* Lord Darcy thought. *His Majesty John IV would never indulge in such menial duties.*

Then Lord Darcy shook his head, as he realized that he was wrong. A crime had been committed in the throne room of Castle Cristobel within the past half hour. A murder that might, if it was somehow tied in to the others, which it most certainly was, affect everyone in the Castle from His Majesty down. The investigation of that murder was, for the moment, the most important thing happening in Castle Cristobel, in the Duchy of Normandy, and quite probably in the Angevin Empire.

Given that, it was altogether fitting, altogether proper,

altogether *Plantagenet*, for His Majesty to do whatever had to be done, and if it was merely lighting the gas mantles, so be it.

As the light increased, Lord Darcy continued with his examination of the body. With a slight shock, he suddenly realized who the victim was. The small, plump body with the sightless, staring eyes, had held the mortal soul of Master Sorcerer Dandro Bittman, until someone had chosen to let it out with the iron point of a pike.

"How did he get in here?" Lord Darcy asked.

"We were hoping you could tell us," Marquis Sherrinford said dryly.

"His name is Bittman," Lord Darcy said. "Master Sorcerer Dandro Bittman. I was talking to him less than two hours ago. As I remember, he excused himself, saying he had a meeting with His Majesty at that time."

"With His Majesty?" Marquis Sherrinford asked, sounding startled.

"I assume that that wasn't the case," Lord Darcy said dryly.

"It was not," the Duke of Navarre assured him. And who, Lord Darcy reflected, would know the King's business better than the Duke of Navarre?

"Then neither of Your Lordships let Master Dandro into the throne room?"

"That is so," Marquis Sherrinford affirmed.

"Well, that lets out the back door, to which, as I've just been reminded, there are only three keys," Lord Darcy said. "Let us find out by which of the remaining doors Master Dandro entered." He walked over to the double doors to the King's Gallery and pulled them open. Two guardsmen who were framing the door on the other side snapped to attention and turned to face each other as the door opened.

"At ease, soldiers," Lord Darcy said. "I'm Lord Darcy, the King's investigator. I need to know who has come in through this door since you've been on duty."

The two soldiers looked at each other and, nonverbally, decided which of them was to speak. The one to Lord Darcy's left came to a brace and said, "Sir, no one has entered or left by these doors since we have been on duty."

"And how long has that been?" Lord Darcy asked.

"Sir, we came on guard at eight o'clock," the guard said. "We are due to be relieved shortly."

"Did you at any time hear any noises from inside the throne room?" Lord Darcy asked.

"Noises?" The man looked puzzled. "No, sir."

"Thank you, soldier," Lord Darcy said, checking his watch. It was a few minutes before midnight. He took a step backward and let the door close in front of him. Then he turned around and strode across the throne room to the Queen's Gallery doors and pulled them open.

Lord Peter Whiss was running down the hallway toward him as the door opened. "What is it, Lord Darcy?" he said, panting, as he reached the doors. "What's happened?"

"One second," Lord Darcy said, and turned to the guards who flanked the door. "How many people have been through these doors since you've been on duty?" he asked.

"None, sir," one of them replied, standing at brace.

"Did you hear any sounds from in here while you were on duty?"

"No, sir."

"Thank you," Lord Darcy said, and motioned to Lord Peter to follow him into the throne room.

"We have another killing," Lord Darcy told Lord Peter. "Walk me to the Doors of State; they're the only unchecked entrance to this room."

"In here?" Lord Peter demanded. "Someone's been killed in *here*?"

Lord Darcy nodded. Lord Peter said nothing further as they walked together to the Doors of State. In the great hall beyond, as they saw when they opened the massive right-hand door, there was a full squad of men deployed around the various posts, pillars, and wall niches, including the usual two at the door. A member of the household staff was scurrying from left to right across the room at that moment, but there were no other civilians in evidence.

"Has anyone been through these doors since you came on guard?" Lord Darcy asked the closer guard.

"No, sir," the guard said.

"And you've been there for the full tour—almost four hours?"

"Yes, sir."

"Did you hear any sounds from inside while you were standing guard?"

"No, sir, but then we wouldn't. The doors are thick and heavy. We never hear anything through them."

"I see. Thank you," Lord Darcy said, and let the doors close. "They're not lying?" he asked Lord Peter.

Lord Peter nodded. "Only the truth, so far."

"You'd know?" Lord Darcy asked. "Even on such short statements?"

"I'd know," Lord Peter told him. "When anyone lies to me, I know. Incidently, they're right about not hearing noises. With all this drapery about, sounds are pretty much absorbed within the room, and the doors are the sort they haven't made these past three hundred years: thick, solid, heavy, and close-fitting. No sound would get through."

"I already asked the guards at the King's Gallery," Lord Darcy said, "but I think you should check their statements. I don't have your ability; if they are telling the truth also, we have an interesting problem."

Lord Peter went to speak to the King's Gallery guards while Lord Darcy returned to the throne and its dead burden. Master Dandro had a look of shocked surprise on his face; clearly he had not expected what happened to him. Lord Darcy could believe that. One does not sit down, even on a throne, if one expects to be skewered to the back of the chair with a twelve-foot pike.

Lord Darcy conducted a superficial examination of the body while he waited for Master Sean and the chirurgeon. Clothing, the same as he remembered: the gold-trimmed powder-blue dress robes of the master sorcerer. The insignias of several holy orders and magical societies were sewn on the left upper arm, the left side of the chest, and other appropriate spots on the robe. Several ribbons were pinned to a ribbon bar on the chest, denoting service awards given him by the Sorcerers' Guild. Truly a useful member of society, if a bit vain about it.

And, pinned in the middle of his chest with a long straight pin, was a folded slip of paper. Lord Darcy removed it and unfolded it. His face was expressionless as he read.

"What's that, another verse?" asked Marquis Sherrinford, who had been watching Lord Darcy's inspection of the body.

Lord Darcy passed it to Marquis Sherrinford, who read it quickly and handed it to His Majesty.

* * *

Eight little wizards praying to heaven
  One's prayers were answered—and now there are seven.

"Damn!" said His Majesty. "Is there no way to stop this madman?"

"I sincerely hope so, Your, ah, my lord," Lord Darcy said.

The King turned to Lord Darcy. "You have some prospect of finding this killer?"

"Yes, Your Majesty. I only hope that I can do so before he has a chance to write another of these little verses."

Lord Peter walked over and nodded to Lord Darcy. "You have a mystery on your hands," he said. "They weren't lying."

"Who?" the King asked.

"The guards, my lord," Lord Peter said. "According to the guards at all three outer doors, nobody entered this room or left it for the last three hours. And, as Their Majesties and Marquis Sherrinford have the only keys to this back door, we have a *real* locked-room mystery on our hands."

"Could this lock have been circumvented magically?" the King-cum-Duke asked.

"Your Sorcerer Laureate thinks not, my lord," Marquis Sherrinford said.

"I will have Master Sean make sure, my lord," Lord Darcy said. "It would have to have left signs, even if it could have been done."

The King shook his head. "Do something, Lord Darcy," he said emphatically. "This is not how I pictured my son's coronation to be." He turned to Marquis Sherrinford. "We are going up to Our apartment. Keep Us informed."

"Yes, Your Majesty," Marquis Sherrinford said, noting His Majesty's switch to the first person plural—or regal—which showed that the Duke of Navarre was no longer present. "One second." He went to the great doors and called, "Guard!"

"What's this, my lord marquis?" the King asked. "You think We need an escort?"

"Yes, Your Majesty," Marquis Sherrinford said firmly.

His Majesty glared at Marquis Sherrinford for a second, and then looked over at the corpse and relaxed. "Well," he said, "you're probably right. The Empire needs Us more than We need to prove—whatever We were trying to prove."

"Yes, Your Majesty," Marquis Sherrinford agreed. He

called in a corporal of the guard and two privates, and instructed them to escort His Majesty to the door of his apartment.

The King went to the rear door and unlocked it, then paused while the guards preceded him into the hall. "Remember," he said, turning back to the room, "keep Us informed. We are depending on you. Lord Peter, Lord Darcy, Our prayers go with you. Marquis Sherrinford, We shall see you first thing in the morning."

"Yes, Your Majesty," Marquis Sherrinford replied. The three of them knelt as their sovereign left the room.

Master Sean O Lochlainn and Sir Moses Benander came in together from the King's Gallery and, looking curiously at the group by the throne, walked over to join it.

"What have we here?" Sir Moses said. An old man with intense dark eyes and a straggly white beard, Sir Moses Benander was the Royal Chirurgeon. A very positive man, who had no use for fools or foolishness, he was acknowledged to be the finest chirurgeon in the Empire. His evenings he spent at aristocratic dinner parties, enjoying the status of being the Royal Chirurgeon. His days he spent at a free private hospital he had founded in London to aid the poor.

"A dead man, Sir Moses," Lord Darcy told him.

"Remember, young man, he isn't dead until *I* say he's dead," Sir Moses said. He pushed Lord Darcy aside and stepped over to the throne. He stared down at Master Sorcerer Dandro Bittman.

"This man is dead," Sir Moses said.

"Indeed he is, Sir Moses," Master Sean said, coming up behind him. "And that's something that neither you with your bone cutting nor I with my spells, nor the finest healer with the most sensitive hands in the kingdom, can do aught about."

"That's so, Master Sean," Sir Moses said, staring down at the grotesque figure of a man pinned to the royal throne by a twelve-foot pike like a moth on a card. A very bloody moth. "And I can do even less than you. All I can do is verify that he is dead, which any fool could see. You can catch the bastard that did the deed."

" 'Tis Lord Darcy who does the catching," Master Sean said. "I supply him with my findings, and he talks to the parish priest and the innkeeper and the woodchopper, and then he runs his finger along the side of his nose three times and says 'arrest the seneschal,' and later on he explains to me how he knew. And it's all painfully obvious—*after* he explains it.''

"Let us hope that it is so this time, Master Sean,'' Lord Darcy said. "But, as I'm faced with an impossible crime, I'm afraid I'm going to have to come up with an impossible solution.''

"Impossible?'' Master Sean stared at the corpse. "The man was skewered with a pike. Nothing impossible about it. It took a strong hand—''

"And a little practice, I'd say,'' Sir Moses interrupted. "A hand—arm, actually—that was only moderately strong could do it, but it would take practice to get the motion down.''

"It's the question of ingress that turns this into an impossible crime,'' Lord Darcy explained. "There are four entrances to this room. One of them, the rear entrance, has three keys, all attuned to the holders, who are the King, the Queen, and Marquis Sherrinford here. Unless Master Sean tells me that the lock has been tampered with, which I'm sure he won't, then neither the killer nor the victim could have gotten in that way. The other three doors are under constant guard, and the guards swear that nobody has entered or left this room for the past four hours, since eight o'clock. And Lord Peter assures me they're telling the truth.''

"But this man has been dead for less than an hour!'' Sir Moses said.

"Lord Peter,'' Marquis Sherrinford said suddenly, "ask me whether I brought anyone in here over the past four hours before I entered with His Majesty.''

"What's that, Your Lordship?'' Lord Peter said. "I don't understand.''

"Ask me,'' Marquis Sherrinford said, "so that I can say no.''

"Ah,'' Lord Peter said. "Now I understand. My lord marquis, did you bring the victim, or anyone else aside from His Majesty, in here at any time over the past four hours?''

"No, Lord Peter, I did not,'' Marquis Sherrinford said firmly.

Lord Peter looked at Lord Darcy. "His lordship is telling the truth,'' he said. "Not that I doubted it for an instant, you understand.'' He paused thoughtfully. "But how do you know *I'm* telling the truth?'' he asked Lord Darcy.

"It would be stretching the bounds of probability to assume

that these killings are a conspiracy between Your Lordship and my lord marquis," Lord Darcy said. "Particularly these particular crimes, done in this particular manner."

"You don't think we'd commit so grotesque a crime?" Marquis Sherrinford asked.

"It's not that," Lord Darcy said. "Lord Peter, if you wanted to kill a man, how would you do it?"

"Well . . ." Lord Peter thought for a minute. "I've never *wanted* to kill a man," he said. "I have killed a few men in the course of my, ah, profession, but never with advance planning. Always in defense of my own life. The Most Secret Service does not condone assassinations, you know."

"But if you *had* to," Lord Darcy persisted. "If you were convinced that, for the good of the Empire, one man had to be removed, how would you do it?"

"I don't know," Lord Peter said. "Something clean and quick, I expect. Most likely I'd take him out to the woods and we'd have a hunting accident."

"That's what I mean," Lord Darcy said. "Even if your mind, or Marquis Sherrinford's mind, ran to murder, they wouldn't run to this type of murder. This is advertised, prominent, thrust at us like a great dare—and totally insane."

"We are greatly complimented, my lord," Marquis Sherrinford said dryly. "You don't think we're gibbering madmen."

"This killer may be mad," Lord Darcy said, "but he most assuredly doesn't gibber. He has now killed three men—perhaps more—and left behind taunting verses, but precious few clues to his identity."

"Will you help me, Master Sean?" Sir Moses asked. "I'll disimpale this poor chap and conduct the superficial examination of the body, and then turn it all over to you for the magical forensics."

"My pleasure, Sir Moses," Master Sean said.

The chirurgeon and the magician worked together, carefully working the pike loose from first the back of the throne and then the body. They lay the pike aside and gently moved the corpse to the tile floor. Lord Darcy went over to examine the pike while they worked on the body. Sir Moses undid the blue robe and looked the dead man over carefully, poking, probing, and muttering as he went. "No bruises or lacerations visible," he said finally. "But several other puncture marks. Small ones, in several places around the chest and stomach area. I'd say the victim was prodded with that pike a bit before the final thrust. The external examination is completely consistant with the appearance—this poor man was killed by having a twelve-foot, steel-tipped spike rammed through his gut while he was sitting on the royal throne."

"Thank you, Sir Moses," Lord Darcy said, laying the bloody pike down on the floor. "Sorry to have gotten you out of bed at this hour, but this couldn't wait, and I always like to have a chirurgeon look at the body as early as possible."

"No problem, Lord Darcy," Sir Moses said. "I was playing cards. Expect the game's still going on, so I'd best get back to it. Unless you need me, Master Sean?"

"No, thank you, Sir Moses," Master Sean said. "But I'd better get busy. The fresher the, ah, event, the better the results, you know."

"We'll leave you alone, Master Sean," Lord Darcy said. "Let me know when you're done."

"Aye, my lord," Master Sean agreed, pulling his symbol-decorated carpetbag over to the corpse and snapping open the lid. "I'll be a while. Say half an hour."

"Fine," Lord Darcy agreed.

"Will you need me anymore?" Marquis Sherrinford asked.

"I think not, my lord," Lord Darcy said. "Oh, before you go, there is one thing . . ."

"Yes?"

"I do need to go over the area around the back door, and since the key is attuned to you, I'll need your help."

"Of course, my lord," Marquis Sherrinford said. "Shall we do that now?"

Marquis Sherrinford drew back the curtains and preceded Lord Darcy to the rear door. Taking a key ring from his belt pouch, he isolated the appropriate key and turned it in the lock. Lord Darcy heard the slight click as the bolt withdrew.

"It's self-locking," Marquis Sherrinford said, pulling the door open. "Part of the spell. There's no way to leave it unlocked once it shuts."

Lord Darcy had the Marquis open and close the door several times, in several different ways. He noted that even if released gently when almost closed, the door still finished closing, and locked itself with a soft click. "It's an efficient spell," he commented.

"Nothing but the best," Marquis Sherrinford said. "What now, my lord?"

"Hold the door open for me, my lord marquis," Lord Darcy requested. "I want to look around in the corridor."

Lord Darcy went into the corridor and knelt down to examine the floor and walls on both sides with a small magnifying glass. For about ten minutes he worked his way around the corridor, occasionally pausing to pick up some small object, before straightening up and putting the magnifying glass back in his belt pouch.

"What did you find, my lord?" Marquis Sherrinford asked. He had been trying hard not to show his impatience at this investigative ritual.

Lord Darcy opened his hand and showed the Marquis the three items he had picked up. "Two scraps of fabric, one white and the other multicolored, even in this small sample, and a somewhat larger block of wood, wedge-shaped, about three inches long."

"And what does that tell you?"

"It's too early to know yet," Lord Darcy said, "but the possibilities are there. I don't hold out much hope for the fabric, you understand, but I fancy this scrap of wood can tell an interesting story. The only question is how to get it to talk."

Marquis Sherrinford took the fragment of wood in his hand and examined it. "A hard wood," he said, "a bit over three inches long, perhaps half an inch thick at one end, tapering to an edge at the other. A little over an inch wide. What sort of story do you expect to get from this?"

"A tale of murder, my lord marquis," Lord Darcy said. He gave a half bow and, taking back the piece of wood, returned to the throne room.

"You will keep me informed," Marquis Sherrinford said, "if you discover anything about this horrible crime—or about the threat to His Majesty."

"I shall, my lord," Lord Darcy assured him.

"Good. Then I will go to sleep. It's almost one in the morning, and I must be at my desk by seven."

Marquis Sherrinford departed and Lord Darcy occupied himself with a detailed search of the throne room, doing his best to ignore Master Sean and the clouds of green smoke he was raising with his forensic sorcery in front of the throne. Lord Peter remained behind so that he could watch these two experts at work, but he stayed out of the way, sitting at Marquis Sherrinford's ornate desk, which fortunately was on the side of the throne away from Master Sean's incantations.

After his circuit of the room, Lord Darcy approached Lord Peter and sat down next to him. "I think I've got all there is to get out of this room," he said. "Now it only remains to hear what Master Sean has to say."

"Have you found anything?" Lord Peter asked.

"Detail—only detail," Lord Darcy replied. "But it will tie together. There's no way to tell beforehand exactly how—but it will. There, for example"—he pointed to an ornamental group of medieval weapons on the far wall—"is where our murderer got the pike that let the life out of Master Dandro."

"That would seem to imply that the killing was a spur-of-the-moment thing, wouldn't it?" Lord Peter asked. "Surely if the murderer had intended to kill when he lured Master Dandro in here, he would have supplied his own weapon."

"Your logic is faultless," Lord Darcy replied. "But in this case there are three facts that mitigate against it being a sudden decision to kill. The first is the rhyme."

"Oh, yes," Lord Peter said. "I forgot about that."

"The second is the ingenuity with which the killer got himself—and his victim—into the throne room. Surely that was not accomplished merely to chat."

"And the third?" Lord Peter asked.

"If, after Master Sean is done with it, you will examine the edge of the iron head on the pike so lately removed from Master Dandro," Lord Darcy said, "you will find that it has been sharpened. Carefully and methodically sharpened, both edge and point, with some sort of stone or file—which is not in here. If it was as dull to begin with as the remainder of the weapons, I don't see it taking less than ten minutes to put that edge and point on it."

"That," said Lord Peter, "presents a very uncomfortable image. One would have to imagine Master Dandro sitting there waiting patiently while his assailant methodically sharpens the weapon with which he's going to murder him."

"It would take a certain measure of diabolical self-assurance, wouldn't it?" Lord Darcy said. "Nonetheless that, or something like that, is what happened. Poor Master Dandro thought he was coming in here for an interview with His Majesty. I imagine he was asked to wait, that His Majesty would be along in a minute."

"On the throne?" Lord Peter asked.

"No," Lord Darcy said. "I can picture the scene. Master

Dandro is waiting in front of the throne for His Majesty to show up. The killer is sharpening the edge of the pike head and talking to Master Dandro. Telling him how His Majesty is looking forward to this meeting. Master Dandro's thoughts are wandering. Will he accept the royal appointment—or whatever he's been told is going to happen. Something wonderful and exciting, no doubt. Then Master Dandro feels a pricking through his cloak. He turns around. There stands the killer, pike in hand, prodding at Master Dandro. 'Sit down,' the killer tells him. 'On the throne?' 'Yes, on the throne.' Terrified, Master Dandro backs up until his calves are touching the bottom of the throne. The killer prods. Master Dandro goes backward onto the throne. Screaming for mercy, possibly—the room, as you have assured me, is soundproof. And then—"

"Yes," Lord Peter said, nodding at the horrifying image Lord Darcy had created. "And then indeed!"

"The man we are looking for is not nice," Lord Darcy said. "He has a cruel and vengeful mind."

"Vengeful?"

"Yes, I think so. He has been badly hurt, or thinks he has, by either sorcerers in general or these victims in particular."

The smoke from Master Sean's crucible and thurible had turned a deep blue and was getting thicker. "I think our forensic sorcerer is just about done," Lord Darcy commented. "I have noticed, in these matters, that it is always darkest before the dawn."

16

"IT WASN'T MAGIC, MY lord, that I'll swear to you." Master Sean closed his carpet bag, carefully fastening the elaborate double strap, and picked it up. "I'm all finished now, and I know scarcely more than when I began."

"What *do* you know, Master Sean?" Lord Darcy asked, stalking over to where Master Sean was standing and joining him in staring down at the pitiful object that had so recently been a Master Sorcerer.

"I know that magic is not involved in this killing in any way. There is a miasma of evil about the act, but it is a secular evil, if you see what I mean. It is the evil of intent translated into physical action, not translated into psychical or magical action."

"I do see," Lord Darcy said. "I trust that the, ah, miasma will not linger about the throne."

"I made a point of dissipating it, my lord," Master Sean told him.

"Of course," Lord Darcy said.

"There were two people in here at the time of the murder, aside from the victim. One was a strong—powerful—person. In a psychic sense, that is. The other . . . well, I'm getting a mite tired of reporting this, but the other was a ghost."

"I understand your reaction, Master Sean," Lord Darcy said. "Two people—now, that is interesting. What about the picture test?"

"You mean the eye test, my lord? Developing the victim's retinal image of the killer? I checked the eyes, my lord, and I'm afraid death was not quick enough for that. Unless death is practically instantaneous, we don't get any results."

"A pity," Lord Darcy said. "But I suppose it was too much to hope for. Tell me about that back door, Master Sean."

"The spells on that lock have not been tampered with," Master Sean told him.

"What about the guards on the other doors?" Lord Darcy asked.

"Well, my lord, what about them?"

"Could magic have been used on them to effect an entrance? Could someone have gone by them using, say, the Tarnhelm Effect to remain invisible?"

Master Sean shook his head. "I won't say it's impossible, my lord, but I will say that it's so close to impossible as to be inconceivable. If conditions were exactly right, for just the right length of time, it would have worked. But the magician couldn't have *known* that they would be, so he couldn't have planned on it."

"And if conditions *weren't* exactly right?"

"Well, you'll remember that the Tarnhelm Effect does not make the user truly invisible. It only makes those in the room with him look everywhere but where he is."

"That's so," Lord Darcy agreed. "I remember you pointing that out to me the last time we discussed it. But it's hard for a layman to translate that into practical terms."

"Well, look at it this way, my lord; you can't see the invisible man, but you can see the *effects* of the invisible man. If you are a guard in the King's Gallery and a magician wrapped in a spell using the Tarnhelm Effect passes you, you will find yourself looking everywhere but where he is. You won't see him, even though he is actually in plain sight next to you. You will glimpse him with your peripheral vision, but your mind will interpret it as an umbrella rack, or a portrait of His Majesty Gwiliam the Second."

"And so?"

"Now, in a larger space, more crowded with objects, that might work. As long as there weren't any mirrors. But in a confined area like the end of a long hallway? Imagine the conversation, as one guard says to the other? 'Wasn't that a portrait of Gwiliam the Second that just walked by and entered the throne room?' and the other replies, 'Funny, I thought it was an elephant-foot umbrella stand.'"

"I think you've made your point, Master Sean," Lord Darcy told him.

"I will have the guards notify the Castle mortician to take away the body before morning—that is, I assume Your Lordship is done with it?"

"You assume correctly," Lord Darcy assured him. "And ask them to have a cleaning crew in here before matins. Blood-stains are hard to remove."

"That is so, my lord," Master Sean agreed. "And then I'll go to bed. And double-bar my door, *and* add a few extra protective spells, while I'm at it."

"I cannot say you are being foolish," Lord Darcy told him. "I wish I could."

The next morning over breakfast Lord Darcy gave Mary of Cumberland the details of what had happened in the throne room the night before. "And the coronation is now—what?—a little more than a week away," he said. "And there's a maniacal poetical killer on the loose, and the threat to His Majesty is still a threat, and the deaths in the *Gryphon d'Or* are still a mystery. And everyone else is sitting around waiting for me to apprehend the killers. As well they might, after all, it's my job." He sighed. "It's a lucky thing I'm not up for a promotion, isn't it, Mary?"

"You're feeling depressed because you haven't solved these murders yet, is that it?"

Lord Darcy nodded. "That is exactly it," he said, pouring cream into his caffe.

"Well, we'd better get busy then, hadn't we?" the Duchess of Cumberland asked him.

Lord Darcy smiled. And then he laughed. "Yes," he said. "I suppose we'd better."

"Good! What shall we do, then?"

"You interview some of the people on that list—the ones who were at the inn when the murders were committed."

"All right. What am I to ask them?"

"That," Lord Darcy told her, "is the hard part. I don't know for sure what to ask them. I'm looking for something out of the ordinary, something that will give me a hint of what went on that night. I'll know it when I hear it, Mary, and I'll have to hope that you will too."

"I'll do my best," Mary of Cumberland said. "What will you be doing while I'm interviewing?"

"I'll be talking to some of the others. And with any luck," he told her, "speaking to a spy."

After their second cups of caffe, Mary of Cumberland went off to find and speak to the people on a subset of Prefect Henri's list, while Lord Darcy sought out Lord Peter Whiss.

"I want to speak to your man in the Polish delegation," he told Lord Peter, standing on the other side of his antique walnut desk and tapping his fingers on its polished surface.

Lord Peter considered briefly, and then nodded. "I guess it has come to that," he said. "I'll arrange it as soon as possible. Check back with me early this afternoon."

Lord Darcy nodded and turned away, consulting his list of names. As he reached the door, the Chevalier Raoul d'Espergnan arrived at the other side, coming in to see if Lord Peter had any orders for him for that day. Lord Darcy recognized the young man as the one who had been sent to notify him of the second wizard's murder when he was in Tournadotte. And further—his name was on Prefect Henri's list.

"I'd like to speak to you, Sir Raoul, if I may," Lord Darcy told the young Chevalier when Lord Peter had verified that he had nothing for him.

"Of course, my lord," Sir Raoul said, doing his best not to look puzzled.

"You can use the inner office—through the right-hand door," Lord Peter offered.

"No, I think not," Lord Darcy said. "We'll stroll together to Between the Walls and sit over cups of caffe, or perhaps mugs of good Norman beer at that little pub with outdoor tables on the square. That is, if Sir Raoul does not object?"

"The *Sword in the Stone*? Certainly, my lord, that will be fine with me," Sir Raoul said. Now he was doing his best not to look worried. What could the Empire's Chief Investigator want with him?

Lord Darcy walked with Sir Raoul through the Castle and out, onto the narrow, winding streets of Between the Walls. There was no particular motive to this, but he felt restless and thought that a little outdoor exercise and another cup of caffe might clear his head and start some productive thoughts flowing. "Relax, Chevalier," he said. "I merely want to ask you some questions about something you may or may not have seen about a month ago."

"A month ago?" Chevalier d'Espergnan thought back. "In London?"

"On your way here from London," Lord Darcy told him. "In Tournadotte."

They reached the pub, and sat at one of the outside tables.

"Oh, yes, my lord," Sir Raoul said. "I remember that trip. Packet boat to Cherbourg, rail to Tournadotte, overnight in Tournadotte, and then on to Castle Cristobel in the morning. It was just before the heavy flooding started. Everything went very well. Got in on time. What did you want to know, my lord?"

The publican came over, rubbing his hands on his starched white apron and smiling down at them with the smile of the happy innkeeper. Lord Darcy ordered a brandy and caffe, and the Chevalier decided that a pint before lunch couldn't do him any harm.

"Cast your mind back to your night in the *Gryphon d'Or,*" Lord Darcy told Sir Raoul when the publican had gone off to fill their orders. "I want you to tell me everything you can remember about that night."

Sir Raoul looked blank for a moment. "The *Gryphon d'Or?*" he said. "I'm afraid I don't remember much after a month. Nothing meaningful or important, certainly."

"Don't try to remember anything specific," Lord Darcy told him. "Neither of us knows what may turn out to be meaningful. Just try to remember what happened as it happened. What time did you arrive at the inn?"

"The train got in about four o'clock," Chevalier d'Espergnan remembered. "I walked to the inn from the station. It took, I imagine, fifteen or twenty minutes. I got a room and went upstairs to take a nap. At around seven o'clock I woke up and went downstairs for dinner. Veal, I believe. Overcooked."

"Did you see anybody you recognized at dinner?"

Sir Raoul's face screwed up with the intensity of his remembering. "Yes," he said finally. "Sir Darryl Longuert was eating dinner at a nearby table."

"Alone?"

"As far as I could tell, yes. As a matter of fact I thought of asking him if he'd mind if I joined him for caffe. But I only know him casually, from the court in London, you know. And I thought he might think it presumptuous. So I didn't."

"Anyone else?"

"Nobody I recognized," the lad said. "Let's see. There was a major from one of the colonial regiments. In full legionnaire regimentals, he was. I remember because I was trying to work out what the various campaign ribbons he was wearing were for. There was a very pretty black-haired lady who was there with an older man who seemed angry about everything. And there was an Italian gentleman."

"How did you know he was Italian?"

"By his dress, I suppose. Short, dark-haired man with a spade beard. Very dapper. Those are the only people I remember specifically. The dining room was fairly full, I recall, but the others are a blur."

"You've done very well after all this time," Lord Darcy said. "What about after dinner?"

"I'm afraid I went to sleep. In the courier service you learn to get as much sleep as you can. So I went to sleep shortly after dinner. All by myself."

Lord Darcy looked up. "Why did you say that?" he asked sharply.

"What?"

"All by myself. Why did you say you went to bed all by yourself?"

"Only an expression," said the young Chevalier. "I didn't mean to imply—"

"Actually, you probably did," Lord Darcy interrupted. "I don't mean consciously, but unconsciously. You were dredging thoughts from your memory about that night, and something keyed in that response."

The Chevalier looked confused. "You think so?" he asked. "But I'm not the sort to, er, kiss and tell, as it were."

"I'm sure you're not, Chevalier," Lord Darcy assured him. "If you *had* enjoyed the company of some local demoiselle that night, you probably would have consciously avoided mentioning it unless I convinced you it was relevant. But 'I went to bed alone' is not the sort of thing one volunteers unless there would be reason to doubt it. Or unless, for some reason, the fact that you were alone stuck in your memory."

"I see what you mean," Chevalier d'Espergnan said. He leaned back in his chair and stared deeply into his beer mug.

"Now why . . ." He mused some more. Suddenly he sat up. "I remember," he said. "I'm rather embarrassed by this, and I'm sure it's meaningless, but I suppose I'd better tell you after all."

"Fair enough," Lord Darcy said.

"It's funny how memory works," the Chevalier said. "I would have thought this completely forgotten. It was just a casual observation at the time. But it must have been stronger than I thought, since it caused that silly statement about going to bed alone." He paused and reflected for a second. "This is going to sound—well, I don't know how it will sound to you. The truth is, I saw one of the inn's maids going into a guest's room with him. And I remember thinking at the time that *he*, at any rate, wasn't going to sleep alone."

"Yes?" Lord Darcy said in a tone calculated to encourage Sir Raoul to continue to unburden himself.

"Not very nice, I suppose," the young Chevalier said, "but I remember thinking that it was odd that she'd picked an old man over me."

"An old man?"

Sir Raoul shrugged. "Compared to me, my lord. And she was a young girl. Not over seventeen, I'd say."

"Twenty," Lord Darcy said.

"Really? Then you know who the girl was? How strange."

"I'm afraid I do," Lord Darcy said. "But I don't know who the, ah, old man whose room she entered was. Do you?"

"It was that Italian," Sir Raoul said.

"You don't know his name?"

"No, my lord."

Lord Darcy thought that over. The only Italian on his list was Count d'Alberra, who was definitely not dead. But perhaps the girl had skipped merrily from room to room that night.

"Would you recognize him if you saw him again?" Lord Darcy asked.

"I'm not sure, my lord. Perhaps."

"Well," Lord Darcy said, tossing a sixth-bit on the table to pay for the drinks, "then perhaps we'll make the experiment. Come along, Chevalier."

17

THE DUCHESS OF CUMBERLAND knocked on the door of Master
Sorcerer Sir Darryl Longuert's suite and waited for a response.
About twenty seconds later she heard the sounds of two heavy
bolts being pulled from within, and the door swung open. Sir
Darryl, with his shirt-sleeves rolled up, and the toes of a pair of
cotton slippers peeking out from under his wide trowser legs,
smiled warmly at her. "My lady of Cumberland," he said.
"What an unexpected pleasure. Please come in. You will
excuse my appearance, and that of my room; I was working,
and not expecting company."

"If you'd like me to return at another time . . ." Mary of
Cumberland offered.

"No, no," Sir Darryl assured her. "I gratefully accept the
excuse of the company of a beautiful woman to take me away
from my work."

"How nicely phrased," Mary of Cumberland said. "I have
actually come here to ask you a few questions."

"Ah!" Sir Darryl said. "How can I help you? Advice on an
affaire de coeur? We elderly gentlemen are very good at giving
advice on love affairs."

Mary of Cumberland laughed. "I have a feeling that any
advice you gave on that subject would be both accurate and

useful. But, unfortunately, it is on another subject that I seek information."

"Ah?" Sir Darryl closed and bolted the door behind Mary of Cumberland and led her into the living room. "A little refreshment, Your Grace? I have some xerez, set into cask in Spain in 1892. It is mellow enough to drink, and quite pleasing, although it will take another fifty years to complete the complexity of its aging."

"Tell me," Mary of Cumberland said, "you have the door double-bolted—"

"There is a madman out there," Sir Darryl said, "who seems to be seeking out sorcerers. I would just as soon not be caught unawares."

"Of course," Mary of Cumberland said. "But when I knocked, you threw the bolts and opened the door wide without even asking who was there."

"I knew," Sir Darryl said. "Of course I knew. After all, my dear Duchess, I am not the Wizard Laureate solely because of my good looks."

"Of course," Mary of Cumberland said. "How silly of me." She sat down and accepted a glass of the viscous, straw-colored liquor.

"Now, what sort of information can the master give his favorite journeyman?" Sir Darryl asked, replacing the decanter and sitting opposite her.

"That's nice of you to say, Sir Darryl, but I know I'm much too much a dilettante to be worthy of consideration for my magical skills."

"Your Talent is strong, Your Grace," Sir Darryl said. "And, if you have never possessed a sufficiency of that narrowness of mind that enables one to focus only on one small thing, why then, you enable us all to profit from the breadth of your knowledge."

Mary of Cumberland laughed. "You'll have to write that one down for me, Sir Darryl. It's the best excuse for an unfocused life I have yet heard."

Sir Darryl smiled and silently touched glasses with her.

"I am here this morning on behalf of Lord Darcy," Mary of Cumberland said.

"Ah!" Sir Darryl replied, taking a sip of his golden xerez.

"We need to know what you remember of your last stay—I assume it was your last stay—at the *Gryphon d'Or* in Tournadotte. About a month ago?"

Sir Darryl nodded. "Yes. I was there about a month ago. On my way here to join the court, as it happens. I had to be here early, you see, to arrange for the ceremonial magic that will surround the coronation. When you're the Laureate, they stick you with jobs like that."

"Do you remember anything specific about your stay at the inn?"

"Let me think. Oh, goodness—was that when the murders took place?"

"That's right," Mary of Cumberland affirmed.

"Well then, it does become important, doesn't it? Let's see. Tournadotte. I arrived there early in the morning, I remember that. Spent most of the day at the train station trying to find out why my baggage wasn't traveling on the same train I was. When it finally turned up, it was too late to go on to Cristobel, so I checked in to the inn for the night. Had dinner there, and then retired to my room to do some work on a manuscript."

"Did you notice anything strange at all, or anyone that you knew?"

"No, can't say that I did. The next day, however, on the train to Castle Cristobel, I ran into Master Raimun DePlessis. He was feeling disliked, as I remember."

"Master Raimun DePlessis? Isn't that the sorcerer who was murdered in a bakery? What do you mean 'disliked'?"

"Yes, that's the man. I'm not sure what he meant by 'disliked.' He just had the feeling that someone on the train didn't like him."

"Well, *someone* certainly didn't like him!" Mary of Cumberland said.

"That is true," Sir Darryl said, putting his glass down on the small, inlaid table that stood between their chairs. "I never made the connection until you just said that. Oh, my dear, I'm afraid I have been badly remiss. I should have told Lord Darcy this some time ago."

"Well, you can make up for it now. Who was it that didn't like Master Raimun?"

Sir Darryl shook his head. "I don't know," he said. "Someone in his compartment, apparently. He left his compartment to come sit with me because he said he couldn't stand the mental, ah, aura, he was getting from this person. But he said he couldn't tell who the person was."

"Do you remember who was in his compartment?"

"I'm afraid I never knew," Sir Darryl told her. "We talked

about . . ." He paused in mid-sentence and stared, stricken, at Mary of Cumberland. "Oh, my dear, my dear," he said. "I *have* been remiss! Your Grace, you must take me to Lord Darcy right away. I have something to tell him. Something of the utmost importance. How silly of me not to have thought of it." He stood up and looked around, too distracted to take note of what he was seeing. "Who would have thought," he said. "And to think I have an appointment— That explains— Of course! Where's my jacket? We must go right away!"

"Of course, Sir Darryl," Mary of Cumberland said, putting her glass down and rising from her chair. "Right now. What have you remembered?"

"I believe I know who is killing those poor sorcerers," Sir Darryl told her. "And why. And even how—or at least how he is luring them to their deaths. We must get to Lord Darcy before someone else is killed."

"You know who the next victim will be?" Mary of Cumberland asked.

Sir Darryl paused for a second in thought. "Yes," he said. "I believe I do."

"We'd better do something to warn him, then," Mary of Cumberland said. "Who is it?"

"Me," Sir Darryl told her.

Lord Darcy and the Chevalier d'Espergnan crossed the outer bailey of Arthur Keep and knocked at the door of the Stephainite monastery. "Is Count d'Alberra here?" Lord Darcy asked the brown-robed novice who answered the door.

"This way, my lord," the novice said, ushering them inside and down a stone-walled corridor.

Count d'Alberra's clinic was now housed in several rooms in the monastery; a light green waiting room, a private office, and a treatment room. A white-robed nurse smiled up at them from behind her desk in the waiting room as Lord Darcy and Sir Raoul entered. "Good afternoon," she said, "have you an appointment?"

"Good afternoon," Lord Darcy said, smiling a wide smile back down at her. "I'm Lord Darcy, Chief Investigator for the Court of Chivalry." He took out his black credential case and showed her the card. "I'd like to see the Count for a few minutes. I'll be brief, I promise."

"Gracious!" the nurse said, putting her hand to her mouth in an involuntary gesture. "Is there any trouble?"

"No, no, nothing like that," Lord Darcy assured her. "Count d'Alberra may have witnessed an event that I'm investigating. I have a few routine questions for him. The Count knows me; just tell him I'm here."

"Well . . ." The nurse glanced at the large standing clock in the corner. "The Count has ten more minutes with his current patient. You'll have to wait until after that. We have strict instructions never to interrupt the Count during a session. Not for *anything!*"

"Fair enough," Lord Darcy agreed. "We'll wait." He gestured Sir Raoul to a seat, and dropped into the seat next to him. With one lean leg crossed over the other, he relaxed and looked around him. The waiting room was carefully and cleverly furnished and decorated to put the waiting patients at their ease. The paintings on the wall were all bright splashes of cheerful color, in the new "Balanced Masses" concept, with form a secondary consideration. The tables and chairs were light-colored and lightweight, less oppressive to a troubled mind than heavy, somber furniture. It was no doubt very modern, very well thought out, Lord Darcy reflected, but it certainly did look out of place in a monastery.

Ten minutes later Count d'Alberra stuck his head out of the right-hand inner door. "Have I patients waiting, Demoiselle Deville?"

"Lord Batheskill is due shortly, my lord," the nurse told him. "And his lordship would like to speak to you." She nodded toward Lord Darcy.

"Merely some routine questions, Count d'Alberra," Lord Darcy called cheerfully.

"Lord Darcy, isn't it? Very well," the Count said, looking slightly cross. "But not in the treatment room. Come into my office."

As Count d'Alberra crossed into his office, Lord Darcy leaned over to the Chevalier d'Espergnan. "Is that him?" he whispered. "Is that the Italian fellow you saw in the hall?"

"It looks like him," Sir Raoul whispered back, "but I can't be sure. It's been a month, Your Lordship. And I wasn't paying that much attention to his appearance."

"But it could be him?"

"Yes, my lord, it could well be."

"Thank you," Lord Darcy said. "Wait here for me." He got up and followed Count d'Alberra into his office.

Count d'Alberra's office was not at all light or comforting;

that was reserved for the waiting room and the treatment room. The office furniture was heavy and imposing, of dark woods and angular corners. A cluster of framed diplomas and certificates hung on the wall, professing, in their Latinate phrases, the training and expertise of the nobleman sitting behind the desk.

"And what can I do for you, my lord?" Count d'Alberra asked, his elbows on his desk and his interlaced fingers under his chin.

"You were in the *Gryphon d'Or* about a month ago, my lord?" Lord Darcy asked.

"The *Gryphon d'Or*? Oh, yes—that inn in Tournadotte. Yes, it would be about a month ago now. Why?"

"We are investigating a murder that took place there at about that time."

Count d'Alberra's hands dropped to the desktop. "A murder? But no! How can this be? What a dreadful thing. Who was it that was killed?"

"One of the guests," Lord Darcy told him, "and one of the employees. We are trying to find out whether anyone who was staying at the inn at that time saw anything, ah, unusual. Something that seemed, if ever so slightly, out of the ordinary."

Count d'Alberra looked thoughtful for a minute, stroking his beard with his right hand, and then shook his head. "I'm afraid I cannot help you, my lord. It was quite an uneventful evening."

"You were only there one night?"

"That's correct."

"Could you outline for me what you did and who you saw during the course of the evening?"

Count d'Alberra shrugged an expressive Italian shrug. "I did nothing of note, and I saw no one. I ate dinner. I went to bed."

"Did you go to bed alone?"

Count d'Alberra slapped the desktop with his palm in mild astonishment. "Well!" he said. "There's an example of your famous Norman directness."

"I'm sorry, Count, if it seems to be a tactless or impolite question," Lord Darcy said, leaning forward and staring intently at the Count, "but I have a reason for asking."

"Tell me the reason," Count d'Alberra said firmly, "and, perhaps, I'll give you an answer."

"You were seen, that night, retiring with a young demoiselle."

"I see," the Count said. "And what does the demoiselle say about it?"

"She is dead."

"Dead?" The Count slumped in his chair briefly, and then straightened up. "You mean she—it was she—the one who was killed?"

"If the demoiselle you took to your chamber was the one I suspect, yes, she was murdered that night."

"Incredible. So young. So alive. Who would do a thing like that?"

"So you did take the young demoiselle to your room?"

"Yes."

"And?"

"Need you ask?"

"I mean after. What happened?"

Count d'Alberra shrugged. "I gave the lass a silver sovereign and sent her on her way. There was, apparently, someone else she intended to, ah, visit that evening."

"I see," Lord Darcy said. "So it was a simple commercial arrangement, was it?"

"My dear Lord Darcy," the Count said with the patience of one explaining to a small child, "I had just met the demoiselle that evening, after all. I wasn't in love with her, nor she with me. She wanted money, and I wanted, ah, comfort. We both got what we wanted. Fair's fair."

"I didn't mean to sound judgmental, Count d'Alberra," Lord Darcy said. "It's not that at all. You don't know who she was going to see after she left you?"

"I do not."

"I see. Well, thank you very much." Lord Darcy got up and walked to the door. "There may be a few more questions," he said, turning around in the doorway. "Thank you for your time."

"I only wish I could have told you more," Count d'Alberra said. "That poor girl!"

The Count came to the door of his office behind Lord Darcy. His next patient was in the waiting room when Lord Darcy came out, staring at a painting of what appeared to be a large red cloud being attacked by smaller green and purple pieces of fruit. Count d'Alberra called him into the treatment room, and nodded good-bye to Lord Darcy.

* * *

"If you will keep trying to locate Lord Darcy," Sir Darryl Longuert said to Mary of Cumberland, "have him meet me in, let me see, in Marquis Sherrinford's office. I will have news for him. Perhaps more than that."

"Where are you going?" Mary of Cumberland asked. They had traced Lord Darcy as far as the *Sword in the Stone*, and were just finishing cups of caffe they had ordered when they found that the trail ended there.

"I have an appointment," Sir Darryl said.

"Are you sure it's safe?"

"Oh no, my dear, it's quite unsafe actually. But I rather think I'm not the one who will be surprised."

"Perhaps I should go with you," Mary of Cumberland offered. "Or we could get a guard, if you think I'd be in the way."

"It's not that, my dear. But I really am quite capable of taking care of myself—now that I know that care need be taken. And what I am hoping will happen won't happen if you're along."

"If you say so, Sir Darryl," Mary of Cumberland agreed grudgingly. "I will go in search of Lord Darcy. But please—take care of yourself."

"I promise," Sir Darryl assured her. "Now you go along. I have some overdue business to attend to." He watched her walk away for long enough to assure himself that she *was* walking away, and then, after glancing at his watch, headed off in the opposite direction.

The herb garden was in a little courtyard flanked on one side of the Arthur Keep kitchens and on the other by the windows of the Offices of State—the Lord Chamberlain's office and the seneschal's office, and on the floor above them, the private offices of the King-Emperor.

Sir Darryl arrived for his appointment in the cloistered walk by the herb garden right on time. One should not be late for destiny. He looked around. There was no one else in sight, which was not surprising. People were not encouraged to rest in the herb garden; first, the herbs were actually used by the kitchens, and second, neither the Lord Chamberlain nor His Majesty were particularly fond of noises outside their windows.

A minute later he heard a rustling behind him. "Afternoon

Sir Darryl," a thin, whiny voice said close to his ear. "Don't turn around."

"And why not?" Sir Darryl asked without turning around. Mastering all of his considerable self-control, he held himself in check.

A hand was laid on his shoulder, and a coil of something cold was at his neck. After a moment he felt a slight tugging at his jacket lapel. "I'm going to kill you," the voice said, "and I'm going to watch you die. You deserve death. I got what I deserved, Sir Darryl, and now it's time for you to get what you deserve."

"I don't think—"

"Run, Sir Darryl!" the voice commanded. "Run! Maybe you can save yourself."

"I think I'll continue to stand here," Sir Darryl said calmly.

"You won't run," the voice yelled, rising in inflection until it was almost a screech. "Then I'll have to kill you as you stand here!"

Sir Darryl wheeled around, to face a medium-sized, stocky man with very bright eyes, who had just pulled a large knife from his belt. "Die, damned wizard," the man yelled, thrusting savagely at the sorcerer's chest.

Sir Darryl made a slight gesture, and the knife flew into the air. The man screamed, a long, animal scream, and lunged at Sir Darryl's throat with outstretched hands.

Sir Darryl made another gesture.

Sir Darryl stepped aside. The man, frozen in position, his arms outstretched, his face fixed in a feral grin, fell into the basil.

"I think you'll be that way for a while, my man," Sir Darryl said to the living statue with a satisfied smile. "And let this be proof to you that a warned sorcerer is an armed sorcerer. I'll send someone for you."

18

THEY WERE IN THE inner room of Marquis Sherrinford's offices; Lord Darcy, Lord Peter, and a masked man. The man across from Lord Darcy wore his domino mask with easy grace, although it looked particularly out of place on his square, stocky face.

"Has Lord Peter had a chance to explain what we need from you?" Lord Darcy asked.

"He has not, my lord," the man answered in a gruff voice, which Lord Darcy suspected was not his natural one.

"He only arrived a moment before Your Lordship," Lord Peter explained. "And he can only stay for a few minutes, lest they get suspicious."

"There is small chance of that," the masked man said. "But in this business small chances have a way of being cumulative, and even small mistakes are often fatal."

"In that case, ah, Sir . . ."

"You may, without error, call me 'my lord,' My Lord Darcy," the masked man said.

"Well, my lord, there are a few questions I would like to put to you."

"So I understand," the masked man said dryly, "else I would not be here."

"Are you aware of any threat against the person of His Majesty?" Lord Darcy asked.

"His Majesty?" The man looked surprised. "To which 'His Majesty' do you refer?"

"John of England."

"I feared that you meant that. No, I am not aware of any such threat. And since clearly you are, I can only hope and pray you are wrong."

"Would you know if there were a Polish plot against the Angevin Empire?" Lord Darcy asked.

"There are always Polish plots against the Angevin Empire," the masked man said. "Were it not so, I could return to my little home in Kent and raise lilacs. But a plot against the life of John the Fourth, I might not hear about."

Lord Peter poured out three glasses of a heavily spiced wine of Picardy which was supposed to ward off chill, and passed them out. "His lordship's sources are limited," he told Lord Darcy, "being with the retinue of His Majesty of Courlandt. What the King, his father, does or orders done is not always related to the son."

"That is so," the masked man agreed. "The Crown Prince is regarded as something of a liberal, and is viewed with distrust by the Crown Council, and the *Serka* ruling committee."

"Do you know anything about the *Serka*?" Lord Darcy asked.

"Oh, yes," the masked man said. "You see, I am a *Serka* agent planted in the staff of His Majesty the Crown Prince. Not that they tell me anything I don't have to know."

Lord Darcy stared curiously at the man. The raw courage that lay behind that mask must be considerable, he reflected. And it was not for him to risk it unnecessarily. "One final question," he said. "Does the *Serka* have any magical devices designed for laymen to use? Things where the spell is operable by someone without the Talent?"

"Oh, yes," the masked man said. "There are all sorts of magical devices for *Serka* agents to use in the field, although we come equipped with plenty of our own sorcerers. There are two with us now, just to redo all the Angevin spells and make sure it is impossible to sneak up upon His Majesty. And, I suspect, to test the quality of the Angevin spells and write a report for the *Serka*."

"Does the *Serka* possess a device—like a blanket—with an avoidance spell woven into it?"

The man nodded. "It's used for assassination," he said. "If you bury a body with one of those over it, it will decompose very thoroughly before it is found."

"Unless a dog happens to chase a rabbit over it," Lord Darcy commented. "Thank you, my lord. You have been a great help."

The man bowed slightly. "I don't see how, but I'm glad," he said.

"What have you learned?" Lord Peter asked, aware that Lord Darcy's words were accurate, and that something in this brief conversation had given Lord Darcy a key to the puzzle.

"I've learned that the dying words of Goodman Albert Chall were not the rambling nonsense that they sounded," Lord Darcy said. "And I've learned that there really is a threat. But—"

"My lords! My lords!" came the sudden call from the main office outside.

"That's the Duchess of Cumberland," Lord Darcy said. "She was doing some investigative work for me." He rose. "She wouldn't be so insistent were it not important."

Lord Peter nodded to the masked man, who disappeared through a side door. "Ask her in, my lord," he said.

Lord Darcy opened the door. "Your Grace," he said. "What is it?"

"Oh, my lord, I'm glad I've found you," Mary of Cumberland said, panting to catch her breath. "I've been looking everywhere. I think Sir Darryl Longuert has gone off to meet the killer!"

"What? And you let him go?"

"I am an out-of-practice journeyman, My Lord Darcy," Mary of Cumberland said. "He is a master. He is the Sorcerer Laureate. I don't see how I could have stopped him."

"You're right, Your Grace, I apologize," Lord Darcy said. "But we'd better go find him. You can tell me about it on the way."

"I'll come with you," Lord Peter said. "You may need an extra pair of hands."

As they started down the hallway, one of the palace guards came thudding toward them from the other direction, his sword flapping noisily against his side as he ran. "Lord Darcy, Lord Darcy," he called. "You're wanted, my lord!"

Lord Darcy turned. "By whom?" he asked.

"Sir Darryl Longuert. He has captured the killer, my lord."

"Well, I'll be— Lead on, Serjeant."

The Serjeant of the Guard swiveled on his heel and dogtrotted back the way he had come, with Lord Darcy, Lord Peter, and the Dowager Duchess of Cumberland close behind.

He led them down and around the inner corridors of the Castle until they came out at the guard room by the main kitchens. Sir Darryl was standing by the door, looking crestfallen, and Master Sean O Lochlainn was next to him, talking to him in an earnest undertone.

Sir Darryl looked up as Lord Darcy came puffing into the room. "I had him, my lord," he said, holding up his closed right hand. "I had him frozen with this very hand. The murderer. He came after me, but I was ready for him. Or so I thought."

"Don't let it get you so upset, Sir Darryl," Master Sean said. "How were you to know?"

"What happened?" Lord Darcy asked. Lord Peter and Mary of Cumberland came into the room behind him.

"He tried to kill me, my lord. The murderer you're looking for. He tried to use these on me"—Sir Darryl pointed to a knife and a coil of wire sitting on the Officer of the Guard's desk—"but I froze him."

Lord Darcy stepped over to the desk and picked up the coil of wire. "I thought we would find something like this," he said. "You see, Master Sean—this is what killed Master Sorcerer Paul Elovitz in the ballroom. The murderer places it around the victim's neck, leaving most of it dangling on the floor, and then frightens him into running away. The wire slices through the victim's throat as it's pulled back, and he effectively kills himself. Very neat, very clever."

"That's what made the marks on the ballroom floor, my lord?"

"That's right. The murderer never let go of his end, you see. And as he pulled it back, it bounced on the floor." He turned back to Sir Darryl. "And then what happened?"

"I froze him, my lord. But he got away. I should have known, but I never thought of it."

"Thought of what?"

"I think, Sir Darryl, that you had better start from the beginning," Master Sean said. "I'm sure Lord Darcy would like to hear all the details." He turned to Lord Darcy. "A general alarm is out for the culprit, my lord," he said. "Now that we know who it is, he should be easy to apprehend."

"Fine," Lord Darcy said. "But who is he?"

"His name is Bowers."

"Who *is* he?" Lord Darcy repeated.

"Tell his lordship about it," Master Sean said.

"It's my fault," Sir Darryl said earnestly to Lord Darcy. "I didn't think of the obvious. Goodman Bowers has a grudge against sorcerers. And, more particularly, against the sorcerers he has so far murdered."

"How so?"

Sir Darryl went to the bench along the wall and lowered himself onto it. "He was once a sorcerer," he said. "A journeyman, almost ready to qualify as a master. He, ah, went bad."

"Bad?" Lord Darcy asked.

"Black magic?" Mary of Cumberland asked, going over to sit next to Sir Darryl on the bench. "What led him astray?"

"It was, as I remember, pretty much the old story," Sir Darryl replied. "There are three or four patterns that these things seem to run to, and this was one of them. He got in debt to gamblers, playing pukka. To try to get out, he plunged heavily with money that wasn't his, and lost, of course."

"Then he tried to win by black magic?" Mary of Cumberland asked.

"No, Your Grace," Sir Darryl said. "That wouldn't have worked. The card houses are heavily protected against such things. A little precognition, for those who can manage such things, is accepted as the fortunes of the cards, since the ability is uncontrollable and almost random. But no formalized magic is allowed by the card houses. Except, in some cases, their own."

"But if magic was being used against him, couldn't he have detected it?"

"Most certainly, Your Grace. But some people are just bad card players."

"Oh. Of course."

"Bowers started doing favors for these people, using his

magic. Under threat of exposure. And then they began asking for things that were not to be accomplished by white magic."

"And he did them?" Lord Darcy asked.

Sir Darryl nodded. "Apparently. Now, many magicians have been in fixes similar to this. There comes a point at which they stop. Confess to their priest. Tell all to their master or grand master. And take their punishment. These people can be salvaged.

"But some others discover that they like it. The feeling of power—of control—is strong. You *know*, somewhere in the back of your mind, that you are destroying yourself. But it is like some of the addictive drugs. You can't help what you are doing, and get sucked further and further into abominable acts. That is what happened to Bowers. By the time the case was discovered and brought to his Bishop's attention, he was incurable."

"And so?" Lord Darcy asked.

"And so he was tried by a court of his peers and found guilty of practicing black magic. For his secular crimes—fixing horse races or whatever—he was sentenced to some years in prison. For his practice of black magic, a Committee of Executors was formed, and he was thrummed. All his Talent was removed. All. And he was sent forth blind into the world."

Lord Darcy nodded. "I see," he said. "Apparently he bore a grudge."

"That's right, my lord," Sir Darryl said. "All of the murdered sorcerers were on the committee."

"And yourself?"

"Yes. But that was almost ten years ago. Many things have happened since then. I had almost forgotten."

"This explains how he was able to get away from Sir Darryl's freezing spell, my lord," Master Sean said. "It also explains some results I've been getting on my magical tests. You see, as an unintentional side effect, the person who is thrummed becomes almost transparent to magic."

"Ah!" Lord Darcy said. "There's your ghost."

"That's right, my lord," Master Sean agreed. "In a sense, our killer was a ghost. A ghost with a grudge."

"Ten Little Wizards," Lord Darcy said.

Sir Darryl nodded. "Yes, my lord. That reminds me." He dug into his pocket and pulled out a scrap of paper. "This was pinned to my jacket by Bowers when he assaulted me."

Lord Darcy unfolded it and passed it around. "Cute," he commented.

> *Seven little wizards practicing their wizard tricks*
> *One misread his formula—and now there are six.*

"I confess that I am surprised, my lord," Sir Darryl said. "This case is going to have to be studied. Usually—indeed, almost always—a person who has been thrummed loses all initiative. He is thenceforth no danger to himself or his community. Clearly in this case we misjudged."

"Perhaps not," Lord Darcy commented, looking thoughtful. For a long moment he was silent, and then he turned to Lord Peter. "My lord, if I'm right, there is immediate danger of another murder. We have to speak to His Majesty the King immediately!"

"I'll go find Marquis Sherrinford," Lord Peter offered.

"I'd rather not do this through the Marquis," Lord Darcy said. "I think that, between us, we can get an audience with His Majesty. And we need his help to prevent what might be a grave threat to the Empire."

"Come with me," Lord Peter said.

19

THE BEDROOM WAS PITCH-DARK. From the heavily canopied bed, the sound of even breathing indicated that its royal occupant was sound asleep. But this was doubtful.

Two men waited silently by the bedroom door; Lord Darcy on the right, and Lord Peter on the left, for what Lord Darcy knew—and had convinced them all—was going to occur. Farther into the room Coronel Lord Waybusch was concealed beside a dresser and Master Sean O Lochlainn waited by the head of the bed.

For three hours, which seemed like three months, nothing happened. Then, gradually, with a sound so slight that only silence-tuned ears could have heard it, the door lock released. After a longer wait the door swung inward.

Lord Darcy held his breath and listened to the slight creak of the door hinges, only inches away from his face, as the door opened toward him. There was a cautious footstep into the room, and then another.

Lord Darcy couldn't be sure whether there was one person entering the room or two. He fancied there were two. Which would simplify things.

The sound of footsteps crept across the floor toward the bed.

"NOW!"

A bellow in Master Sean's voice—the agreed-upon signal. Lord Darcy slammed the bedroom door and twisted the lock closed in a practiced gesture.

The room suddenly erupted in bright-white wizardly light as Master Sean activated an already-in-place illumination spell. There, in the middle of the room facing the bed, frozen in the sudden glare, were two men. One of them clutched an ancient, two-handed sword with a basket handle, its blade flat against his chest, its point three feet over his head.

For a second they were too startled to move, and then they both bolted; one toward the door and the other—the one with the sword—toward the bed.

Several things happened at once. Lord Darcy and Lord Peter dove for the man heading for the door, and after a moment's resistance, he lay still and raised his hands. "I will not fight you," he said.

The other man reached the bed, his broadsword raised high above his head, and screamed "Die! Die! Die!" in an insane liturgy as he swung it at the sleeping form.

The man in the bed threw his covers aside and gestured in a complex motion with both hands.

The sword glowed bright red and sprang from its holder's hands, thudding firmly and deeply into the ceiling. The man flopped over onto his back and sprawled, motionless at the side of the bed.

The man in the bed got up and rubbed his hands together. "Dot was very good," he said. "A good, strong spell you weave, Master Sean O Lochlainn. You Angevin sorcerers are not all cupcakes."

Master Sean grinned. "It was very effective, Your Majesty, wasn't it?"

His Majesty the King of Courlandt and Crown Prince of Poland shrugged. "In Poland," he said, "we got good magicians too."

Lord Darcy pulled the man on the floor to his feet. "I think, Count d'Alberra, that you have a lot to answer for," he said.

The Count straightened his clothing and dusted himself off calmly. "You win a few, you lose a few," he said, smiling at his captor. "But I don't think you will be asking me any questions. I wish I knew how you knew it was me—but I will never find out. You're a clever man, Lord Darcy." His grin twisted sideways and his jaw clamped.

"Watch it, my lord!" Lord Peter said sharply, reaching across to grab at Count d'Alberra. "He's taking poison!"

But before either of them could do anything, Count d'Alberra, with a high-pitched gargling sound, fell to the floor. He kicked twice convulsively, and then he was dead.

"Well!" Lord Darcy said. "Now that all the excitement seems to be over, we should be going. Coronel Lord Waybusch, would you take the prisoner, please. And arrange for the body to be disposed of. Oh, yes; one last thing." He opened the bedroom door, which lead to the living room of the Polish suite. "Johnson!" he called.

A little man crawled out from under the living room sofa. "Yes, my lord?"

"Did you see who let them in?"

"Tall, skinny man with short-cropped blond hair," Johnson said. "Came from the third door on the left down that hall."

"Very good. Your Majesty, did you hear that?"

"Ja. General Vitapeski. Who would have thought? We will take care of him."

"No doubt. Good night, Your Majesty."

The Crown Prince of Poland walked them to the door. "Tonight," he said, "I think I sleep with my wife. Protocol be damned. Tomorrow I think we move to another suite. I no longer like this one."

"The seneschal will be délighted," Lord Darcy said. "Come, my lords, let's let His Majesty get some sleep."

20

"WELL, MY LORD DARCY," the Duchess of Cumberland said, "I think you'd better tell us all about it."

It was the next afternoon, and they were assembled, at the Duchess's invitation, in the main room of the de Cumberland suite in the White Chateau. Her Grace's stepson, the Duke of Cumberland, had greeted his guests as they arrived and then discreetly gone back to cleaning his fishing gear. The invited guests, besides Lord Darcy and Master Sean, included Marquis Sherrinford, Lord Peter, Coronel Lord Waybusch, and Sir Darryl Longuert. Duke Richard was not present, but Lord Darcy, as his eyes took in the Chinese screen that walled off one corner, had a feeling that there might be royalty in the room nonetheless.

"What do you want to know?" Lord Darcy asked.

"Everything!" Mary of Cumberland said, looking up at him innocently.

"How did you know it was Count d'Alberra?" Marquis Sherrinford asked. "And, for that matter, how could it have been Count d'Alberra? He came here from Italy with letters from His Holiness. How could he be a Polish agent?"

"And why would a Polish agent be trying to kill the Crown Prince of Poland?" Lord Peter added. "And how did you know?"

"All right," Lord Darcy said. He leaned back in his corner of the couch and sipped at his ouiskie and water. "Let me trace it out for you.

"What threw us all off was the reference to 'His Majesty' in Albert Chall's dying words. He overheard someone—it was probably the man we know as Count d'Alberra—say the target was 'His Majesty,' and it never occurred to him, or de London, or any of us, that it might not be His Angevin Majesty who was being referred to."

"Curiously enough, it is only his enemies who insist in calling him 'His Majesty' in Poland," Lord Peter said. "It's sort of a joke."

"Yes, well, we heard him being called 'His Majesty' enough times here to have thought of it."

"So the whole plot was to kill the Crown Prince of Poland," Marquis Sherrinford said.

"Yes," Lord Darcy agreed. "And have it blamed on us."

"But he was going to be killed by a madman," Coronel Lord Waybusch said.

"Yes, but an *Angevin* madman. It makes all the difference."

"Tell us about the Count d'Alberra," Mary of Cumberland said.

"A learned man, a brilliant doctor of the mind," Lord Darcy said, "who was killed a month ago in the *Gryphon d'Or*. The person who died last night was a *Serka* agent who took his place."

"Ah!" Coronel Lord Waybusch said.

"Wasn't he taking an awful chance?" Mary of Cumberland asked.

"A chance, yes," Lord Darcy said. "But not so great a chance. He would have known that not very many people from Italy were coming to the coronation. And I imagine his research showed him that the real Count had never before left Italy, and would be known by almost nobody here. And then, I imagine his resemblance to the real Count is striking. Besides, whatever else he was, he was a brave man and not afraid to die for his cause, as he showed last night."

"An evil cause," Coronel Lord Waybusch said. "A cabal to kill the Crown Prince of Poland and blame it on an Angevin madman."

"That poor man," Mary of Cumberland said. "Is he incurably mad?"

"The Archbishop of Paris is afraid so, Your Grace. But we

will have skilled healers look at him. He is a man who started with a grudge against wizards, and had it fostered by a skillful mental scientist. For, even though the man who died last night was not the real Count d'Alberra, there is no doubt that he was a skillful mental scientist. Look at the success he had in treating Marquis Sherrinford's headaches."

"On that account I shall miss him," Marquis Sherrinford said. "I will have to send to Italy and get the real Count d'Alberra's writings, as I assume that the counterfeit used the same techniques."

"I would think so, my lord," Lord Darcy agreed. "A necessary verisimilitude."

"It's no wonder that my Polish agents didn't pick up any sign of the plot," Lord Peter said. "A cabal of one Polish group against another Polish group is going to be carefully hidden. Especially when the target is the Crown Prince. And a very clever idea it was too. Any move against Prince Stanislaw in Poland would be immediately suspect. But to have him killed at Castle Cristobel would remove him from the line of succession and worsen relations with the Angevin Empire at the same time."

"That also explains one thing that was troubling me," Lord Darcy said. "Why the murders were made to look like impossible crimes."

"Why?" Marquis Sherrinford asked.

"So that the final murder—that of the Crown Prince—would look like an impossible crime. Otherwise it would have occurred to everyone immediately that someone on the Prince's staff was a traitor. But with people being killed in locked bakeries, in the middle of freshly shellacked ballrooms, and in a locked and guarded throne room, it becomes possible to have someone killed in a locked bedroom in a guarded suite."

"How were those done, Lord Darcy?" Coronel Lord Waybusch asked. "Magic?"

"No, my lord," Master Sean assured him. "I was able to rule that out, remember. Otherwise, don't you see, they wouldn't have been impossible crimes."

"The bakery was easy," Lord Darcy said. "Just because we had to break into it, doesn't mean you couldn't close the door going out. A rod inserted through the door to hold the wooden bar up as you close the door, and then withdrawn at the last instant to allow the bar to fall into place, would do very nicely.

Or a stout cord running around the bar and over the door to the outside. I don't know which method he used, but I fancy it was one of those two."

"And the ballroom?" Coronel Lord Waybusch asked.

"The thin wire that Bowers used to try to kill Sir Darryl was used there. It's about twenty feet long. It was put around the victim's neck and held on to by a wooden handle at one end. As the victim ran into the room, he sliced his own throat."

"Nasty!" Mary of Cumberland said.

"Indeed," Lord Darcy agreed. "This whole plot was a nasty-minded piece of business."

"And the throne room?" Marquis Sherrinford asked.

"I'm not sure," Lord Darcy said. "I am still investigating that. I'll make a report when I have an answer."

"Glad you're not infallible, my lord," Coronel Lord Waybusch said. "It makes you more human, don't you know."

The conversation continued for a while longer and then broke off, as the busy men went back to their duties. After all, the coronation was less than a week off.

After the last of the visible guests had left, a royal hand pushed the screen aside. "My Lord Darcy," the familiar Plantagenet voice said.

Lord Darcy dropped to one knee, and the Duchess of Cumberland curtsied low. "Your Majesty."

"Once again, my lord, We have occasion to be grateful that, long years ago, you chose to indulge in your knack for puzzle-solving rather than merely manage your estates or practice beekeeping."

"Thank you, Your Majesty," Lord Darcy said.

"One question," His Majesty said. "Tell me the truth about the throne room death. You do know how it was done, don't you?"

"Yes, Your Majesty."

"How?"

"There is only one possibility. The pseudo Count d'Alberra was practicing more than his mental science on Marquis Sherrinford. His Lordship was hypnotized. He let the Count and the victim into the throne room that night, and the recollection of it was wiped from his mind. Then he went back to the ballroom, and the Count used a wooden wedge to keep the door open."

"You have proof of this?"

"I have the wedge," Lord Darcy said.

"We see," His Majesty said. "We had best not tell Marquis Sherrinford. It would only distress him."

"I agree," Lord Darcy said.

"Once again you have done a good job for Us, Lord Darcy," His Majesty said. "We are pleased." He turned and walked to the door. "Good day, Lord Darcy, Mary of Cumberland. We are lucky to have such subjects."

"May God keep Your Majesty," Mary of Cumberland said as the King closed the door behind him.

"Well, that's that," Lord Darcy said. "I'm glad it's behind me."

"You say that now," Mary of Cumberland told him, "but you'll be bored in a week."

"You're probably right," Lord Darcy admitted. "But human nature being what it is, I don't think I'll be bored very long."

"Come," Mary of Cumberland said. "Cook is making her special omelets for lunch. And it looks like the weather is clearing; perhaps after lunch we'll go for a walk."